DURSTAN
THE MONK WHO
CAST A SPELL

SHARON BRADSHAW

Copyright © Sharon Bradshaw, 2019

The moral right of Sharon Bradshaw to be identified as the author of this work has been asserted in accordance with the Copyright, Designs and Patents Act of 1988.

All rights reserved. No part of this publication may be reproduced, stored in a retrieval system, or transmitted in any form or by any means, electronic, mechanical, photocopying, recording, or otherwise, without the prior permission of the author and copyright owner of this book.

This is a work of fiction. All characters, places, and events portrayed in this novel unless in the public domain are products of the author's imagination or are used fictitiously.

ISBN: 978-1-913127-03-9

Printed in the UK by Ingram Spark

Other Books by Sharon Bradshaw

A Druid's Magic
(the prequel to *The Monk Who Cast A Spell*)

From Now 'til Then: An Anthology of Love Poems

www.sharonbradshaw.com

Contents

Chapter 1: Druids Walk The Land — 9
Chapter 2: The Ancestors' Gods — 18
Chapter 3: Watching The Shadows — 27
Chapter 4: Viking Longships On The Horizon — 34
Chapter 5: Erik And His Sons — 41
Chapter 6: Abbot Faisal's Bell — 51
Chapter 7: The Goddess Speaks To Durstan — 61
Chapter 8: After The Viking Raid — 70
Chapter 9: Roy The Blacksmith's Story — 78
Chapter 10: Mull — 89
Chapter 11: Cormac The Fisherman — 102
Chapter 12: Beth — 110
Chapter 13: Eoghan — 121
Chapter 14: Lora's Story — 128
Chapter 15: The Threads Of The Wyrd — 137
Chapter 16: A Shell Necklace — 146
Chapter 17: The Yule Feast — 153
Chapter 18: Matters Of The Heart — 163
Chapter 19: Love Is The Answer — 169
Chapter 20: A Marriage Proposal — 177
Chapter 21: Future Plans — 184
Chapter 22: Druid Brionach's Tale — 198
Chapter 23: Fighting For Their Lives — 203
Chapter 24: Durstan — 214
Chapter 25: The Gods Are With Eoghan — 221
Chapter 26: Ailan's Magical Charm — 229
Chapter 27: The Only Truth Is Love — 238
Chapter 28: May Woden Go With You — 245
Author's Note — 249

"Behold Iona!
A blessing on each eye that seeth it."
ST. COLUMBA (born 521AD)

"In this year dire portents appeared over Northumbria and sorely frightened the people. They consisted of immense whirlwinds and flashes of lightning, and fiery dragons were seen flying in the air. A great famine immediately followed those signs, and a little after that in the same year on 8 June, the ravages of heathen men miserably destroyed God's church on Lindisfarne, with plunder and slaughter…."

THE ANGLO SAXON CHRONICLE: 793AD

Chapter 1

May, 794 AD

Druids Walk The Land

The sun was beating down on Edgar's back. It was alright for the Druid to say that the Gods had given the golden orb to men as a blessing, but when you had walked as far as Edgar had that morning without meat or ale, it was surely not from a merciful God. He had to put as much distance as he could between the enclosure and himself. They would hang him at the Lord's Court for what he had done, even Edgar Addle-Head knew that.

Edgar ran quickly through the trees, avoiding low branches, and across the sand when he remembered going that way before. He had no idea where he was and must be lost, but if that was the case, then maybe the others were lost too? He trotted happily then into the dense part of the forest. It seemed as good a way to go as any. At least he hadn't come across the mountain where Father had taken him. It would be too far away, and he wanted to go home to the enclosure. He could feel the magic of the oak as the Druid had taught him, and knew he wasn't alone. The tree spirits were travelling with him, but how he hated it when they called him names! He had fought Bhaltair for shouting about his head, and pushed the younger boy into the dung heap. Edgar smiled to himself. It was a long time ago, but he could still remember how good it felt doing that. Bhaltair ran away, screaming like a baby for his Mother, and Edgar Addle-Head had been beaten when she found him.

Edgar looked around warily as he half-ran, and walked. He remembered the stories the Druid had told him about the Ancestors, dressed in animal skins. They had stolen the souls of the bears and wolves for their power. They roamed the earth in shadow, and there were a lot of shadows here between the trees. Edgar hoped that none of those who had practised cannibalism were lurking amongst the branches, or if they were they wouldn't be hungry. He didn't want them to eat his skin or chew his bones. He'd heard tell of it happening to others when food was scarce. Perhaps though he wouldn't taste so good, and they would leave him alone? Edgar shook his head savagely to rid himself of the bad thoughts, but it only made him feel dizzier. A fat, black fly buzzed disconsolately around his head, drawn by the taste of sweat. There were a lot of insects following him and biting his skin.

She had always been beautiful. Edgar thought she was. He did, didn't he? That's why he hadn't been able to resist, and when the Gods took him to the edge he had cried out to them. He hadn't known such a bittersweet moment before that. If only Shella had gone willingly into the dappled shade of the oak and laid there quietly, there wouldn't have been any need for him to put his hands around her throat, or squeeze them tighter. Edgar Addle-Head couldn't forget the loud crack her arm had made when he pushed it behind her back. He had punched her face then, and Shella had looked ugly when he did that. She had spoiled it, the way things often seemed to be. She had screamed when all he wanted was for her to whisper sweetly to him, as she had done with the other man. None of it was as he had planned. Edgar knew that, but he still couldn't understand why she had struggled so hard. She knew him, and he had always loved Shella. It puzzled him and he was vexed now by what she had done. He had meant her no harm. It was her own fault. When she had fought, it was only natural for him to press harder.

Edgar Addle-Head felt the niggle at his temples which had been coming more often of late. He had never really understood things the way the others did. He supposed that's why they called him Addle-Head, shouting that he was stupid, but Edgar wasn't! Mother had told him so. She said he was different to the other boys. If Oonagh was here she would talk to them, and smooth it over as she always did. Mother was good at convincing others. Edgar knew that, and he didn't know what he was doing. Did he? All he had done was take a coracle and row across to the island. He knew Shella was there. He had rowed Mother across the water many times in the past and no one had complained, not even her. He liked the sea. It was his friend. The dolphins and seals were best friends. Edgar smiled to himself. He talked to the fish. They would sometimes jump from the water as he rowed, and chase after the boat. It was all part of their game. He had wanted to play a game with that girl, so why not? She had made him do it! Edgar could feel the anger surging through him, as his feet pounded the hard earth under the pine trees.

It was cooler now and the light was changing. He frowned as he ran, still trying to swat the flies away from his face. She…, Shella. It was the name he had given to her when they were children. She had found the shell first and it was beautiful, like her, perfect. Mother said it was a gift from the Sea God, and would have come from deep within his bed. Edgar had held out his hand when he saw Shella holding it. He wanted the shell badly and she had dropped it, crying as she ran away. Edgar Addle-Head lost the shell in no time at all. He had taken it everywhere, and carried on calling her Shella, long after the others had stopped doing that. Edgar thought secretly that none of the others would have done what Edgar Addle-Head had made the girl do, but then Shella would have gone willingly with them. She had laughed at him with her friends when they were young. It made Edgar's ears and eyes hurt now, as he remembered the harsh sound their words had made. He didn't like Shella very much then, and it stopped him from feeling sorry that he had hurt her.

The wolfhounds were baying louder. He could hear them in the distance. Edgar didn't think he could run any faster, or for much longer. He was too tired and thirsty. He had gone further from the Hall than he had ever done before. He might as well stop to let them get at him. He suspected they would eventually, however far he went. Edgar liked the dogs at the enclosure. He played with them, but not these animals. Eoghan's dogs would tear his limbs. He had seen them do it last year when they had caught a deer. Eoghan and his friends had thrown stones at the creature to begin with, cornered it, and let it run again before they released the dogs. Edgar hoped it wouldn't hurt too much. The deer had cried a lot. Edgar wiped a tear from his cheek, with his grubby hand.

The Druid said that all of us have a certain time for one life, but there would be others to look forward to. Edgar wondered if this one had reached its end. He thought he could smell the dogs now, their sour scent, but he had had a longer lifespan than his brothers. The last one didn't have a name. Father had taken him to the sea after he had drawn his first breath, and held his head down because he had twisted arms and legs. Father said the Gods must still be angry with Mother, to have sent another devil child to her womb, and they wanted it returned to them. Edgar couldn't bear the sound of Oonagh crying afterwards. It was worse than the time before, when that boy lay sick in their hut from Beltane to Lammas before his crying stopped, but the Gods had been kinder then. They had quietly taken his life away. Edgar remembered the meat he had eaten at the feast to celebrate the passing to the Otherworld. He would drool now, if his mouth wasn't so dry.

Oonagh said that Edgar was blessed. The Druid had told Father that he should let him live, however he might be, because there had been a bright star in the sky three nights before he entered the world. It was a portent from the Gods which should not be disobeyed. The Druid had asked the waves to carry the baby's soul, the one who didn't have a name, safely into Llyr's hands and the wind to take him onwards to the sea God. Edgar smiled. His older brother, Branach, lived. Mother would only have to cry one more time. Father didn't bother her anymore at night. Edgar's smile changed to a savage moan as he stumbled through the thicket, and his breath came in ragged gasps.

He saw the tall stones protruding from the undergrowth and swerved to a halt. He knew where he was. It wasn't too far from the Hall. Edgar Addle-Head must have gone in a circle. He scrambled as fast as he could into the cairn, unsure of whether he was more afraid of the dead or Eoghan's dogs. He didn't notice the rough stones graze his skin and draw blood. It was cold inside the cairn, and the darkness engulfed him. The air felt hollow. There was a strange otherworldly smell of decay which made Edgar Addle-Head shiver, but he laughed loudly when he thought that the dogs wouldn't follow him in here. He was safe at last! This was a place for the dead, not the living, and the Gods would be angry with the dogs if they came inside. Even the insects wouldn't fly in here. He was safe! The Druid had told him that the cairn was where his bones would be kept at the end of this life, but he would have to get out soon. He hadn't yet taken his last breath. The men would give up looking after a while. They had to. Edgar Addle-Head would lie still now, be a mouse, and try hard not to breathe in case they heard. His heart plummeted when he heard a horse snorting. It was too close to him, and he began to shiver.

A man's voice broke through the cracks in the stones. "He's got to be around here somewhere, Eoghan. Look! There's another set of tracks between those trees." The words were only slightly muffled. Edgar could hear more than one horse and dogs too, barking and yelping, as they fought each other.

"You're right, but they disappear again beyond that point. It looks as if he might have gone into the cairn. I can't believe even Addle-Head would be that much of an idiot unless the Gods have taken him, but I don't expect they want him!" Edgar could hear Eoghan laughing heartily.

The first man replied, "you are the Lord's son, Eoghan, but I'm not going in there after him if that's what you're thinking. Any man who enters the cairn, even one of the Christians, won't come back to this life from the Otherworld unless he is Druid. And that I'm not. More's the pity Brionach isn't here. He could do the job for us, and have saved us all this trouble even though we've enjoyed the chase!"

Edgar knew they were speaking the truth. He was going to be taken by the Gods, or these men. Perhaps even the Christian God Oonagh didn't like very much? He felt the urine's warmth seep into his leggings. Mother would be angry with him. All because he had only wanted to see for himself what it would be like, to be the same as the others, and join in with what he had seen Shella doing with one of them in the meadow by the stream. A pair of luminous eyes glowed in the darkness inside the cairn. Edgar screamed and tried to move away from them. He kicked over a small urn of ashes in his haste. It was decorated as an offering to Woden, and he thought wildly of his younger brother's death fire. A half-broken antler comb had fallen out of the pot. Edgar tried to grab it, but clutched instead a dagger with the blade broken halfway down its length. He was choking now in the ashes which saturated the air. The cairn was full of them, old bones, and the scent of something else.

All he had wanted was a chance he thought wildly when the dog was on him. It hadn't been afraid after all, to pass the first stones into the cairn. The dog's jaws clenched tightly around his calf before a second, then third dog began to pull his body outside. Edgar heard the men laughing in the distance as he screamed. The dogs' sharp teeth bit into the soft flesh of his arms and legs, then agonizingly a fourth dog tore into his groin. The last dog, the strongest, bit the scream from his throat.

Eoghan watched the spectacle, with enjoyment. This was much better sport than he had dared hope, and had helped improve his mood. He had woken abruptly at daybreak, sat upright without knowing where he was, and fallen back onto the straw with a groan. His stomach was turning somersaults whilst Thor's hammer pounded at his brain. "Never again!" He said, slowly rubbing his temples. The hut was spinning and gathered momentum until he vomited copiously into yesterday's rushes. He wiped his mouth with the back of his hand, and spat out the residue before lying down again, feeling marginally better. If he could sleep, it would be over quicker.

Eoghan groaned, again. There wasn't time. He had to get up now. It was light. He had promised his Father, Lord Duncan, that he would go after Edgar and bring him back to the enclosure for punishment. Eoghan consoled himself with the thought that it would be better sport than hunting a stag, and if the Addle-Head didn't make it back to the Hall, that surely wouldn't matter too much? Eoghan hadn't decided yet how it would end, but he would enjoy thinking through the possibilities while they rode after him.

Eoghan swung his feet unsteadily onto the ground on the other side of the bed. Dara would clean up his sleeping place when she came in. It would be a good lesson for her after she had refused him last night. He could remember that much. If he hadn't drank so much ale, that would also have had a different ending. She was a slave, and it wasn't her place to deny the Lord's son. He would think of a fitting punishment later. He smiled. It was going to be an enjoyable day, once Thor decided to leave him in peace.

He flung open the animal skins which covered the entrance to his hut near the Hall, and walked out into the sunlight. The spring morning struggled to warm the muscles on his bare chest, but Eoghan hardly noticed. He put his head into a nearby trough, shaking the cold water vigorously from his face and thick, black hair. Thank the Gods! He was starting to feel better. Breakfast was what he needed.

"Dara, where are you, lazy bitch? I need food." A petite, dark haired girl who was barely fifteen years old ran across the enclosure towards him. Eoghan watched appreciatively, as her body swayed with the exertion. There wouldn't be any argument tonight. She would not dare say no to him again. He knew Dara would fight him. The Irish Celts always did. He grinned. It would be good sport before he had his way. The day was turning out well after all.

Eoghan roused himself. The beasts were out of control. They were quick when they were ready to kill. They followed their instincts, and may the Gods help him, he had left it too late. He should have paid more heed, instead of thinking about a slave. Edgar's body had become a lifeless lump in a sea of blood. Eoghan gave the order sharply to his men, to separate the dogs, and several hefty kicks caused the frenzy to subside. Perhaps it would have been better after all to have brought Edgar to justice in his Father's Court, as he had been told to do? Duncan had said quite categorically that there shouldn't be any more mistakes. Eoghan could see a broken dagger near the body, but his Father wouldn't believe that he had been so afraid for his own safety, that he had been forced to murder a half-wit. Eoghan groaned. He didn't yet have enough men following him to stand against the Lord, and had on too many other occasions failed to follow his Father's command. A curse on Edgar Addle-Head, wherever the Gods may have taken his soul!

Chapter 2
April, 794 AD

The Ancestors' Gods

The flames from the peat fire at the centre of the floor flickered in the draught, coming through the cracks in the timber walls. It was hard to believe that God wasn't angry. Rain had lashed Iona from early morning, and was still beating the side of Durstan's hut. The women hadn't been able to go back to Mull. A coracle was sturdy enough in 794AD but not in heavy seas. The Monk's right arm lay across a girl's slender shoulders. She was sixteen years old, with black hair cascading softly around an unremarkable face. Durstan was drawn into the depths of her blue eyes. The way the light in them changed, reminded him of how the sea sparkled on a summer day.

Ailan was shaking with laughter, as the Monk dropped morsels of honeyed cake into her upturned mouth. "I want to kiss you," Durstan said, miserably. Ailan stroked his cheek, and his lips moved to her fingers.

"It isn't right, Durstan. You can't kiss me because you made a promise to your Christian God when you didn't understand the meaning behind the oath? You can't be bound by that. Abbot Faisal should have explained the vow properly to you when you were older, not taken it from a seven year old boy who knew nothing of life. We're not doing any harm, and this Christian God of yours surely can't want to deny nature itself? Listen to the storm! It's not as if we are trying to stop the thunder and lightning or be disrespectful to Him, only make love from what's already here tonight." She looked up at the Monk, with the question fixed in her eyes.

"Everyone has to make their vows to God as soon as they arrive at the Monastery. I wouldn't have had a choice, even if I had been able to argue with the Abbot. My Father left me here, and that was that. I would have been outcast if I hadn't agreed to say Faisal's words. Things changed when I met you, Ailan, but Faisal is like a Father to me now. Iona is all I know, and I feel as if the sky will fall on me if I break the vow I made, despite how much I would like to." He took Ailan's hand in his. "It's hard not to believe Faisal, when I'm in front of the altar listening to him. He tells us all the time that women are sent by the Christian Devil, to tempt and lure rightful men away from their one true God. We are to practise chastity, to protect the Church which is our home and family, and we should do so willingly to obey our God. When I'm with you again, my feelings for you become the stronger, even though the faith inside me is still important. I'm afraid of what's happening to us, Ailan. If I lie with you tonight it will change everything, because it has to." Durstan smiled sadly, as he dropped another piece of cake between her lips. He imagined the touch of them on his skin, and was mesmerized by the row of tiny, pearly teeth as Ailan savoured the sweet taste of the cake on her tongue. It had been meant for the Abbot's table, but Durstan had taken it from the kitchen when no one was looking.

Ailan stared longingly at the Monk's broad shoulders, and his black hair draped across them. "I have my Gods too, Durstan, the Old Ones. They've been on these islands for as long as I've known, and well before that. They're more powerful than the Jesus you talk about. The Lady Brigid smiles on me and I'm happy being here with you tonight, Monk or not. I don't know the answer to any of what you are saying because it's straightforward to me. The Goddess doesn't frown on love. Maybe later you'll feel able to kiss me properly. Our first night together is far from over yet!" Ailan leaned back against Durstan's robe, ignoring the coarseness of the cloth.

His heart was beating quickly, and he could feel control slipping slyly away into the shadows. He hadn't long been a man at seventeen years old. When he had seen animals coupling in the fields more times than he could count, he had assumed it was only for procreation. He didn't know that there would be feelings to be taken into account. Some of the Monks whispered after Nocturne late into the night, about the women they had known before they came to the island, and the pleasure they had taken. They seemed to be reluctant to accept their vows and, as for the rest of it, all Durstan truly knew was from the time he had kissed another girl a couple of years ago. He had been seen then and thrashed by one of Faisal's disciplinarian Monks, Aelfric the Saxon, who had been in more shield walls than he could remember. But Ailan couldn't be one of the Devil's whores. The blood pounded angrily through Durstan's veins. "The first time we met I saw you washing the Abbot's undergarments in the stream, and you looked to be enjoying it!" He couldn't hide the jealousy in his voice.

Ailan said, indignantly, "that was my first morning on Iona, Durstan! I'd had to listen to a lot of tales about the Monastery from the women who crossed the water with me. As you well know, I had my skirt tucked up high because I thought all of you were inside the Church, praying to your God. You do a lot of that here. How was I to know that the Abbot had told you instead to go into the barn, to see to a mare who was foaling?" Ailan had the strangest feeling that Durstan was looking into her heart, and he was smiling again. "This isn't funny, Monk. Stop teasing me. It was a hot day. That's how I usually work when I'm washing anyone's cloth, Lord Duncan's included. If I have to tell you the all of it, I like to feel the Sun God's touch on my skin."

"I won't forget how you looked, Ailan. I stepped back around the corner of the kitchen, to listen for a while longer to you singing. I guessed you would stop as soon as you saw me, and your voice is beautiful."

Her eyes shone with happiness. "I was singing to the stream. My Mother taught me the words. She heard the Goddess whisper them to her when she was worshiping at the shrine. You are right though, Durstan, I did stop as soon as I saw you. I remember I tried to talk to you, but you looked so bemused. It was as if you hadn't seen a woman before, let alone one working. It's quite normal for us to do that."

Durstan grinned. "Admit it! You were embarrassed, even though it did take you a while to pull your skirt down!"

"Stop talking like that! I'm ashamed now. I was only having a bit of fun, and why shouldn't I? People do sometimes do things to have fun, Durstan. I didn't mean any harm. Anyway, I didn't do it very well."

"You're wrong about that," he said, taking the opportunity to pull her closer. The scent of her skin was intoxicating, and he could barely hear the words she was saying against his chest.

"I liked the look of you, Durstan. There's kindness in your dark eyes. You remind me of a great bear, a gentle one. I admit I'd never seen the like before, that first time I set eyes on you. You were bedraggled and dirty, with the mare's blood on your robe!"

Durstan laughed. He kissed the side of her head, savouring the softness of her hair. Ailan had stolen his heart, and she knew it. After the first time at the stream they had met whenever they could, but there was little on Iona which escaped the Abbot. It was the larger of the islands which belonged to Lord Duncan, Durstan's kinsman, and Faisal's word at the Monastery was absolute. Close association between a Monk and a woman was mostly forbidden, so they had been cautious not to flaunt their friendship. Nevertheless Durstan had been taken from tending the sheep, to work alongside Roy the Blacksmith at the furnace. Before this happened Ailan would hide her coracle in the undergrowth by the shore when she had finished work for the day, and run back through the trees to see Durstan in the fields. They didn't usually have long before the bell sounded again for prayer and Ailan had to leave, but it was enough for them to take the risk. Tonight was the first time in several weeks that they had been alone, and waiting had intensified their feelings.

The fire crackled in orange and golden sparks, complaining of the sharp gust of wind which had found its way through a crack in the timber wall. Ailan flinched when she felt the cold air on her skin. Durstan's strong arms tightened around her, but she sensed his fear. "We're safe enough in the hands of the women, Durstan. They'll not tell anyone where I am. I know Caitir can be spiteful and has cast a spell for you, but she would run the wrath of the others if she dared to breathe our secret. They despise Faisal as much as I do. He's an evil man in his rich white robes, and gold cross from over the sea. It's in his bones.

The people at Duncan's Hall talk about Columba, the Sainted Abbot from years ago. I know lots of stories about the miracles he did, and they are good stories, Durstan. There's talk of him killing the Druids when he came to Iona because he wanted it for the Christian God, but who knows if that's true? He sounds much nicer than Faisal. I expect though your Church will still make a holy Saint of him. It's difficult to believe that Faisal is likely to become akin to a God. The women say that he has a viper's poison for blood, and I don't think they're wrong. Surely not all of your Christian Monasteries can be as bad as this one?"

Durstan sighed. "I don't know, Ailan. Sometimes it's alright here. Then, it'll start again. John was beaten last week for laughing when he came out of church. He said afterwards that he was happy to have felt the warmth of the sun on his face. It can be as cold as death inside the church. There wasn't any evil in what he did, but we are taught by the Abbot not to feel sensual pleasure so that we can remain fully devoted to Christ. I have heard tell though that some of the Monks in other places are married, but I don't know any more than that."

"I can't forget those long, red welts you had on your back, Durstan. All because watching me coracle to Mull had made you late for your damned Church." Ailan shuddered. "I don't understand how you can accept that such violence is part of your God's love, or want to stay here. Anyone would think this Christian God of yours didn't want you to be happy."

"Hush, Ailan. Faisal was making an example of John, to remind the rest of us what could happen if we stepped out of line, and he's alright now. So am I. I'm fortunate that Faisal is leaving me alone. I expect that's because of Mora, my sister, being married to the Lord. I've also heard tell that Duncan is taking more of an interest now in what's happening here, and the Abbot seems to enjoy parading me in front of his visitors as a prize which he's captured for the Church. I've heard him pretend to have more influence over Duncan because of me, but there's nothing I can do about it, Ailan. It's unlikely Faisal will let me leave Iona, nor do I want to be outcast if I take a coracle and go without his permission. I can't see that my kinsman Duncan would want an argument over my freedom, if I should escape. He would be taking on the Christian Church, if he decided to help me against the Abbot's wishes.

All that aside, I wouldn't have missed a single minute of any of the time I've had with you. I don't believe that God intends to hurt us. The problem is Faisal, and the way he is. God does smile on me. I enjoy working with Roy. He has me pumping the bladders for the fire, and you've not seen the like before of the gold filigree work he does, the artistry in it. He's said he'll teach me as soon as we can persuade Faisal to let me try. I'm happier too being able to see the others in the huts behind the enclosure. I have a bit more freedom helping the Blacksmith, and can talk with men who aren't Monks. The carpenter's boy and wheelwright often work nearby, and I've listened to their stories." Durstan slid the sleeves of his robe along his arms so that Ailan could look at the muscles he flexed. "I'll be a giant of a man soon, like Roy. You'll see. No one will dare come near me!" He gazed into Ailan's liquid eyes as she ran her fingers slowly along each arm tracing a path, but he knew that he hadn't convinced her.

"Try to be happy for me, Ailan. Roy can be a hard taskmaster when the mood takes him, but he has a kind and gentle heart which keeps me away from Aelfric. I've seen him secretly share a crust with a hungry bird, and don't forget he was the one who refused to administer any more discipline after what happened to me, even though that task is usually part of the Blacksmith's duties. He told Faisal that it was distracting him from his real work. If the Abbot agreed to release him from it, he would have the finest swords in all of these islands for trade. It was an offer which Faisal couldn't refuse. Roy's the best Blacksmith and, despite pressure from the Abbot, he's not become a Monk so can leave here at any time." Durstan paused. "I was given to him, to be encouraged to forget about you. The magic of the forge and a women's charms are said not to mix, but I would never do that, Ailan. I'm grateful now to have had the chance, to learn how to work iron on the anvil when it's red hot. It's an incredible sight. How we can make it into anything: tools, nails, daggers, shields, only name what you want. It's magical how the change occurs, and the nature in it is beautiful to see.

The truth is whatever I'm doing, wherever I am, you are never far from my thoughts. I worried about you travelling alone to Mull when the other women had gone. I know it's only a short distance over the sound but the waters aren't always safe, especially at twilight when the sun loses its power over the darkness."

"I grew up in a coracle, Durstan, and can row as well as any man. You know that. Besides, the Lady Brigid protects me on the water and my Mother's spirit travels alongside, so there's nothing to fear. Don't you remember? I didn't once say to you that I was worried, or the Gods had stolen the Moon when it was getting dark." Ailan smiled, and playfully traced the tonsure line in his hair.

Durstan pulled her hand into his own. "I'm sorry that

you had to do it. I prayed to keep you safe, and I watched for as long as I could see you, longer…"

"Hush, Durstan. It's done, and we're both safe. There's no good wishing it was different. We can't make it so. Like you, I wouldn't have missed any of the time we've had together."

Durstan leaned over the fire to poke the embers when Ailan shivered again. The night was cold because of the pelting rain and blustery wind. The flames rose higher to lighten some, but not all of the shadows behind them.

Chapter 3

Watching The Shadows

As the firelight flickered across Ailan's face, Durstan could see that she was frowning. "What is it, my love?" He said, with concern.

"Nothing really, only… I wish I didn't have to leave my brother behind. I know that Tam will be alright with Saille, but she already has enough to do. She has Dacey too. She deserves a good man, Durstan, who will care for them both. She's been lonely since the Gods took her Husband. It isn't easy being a slave with a daughter, even at your kinsman's enclosure. Perhaps Lord Duncan will find another man for her, or let her choose for herself?"

"Tam will be fine, Ailan. You'll see, and from what you've told me about Saille, she'll have fed and played with them both until they couldn't keep their eyes open. I'm sorry about your Mother and Father," he said, softly. "I wish you and I had known each other sooner."

"It was a bad time for a lot of people on Mull, Durstan, three summers ago." Ailan's eyes filled with tears. "Father thought Woden would spare us if he jumped with the other men from the tall rocks into the sea, as a sacrifice. He could feel the plague inside his bones. The Gods had already taken others, and he was afraid. Mother said it was the only thing left for him to do. The charms and protection spells they had used didn't work. It was as if we'd angered the Gods. How was he to know that Mother would die soon afterwards from the same illness?" She paused, "and now… I don't know anymore, Durstan. I miss them both so much."

Ailan's tears fell steadily down her cheeks, as Durstan held her gently. He couldn't say so now but he would have tried to persuade her Father to place his trust in the Christian God instead. He didn't expect men to sacrifice themselves in that way for Him. He wasn't one of the Old Gods! Ailan's Father may well have lived and been cured in exchange for his faith. Faisal was right when he said that it was necessary for knowledge of Christ's ways to spread. Too many still believed in the power of the Old Gods, including some of the Monks who were not averse to using a charm or spell during difficult times.

Ailan wiped her cheeks and eyes roughly, with the back of her hand. "I wish the Abbot would let Tam come here more often. It's not as if I don't have to coracle to Iona. Lord Duncan says that I must, to help the other women. That all of us have to work if we want to stay at the enclosure, but Tam's only six years old. He's too young to be left alone so much, or even swear allegiance to his Lord. There's another year before he can do that. May the Goddess protect him from being sent here as an oblate! I've been praying to Brigid, to make sure that his fate doesn't lie in that direction. I'd rather Tam be given a knife, to learn to fight alongside the men, and I am thankful that Saille will look after him tonight," Ailan said, trying to smile. "I'm sorry for being sad, Durstan. I don't mean to be. Everything seems far worse in the dark." Her voice softened. "It's good to be able to tell you how I feel."

Durstan tried to hide his concern. When he had played with Tam on the couple of occasions the boy had come to Iona, he found him withdrawn. "I wish I could make life easier for you, Ailan. Faisal is at fault! He puts up with the craftsmen's children from the huts behind the enclosure because he wants their Fathers' skills. He's taken advantage too of the Lord's generosity in having you here. I don't believe he likes children. They don't fit into his politics and scheming but things can change, with or without charms and magic, or us knowing the path of the wyrd. We have to trust in God, and your Gods, to help us. At least we're safe in here tonight. Even if any of the Monks did see you slip into the hut, it's unlikely it'll get back to the Abbot. Those closest to Faisal will be inside now, well out of the storm. They won't venture out again unnecessarily. It's hard enough as it is to have to open our eyes twice during the night, and worse in winter when there's ice in the church. If snow comes or there's a cold rain, the Abbot often stays near the fire in his own hut. The excuse may be nothing at all, or he'll plead an ague. You should hear the Monks' scornful whispers when he does that. No one wants to leave their bed. As for tonight, Faisal wouldn't think of you leaving the visitor's hut to take Andrew's place in here, or that you could even suggest so devious a plan." Durstan grinned. "As a woman you are of little, or no intelligence!"

He realized his mistake when he saw the anger in Ailan's eyes, and said, quickly, "I thought Andrew would have been more difficult. It was bad enough when Faisal said I was to share the hut with him a few years ago. A storm had damaged the one I slept in, and I was homeless. He was the only Monk left who had a hut to himself, because he was the best scribe at the Monastery. I'm fortunate that he eventually became my *anam cara*. It was beyond question then. He wouldn't be able to disclose any of the private thoughts I shared with him. We should be able to choose our own soul friend, Ailan, but Faisal decided a long time ago that he would do it for us. Some of the Monks still resent that. I suppose I did at first, but it's a comfort now to be able to talk openly to Andrew even though we don't always agree. He's seen more of the world than I have, and doesn't like change. Maybe it's age which is responsible for that?" Durstan smiled. "Forty four years is a long life for anyone. When I told him that I wanted to be here with you tonight, he didn't say a word. He collected what he needed, and left. I expect he'll have used it as an excuse to share Osfric's hut. You know Osfric? He's one of the boys Andrew has been teaching to write a manuscript." Durstan hesitated. "Andrew will think that all you and I shall do tonight, is share the warmth from the fire. He's right but he's missed the most important part, about watching the shadows for anything which might prevent us, from falling more deeply in love."

Durstan stared at Ailan. She was beautiful, but the spell cast by the firelight had to be broken. "We have to sleep now, sweetheart. Otherwise neither of us will be able to work tomorrow. I shall have to go when the bell sounds for Nocturnes, but you won't be afraid. Will you? You're safe in here, next to the fire. I can't get out of going to the church. Even if I said I was ill, I would still have to go."

Ailan's reply was faint. "No. I know you'll come back."

Durstan lowered her gently onto the sheepskin which would be underneath her body for warmth, and pulled another carefully over her. "It gets cold before dawn when the fire is low, so keep well covered."

She lay gratefully under the fleece. She wasn't used to having such attention, and she came to a decision. "Lie next to me, Durstan. I want to fall asleep beside you, please. There's no harm in it!"

The Monk's heart exploded and, in a split second, the

man within him didn't resist. He pulled his sheepskin next to hers beside the fire, and laid down with the thought that the night was truly wonderful. Any doubts he might have had about God's will vanished. There wasn't any evil here, and they talked quietly about nothing before drifting into a dreamless sleep, without either of them realizing their words were no longer there.

Durstan awoke with a start, to the sound of the bell pealing. The clanging was pounding through his head. He groaned, as he turned over heavily. He had only been asleep for a couple of hours. His body knew it, but Ailan seemed still to be asleep. Durstan could see her face etched in the half-light. Without thinking about what he was doing, and barely awake himself, his lips grazed hers. She murmured and pulled him instinctively downwards into an embrace. Durstan felt for the first time the full softness of her breasts against his chest.

"Are you asleep? Come on. Get up, Durstan! I'm wet to the bone out here. We're the last ones, again. You know what it'll mean if we're late, and Faisal is angry." Andrew's voice was muffled by the rain. Durstan pulled away from Ailan, as if a sharp knife had entered his chest, and he left the hut without a backward glance.

She dragged the sheepskin closer around her body, and with eyes still closed, reached across for Durstan's. She hoped from somewhere not too far away that he wouldn't be gone for long, as the night was passing quickly. She could smell the sheep's scent on the skin, and him. She pulled it closer to her face. Most of the women on Mull would have considered Durstan as a Husband, if he had not been wed already to his church. A handfasting with him would also be impossible on Iona. He was a Monk under Abbot Faisal's rule and the women had been dissuaded, but not Ailan. She wanted more, much more, because she loved him.

She fell into an uneasy sleep whilst Durstan and Andrew slid unobtrusively into the back of the church. Faisal was uttering the first prayer. Durstan didn't see the Abbot standing in front of him. He belonged to Ailan. Although he had chosen to worship the Christian God from Rome, not Ailan's Old Gods, Durstan thought that they might still be with him in the Ancestors' blood flowing through his veins. It wasn't inconceivable that these men's thoughts and beliefs were a part of him. He wondered if that could be the reason he was now contemplating committing so grave a sin.

The night did pass quickly. The rain had gone by morning and daylight shone brightly in dawn's cloudless sky. It was a beautiful setting for the Abbot's unholy bell when it began to peal again. Durstan hated the sound of it. The bell ruled his life. Everything he did from morning until night, day after day, and it had done so for years. The Monk shook Ailan's shoulder to awaken her. He felt miserable. Night had disappeared and he had failed to follow his instincts, by loving her completely. He kissed her forehead. "You have to get up, sweetheart. It's time. I'm so sorry. I've been a fool." Ailan opened her eyes slowly, to see Durstan leaning over her. She reached up and put her arms around his chest. They didn't quite meet at the centre of his back. "Mmm… It's so good to wake up with you," she whispered. "I felt safe last night, knowing you were there in the dark. Sometimes at the enclosure, Durstan, I'm afraid of some of the men when they have too much ale inside them. It was so different being here, with you."

Durstan kissed her mouth hungrily. His hands sought every part of her, lingering in those places he hadn't touched before, as Ailan's fingers stroked his chest. When she lowered her hand, he groaned. His body responded while the bell continued to peal. They would have to leave the hut. Otherwise they would soon be discovered. Durstan's anger at himself was growing stronger. Why had he been so stubborn, and not instigated this last night? He pulled Ailan's hand away when every fibre of his being was telling her to carry on. "We have to stop. There isn't time. I'm sorry, my love." Ailan's eyes met his with a different understanding when he said, "but it's your Beltane next week. The Abbot has to turn a blind eye to the wildness of the fields on that night. Women come here to be with the Monks. Faisal doesn't question it. The Old Gods are at their most powerful when there's a solstice, and they were on Iona long before Rome arrived. People wouldn't accept it, if he refused them. Faisal knows that. I've felt the magic in the air myself on Beltane night. People look forward to it, probably because so much here is forbidden. As you said, it's nature's path." He paused. "I was wrong, Ailan, so what I'm asking is… Will you celebrate the night with me in the old way?"

He held his breath, as she stared longingly into his eyes. "Yes, I'll celebrate Beltane with you. I know what's done even though I haven't yet taken part. I'll stay behind at the end of the day, to be with you, Durstan. I promise you, my love, as the Goddess is our witness."

His lips met hers, and he kissed her gently. "I also haven't taken part in it," he said, feeling his face redden with embarrassment. "I was waiting for you." He kissed her mouth roughly this time, and wondered how he would live with himself until Beltane.

Chapter 4
October, 794AD

Viking Longships On The Horizon

The wind from the sea was bitterly cold. Durstan's sodden robe clung to his skin. The sharp stones from the low wall on Saint Columba's beach pierced his legs whenever he moved. Thinking about Ailan wasn't a distraction, and he grasped the wooden cross hanging loosely around his neck in despair. The black dye on its leather cord stained his hand. The Vikings had been raiding throughout the summer, but it was inconceivable that they would come so late in the season when visibility had been reduced to a short distance. Abbot Faisal said that an early warning from a watcher, that the longships were approaching, would give the others enough time to hide safely in the wood behind the Monastery. Durstan wasn't convinced. The tales told by the fishermen and travellers showed that these were desperate men, seeking glory and reward from their Gods, Thor and Odin.

Durstan shifted his legs in an attempt to find a more comfortable position. Faisal had told him to sit on the wall, since it was far too important a task to leave to one of the oblates. In reality, there had been too many complaints from the older Monks whose duty this was. Durstan was also gaining a reputation for having the Blacksmith's magic in his bones. The Abbot was no doubt relying on this as an extra charm, to protect them from the men from over the sea. The others had different excuses not to watch. They pleaded illness. Some argued when they dared that they were already in God's hands. Our Lord would churn the waters if He wished to, and the Monks' prayers were sufficiently fervent. Perhaps the Vikings would not sail again this year? They would not be so foolish as to challenge the Christian God!

Durstan spat the phlegm from his throat onto the ground. The Monks were using pagan charms for protection, with the Abbot's knowledge. They were frightened, and so was Faisal. It was always the same when something was not to their liking. The Irish Monks called on the elves of their ancient legends, and carried charms associated with them. Some had a stone, twig, or shell. It had reached the point where no one knew what to believe any more. So far as the Vikings were concerned, Faisal saying that faith in the Christian God was all the Monks would need for protection was patently untrue. The Vikings were well beyond influence, and Durstan felt afraid when he was out here alone, with only the wildness of the weather and sea for a companion.

He barely heard Andrew's shout in the rush of the wind. "I've brought you some food, Durstan. Are you dreaming again? God will know if your thoughts are blasphemous, and you're looking for a Viking kiss? The hair on their beards is not a pretty sight." Andrew made an attempt at being jovial, as he passed the loaf to his friend with a piece of fish and pot of ale. He hoisted up his spindly frame onto the wall, breathing heavily from the climb.

Durstan spoke with his mouth full. "Thank, God! It's not a fasting day. I thought I would perish out here doing such a useless task. Woden himself would say it was too dangerous to sail in these seas. The water is rough enough to drown all of their cursed longships with the Vikings in them, their Ancestors, and sons waiting to be born." Durstan glanced at Andrew. He was shivering uncontrollably. His robe was already soaked through from the sea spray blowing across the rocks. God would have been merciful, had He given them a little shelter, and Andrew was rubbing his eyes in an attempt to see better. The years which he had spent working in candlelight on the Monastery's manuscripts had ruined them. Durstan couldn't understand his fascination for writing, or letters as Andrew liked to call them. The intricate patterns on the calfskin pages were beautiful, but so many animal skins had to be used to make a parchment for one thin book. Durstan had seen animals killed solely for this purpose. His heart was against the loss of life, and in the animal's cries. If Andrew had spent more days working in the fields he would have felt the same, and would have been a stronger man. Durstan frowned. There would be little for him to do at the Monastery, once his eyes failed completely, and that could happen at any time. His squint had become more pronounced in the last few weeks. Faisal wasn't keen to feed anyone who couldn't work. There might be some lighter work in the medicinal garden or kitchen for him to do eventually, but that also wouldn't be possible if Andrew couldn't see the plants. All that was left now was to trust that God would answer Durstan's prayers for his Brother's safety.

"I've been here for three hours, Andrew. Faisal said that I was to wait for the bell at dusk before I came back to the enclosure." Durstan shouted the words into the wind, as he scanned the small area of sea which was still visible. Rain had darkened the water. There was little to see, and the Monks sat side by side in silence, both lost in thought.

"God help us, Brother. You're wrong. Listen!" Andrew grabbed Durstan's arm. "I can hear better than you, and that's not nature playing with the wind. It's the rhythm of oars splashing in the waves, and a boat coming closer. They thought they would surprise us when the weather was against them." Durstan's heart sank. Andrew had already climbed down from the wall, with the intention of running back to the Monastery buildings, to warn the others of a raid.

Durstan scrambled after him across the rocks and sand, until they reached the low thatched wooden huts which formed a circle around the stone church. The Monks shouted as they ran, and into the doorways they passed. "Vikings! Run for your life!"

Men and boys left the huts in disarray, and panic. Many of them were carrying food. There was little to spare on Iona unless you were sitting at the Abbot's table. The altar dressings, crucifix, and jewelled chalice were left behind. Those who had tried to carry the earlier ornaments to safety in the first raid on Iona had been hewn down from behind. The weight of the gold had delayed them. Their blood spread as a pink mist in the early morning light. Many of the men who were running now recalled it sufficiently clearly, to spur them on to find a safe place to hide.

Durstan approached two of the Monks who were standing still, watching the activity in the enclosure. He grabbed the nearest one by the forearm. "Why aren't you running? Follow the others across the vallum ditch, and hide yourselves. The Vikings won't search far inland unless they are desperate for slaves. The riches on the altar may be enough for them this time." The man stared into the distance. Shock glazed his eyes, and Durstan tried again. "Iain, snap out of it and run, or it'll be your death!" The man's eyes drifted into focus. He pulled the other Monk behind him, as he started to run along the nearest path to the vallum.

Durstan looked around for Andrew among the few people who were still left to scatter. Monks were pushing and shoving each other in their haste to escape. Heavy rain made it difficult to see properly, and the sky was as dark as a kitchen pot. Durstan thought he could make out the Abbot's white robe in the distance. The hefty bulk of Aelfric the Saxon was beside him. They were at the front of a group of Monks who looked to be carrying the Abbot's possessions. Durstan grimaced. Faisal would be the first to be hidden in the undergrowth, but he could see Andrew now. He was leaving the church with the manuscripts he had been working on for the last three years. One was a compilation of the Saints' lives and the other a smaller book of Columba's miracles. He held the books awkwardly because of their size, and the weight of the wooden casings. They were covered in gold, garnets, and precious sapphires. He would be a welcome sight to the first Viking who came upon him.

Durstan ran across the pebbled area in front of the Church. He pulled both of the books from under Andrew's arms. "For the love of God, Andrew! Your life is more important than these words, or whatever charms you think they possess. Their magic has already stolen your eyesight. Isn't that enough?" Andrew was looking at Durstan as if he had been sent by Almighty God, as a miracle.

The guttural sound of men disembarking from the longship travelled to them on the wind. Roy the Blacksmith was carrying an elderly Monk across his shoulder who was too ill to walk by himself, and at the same time, dragging a young child by the wrist. The boy was babbling strangely, as if he didn't know where he was. Durstan remembered him. He had been at the Monastery since the last Saint's day, and had been taken a week ago by the Devil who had entered the Church at the same time as he did. The boy had fallen to the ground, frothing at the mouth. His limbs were out of control, and the Abbot had rightly been afraid. Faisal ordered his immediate removal from the sanctified ground, with prayers said for protection. None of the Monks had wanted to touch the boy but they were equally afraid to disobey the Abbot, so it was done. Durstan had heard later that the child was to undergo trial by ordeal for consorting with the Devil. The boy had been locked inside one of the huts outside the enclosure. Everyone was afraid of the Devil's hands being placed upon them. It could happen at any time, but Roy refused to turn away from anyone who was in trouble, especially a child. The smell of fear was in the air. The Devil in the child had been unable to harm Roy, so maybe Faisal was right? A Blacksmith makes his own magic, and it's a powerful one that most cannot match.

The Abbot's bell was ringing dolefully from the wooden tower next to the Church. There would be little hope for the unfortunate Monk who was pulling the rope on Faisal's instruction. The Abbot would want it told later in tales around the fire, that his bell had rang out a warning for as long as possible. It would be another example of Christianity's intention to prevail against the non-believers. Durstan couldn't think of anything which would help the other Monk. It was too late. If he ran back to the bell tower to take him by force, it would mean death or worse for both of them. He could see the first of the Vikings approaching. Their features were lit by the flaming torches they carried.

"Andrew, for the love of God, move!" Durstan was afraid

for a moment that his friend was thinking of going back into the Church for the Saints' relics which were kept behind the altar in a jewelled chest, but Andrew's thoughts were elsewhere.

"Durstan, what about Osfric? We can't leave him! I thought he had gone with his friends, but he'll be the one ringing the bell. I saw him earlier, heading towards the tower."

Durstan could see the terror in Andrew's eyes. He desperately wanted to throw the older Monk over his shoulder and escape, but was hindered by the books' magic. It would equally break his friend's heart if they should be left behind. "There's no time to go back, Andrew. For the last time, come on!" He pushed him as hard as he could from behind using the weight of the books. Tears mingled with the cold rain streaming down Andrew's face, as he ran. The Monks slipped and slid across the vallum at the same time as the first Viking reached the Church. Andrew turned to grab the front of Durstan's robe in an attempt to make him go back. Durstan wrenched himself free. He pushed Andrew again, none too gently in front of him.

The older Monk muttered, as he ran through the low undergrowth in front of the trees. "May God protect him. I love that boy. I can't stand any more of the life here, and not without Osfric." Andrew stumbled on a tree root. Durstan saw him wince with pain when the muscle tore in his ankle. His heart went out to his friend, but they didn't have a choice. They had to run. He pushed Andrew again, as he prayed for forgiveness from whichever God might be listening.

Chapter 5
October, 794AD

Erik And His Sons

Erik shaded his eyes from the glare of the midday sun reflected in the whiteness of the snow. He looked fondly at his Wife who was trying to calm their eldest son, and stop him from disappearing across the glacier with his younger brother, Dag. Gudrid was holding onto Vidar's arm as tightly as she could, but clearly the boy was the stronger. Snorri, their youngest son, sat quietly on a flat rock outside the hut watching his Mother. He wanted to see what she would do when Vidar managed to wriggle free.

Erik shouted at the boys for being disobedient, and said more quietly to his Wife, "take no notice. They have Thor's fire in their blood, and want glory. It's their birthright. They're Vikings! You'll have to let them go soon, Gudrid, or they will go anyway. They can't help themselves. They belong to Odin and the Gods, not a woman." Erik put his arm around her shoulders. He marveled at how she had kept her figure when she had borne him three sons despite the whelp, Snorri, not being of the same mould as the older ones. Gudrid's blond hair was still magnificent. Erik thought of how it had fallen across his body last night when the children were asleep.

She looked up into his brown eyes, searching for what

he would be prepared to tell her. "Will you travel far this time, Husband?"

"No, only to the islands the traders call the Hebrides, off the coast of Dalriada. It's one of the places we went to earlier. I've heard that the Monks are keeping silver plate and jewels again in their wooden church. They make marks like runes, and call these spells writing, but the real magic is in the wooden casings covered in gold and jewels. I'm hoping it'll be much the same as we took from them last time, and the other Monastery further along the coast at Lindisfarne. If I'm right, there should be plenty for us to plunder and live on in the lean months." He crushed Gudrid's lips beneath his own. "Their winters are far gentler than here in Norway. We should think of settling there, and take the farmland from them. It would be a much easier place for you to live with Snorri, if the boy lasts the winter."

"I wish you wouldn't tempt the fates with your words, Erik, and that you didn't have to go again," Gudrid said, angrily. "Why are you never satisfied? The Gods will provide for us here at home, and they listen to what we say. You know that! I worry that you may not come back this time. What would happen to your sons, and me? I couldn't look after them, not without you. You've seen how they are. They need their Father, and a strong arm. Besides, Erik, I still need a man to warm me at night." She smiled persuasively until she saw the stubborn look on her Husband's face. "It was only yesterday that your sons of Odin tormented and killed the seal pup Snorri had tamed. I know it was only an animal, but they didn't take any notice when their brother begged them to stop. They laughed at his tears. How he cried, Erik! He's a child. Three summers, that's all. I know you have little patience with him but those two have no mercy in their hearts, even for a boy who is of their blood. Snorri was so angry, he hit them one after another, as hard as he could with his little fists. All it did was make them worse. They picked him up, tossing him between them as if he was a feather. I couldn't stop them," she said, sadly. "I had to run for one of the men to finish it."

Erik was laughing so hard tears came to his eyes. "Gudrid, Gudrid, my sons are behaving as they were raised to in the spirit of our Ancestors. How will they be able to stand in a shield wall if they are afraid to kill a child's pet, or tease a baby who annoys them? As for me raiding again, we're going to take whatever we want from a few Monks. Do you think they will be a match for my fighting skills or the other men, that our mighty Odin will let them cause me harm? What will they do? Threaten to strike me down with their Jesus God?" He punched the air with his fist. "I think not! This'll be another tale to be told in the halls of Valhalla when I sit at Odin's table, but I'll come back this time with a jewel for you, my love. I promise. A ruby, if I can find a good one. You will have to try to take it from me. I won't give it up easily." He pushed her arm playfully, imagining how he would make her beg for the jewel, and satisfy him afterwards.

"Erik, you make me so mad I could scream to Freya! You and that damned table where you'll be sitting drunk as only Viking men can be, womanizing and worse, I'll be bound. I know all about you seeking glory, to pay for your time feasting with Odin in the Otherworld, but I can't help worrying. That's then, this is now, and don't bring any more of those slave girls back with you. I won't tolerate it," she said, firmly.

"But you need the help of another woman. You were

glad of the last one, for a time. Don't you remember?" He said, mischievously.

Gudrid snapped. "Not with you in your bed, thank you, Husband. I can manage that task alone, as you well know."

Erik grinned. "Is that why I found her on the ice, with an axe in her back? I thought for a moment Snorri had finally become a Viking." She stared at him unsmiling, before they both laughed. "You are my only Viking Princess. Why would I prefer a skinny slave girl's thighs to yours? I desire a woman with meat on her bones, fire in her heart, and loins. The only value of a slave is to sell her onto the highest bidder when I have done with her. You know that, Wife. None of them compare to you, and never will."

Gudrid became serious again. "No, Erik, I don't. I'm asking you not to take any more girls. Just leave them be. I am your Wife."

"Enough! Don't raise your voice to me in that way again, woman. You are not behaving as a true Wife should. If there is any more talk like this, I shall have to roll you in the snow, and leave you outside my hut at night to toughen you up. It's not enough to have Freya's fertility. You need also to have strength to survive, for your sons and Husband. You have already given me a sickly son in Snorri, to look after. He gets the best food we have but still doesn't look nurtured." Erik shivered. "That faraway look in his eyes frightens me. I fear he is already halfway to the Gods, and won't have the opportunity to find glory, to follow behind with his name. They will take him back this winter, if we aren't careful. He doesn't run with the other boys. His strength isn't there. By the Gods, if I can save my son albeit the weakest one, by slaughtering a few miserable Monks then I shall. I'll raise him yet to be Viking, and not disgrace the Ancestors. Odin will smile on us too, if I can rid the earth of a few more of these so-called Christians, with their one God. Thor's hammer is mighty when it falls on those who challenge him. I've heard that they dare to say their God is greater than him." Erik touched the carved hammer which he wore around his neck as an amulet, to seek his God's protection.

"You'll have plenty to occupy you whilst I'm gone, Gudrid. I need a new sail for my ship, if I'm to go to sea again next spring. The old one has been torn to shreds by the wind, is barely there in places, and I'm disgraced by my Wife. The men laugh. They say she cares so little for me that she delays spinning and weaving cloth. That doesn't make a man feel as he should. You offend my manhood by your behavior. See if you can teach Snorri to help you while I'm away. He'll be able to stay with the women if he can manage that, and I can't make a son out of him."

Gudrid smiled at him. She was glad to have his arm around her waist, despite his harsh words. "Ssh, Erik. Please don't tempt the Gods again. They listen to us, and I can't help but worry when you are gone. The snows are worse this year. It's early for the river to be frozen. We'll have enough to eat in the dark months if we're careful, and save some of what we have," but Erik wasn't listening. She clung to his arm, and was comforted by the breadth of his shoulders. She knew in her heart that she was safe with Erik, despite his faults.

A cold breeze was blowing again, across the open space where they were standing. Erik and the older boys had cleared the snow away from the front of their timber hut, heaping it behind in large mounds. The thatch on the roof had been white for several weeks. The men from the other huts had done the same, to create a large area in the centre of the settlement where people could stand and talk, before the weather deteriorated and the blizzards forced them inside. Gudrid had seen it often enough, to know that the men would vomit there after a night of heavy drinking. The women would have to clear it away before the younger children walked through in the morning. Fights would break out in the communal area, if two men simply glanced at each other, and their boredom needed to be alleviated. There would be blood then to be washed away before it attracted the wolves.

Gudrid called out to Snorri, telling him to come inside the hut. She was afraid he would catch another chill. He had pulled the bear fur higher up his chin. It would be moist from his breath. He had said yesterday that he felt safe inside the cocoon it created. She had seen in his eyes that he hated Vidar and Dag. She had told him that the seal pup's Mother hadn't taken to it which sometimes happened, so the baby had been left on the ice for him to find. He was only a little boy, and had straightaway fallen in love with the pup. When she held him after his brothers had killed it, he whispered that he wished they were dead instead of the animal. Let them wait until Snorri was grown, they would find out then what it was like to suffer. He couldn't stop crying, and told her that all he could see was the seal dying, even though he knew that his Father wouldn't approve. Gudrid sensed that he was ready to cry again. She took him quickly inside the hut before her Husband had the opportunity to be angry with them both.

Erik looked around. Vidar and Dag had disappeared into the white landscape, despite his words. He would deal with them later, but not too harshly. All they were doing was practising at being men. He was proud to be able to tell anyone they were his sons. They had by themselves almost cut their Mother's cord. He was going to have to speak to Gudrid about them coming on the first raid next season. Erik's heart sank. She wouldn't be happy, but it had to be done. They might bring home something of value. Perhaps even kill a man, to cover themselves in glory? They would win arm rings if they could prove their bravery. Yes, it had to be done! He chuckled to himself at the thought of Erik and his sons. He nodded. It sounded right.

He was deep in thought, and didn't see the man approaching him. The snow hid the sound of his footsteps. "Erik, my Lord, why are you out here alone in the storm? Where is your woman, Gudrid? Why doesn't she stand by your side, or are you afraid of her tongue?" Harald clapped him hard on the back in friendship, and amusement. "It's time to do our duty by Odin before the weather worsens. My bones ache from the cold. I shall not be sorry it'll be the last outing this year, but by the Gods' will and with the wind at our back, we'll have a speedy return. We can let the women wait on us afterwards, and have enough to feast on until the thaw when we'll be doing men's work again." Harald laughed heartily. "It's a good life, my friend."

Gudrid came outside when she heard the men's voices. She had sworn an oath to Erik that she wouldn't cry but she was tired, and tears coursed down her cheeks when he walked away from her. She stood close to Snorri with a hand on his thin shoulder. He had followed her, hoping to say goodbye to his Father from the doorway. He didn't receive more than a quick glance from Erik. The other two boys were nowhere to be seen. They would be back when they were hungry, or to sleep if they had caught an animal and lit a fire hot enough to cook the meat.

Several of the other men had left their huts, creating a

hub of noise. Children were running and shouting, paying little heed to the weather. The colours in their clothes threaded in and out of the snow. Gudrid couldn't help but think that the Gods were trying to prevent the men from leaving. Snowflakes were falling thickly, too fast, but they would still go. There wasn't a choice, if all of them were to live through the winter. She knew that in her heart, despite her earlier protestations. It would be a late adventure for them, to help prevent boredom setting in. Erik had told her in a quieter moment that his new leather boots would keep out most of the water, so he was unlikely to suffer with foot rot this time. The longship had been well sealed against the sea, but there would still be many other dangers for them to overcome.

The sacrifice had been made to Odin last night, as required by the God. The cow's blood had stained the snow red before they ate its meat. The men were fortunate that the auspices had been with them, when the entrails were read with Erik's runes. There wasn't another cow to be spared if they had decided not to go, but Erik had said he was happy to carry on. As their leader, his decision was final. He had enough capable men to travel in one ship, twenty of them, with plenty of space for the oars and plunder when they took it.

Gudrid had overheard Ivar opposing the raid. She had listened through a crack in the timber wall when Erik and the men were gathered in the large hut yesterday morning. They had laughed at Ivar, and said his manhood was soft. How would he Father another son? He would end up being Odin's slave girl, if he was allowed into Valhalla.

Ivar had called them fools. He said there was little point in setting sail if the blizzard drove them home again with chilblains on their feet, ice burns on faces and backsides.

Erik had been disappointed by Ivar's half-heartedness. It was the first time he had shown a reluctance to raid. "You don't have to come, old man, if you're afraid. Or maybe your main concern now is the young Wife you've taken?"

Erik didn't know that Ivar had felt afraid, the last time they sailed. His arm was losing the strength of its youth. He had resisted the thought of standing in another shield wall, since it might well be his last. He wasn't ready to die even though he was a brave man, with thirteen arm rings to prove it. Odin wouldn't turn him away when the time came, but he couldn't help thinking now that a raid was for younger men. It was a pity his first Wife had died in childbirth, with the son she was carrying. If he had another son with Asta, the men would respect him again. A daughter could only spin and weave, but a boy was different. What couldn't he do?

Ivar had secretly been plucking white hairs from his beard for the past year. It was true that he could read the runes as well as the next man, but there had to be a time for a Father to give his sword to his son. He thought that Erik may have realised he was feeling this way, but he couldn't be sure. Ivar had sworn an oath to follow him. It had been made before age beckoned, and there was little choice. He wouldn't be free of it until Erik released him, or he died. At least in going now he would have the opportunity to die with a sword in his hand, and honour. To refuse to go with his Lord would disgrace his family name. He may well be outcast, and definitely not rewarded with any of the plunder. But there shouldn't be a shield wall this time. It wouldn't be necessary, to overcome a few defenceless Monks.

He raised his right arm, and clasped Erik's. "I was testing you, my friend, to see the strength of your resolve. Now that

I am sure you are as committed to this as I am, the pretense is over. Of course, I'm going with you. I said goodbye to Asta last night!" The men laughed good-naturedly at his response, and let him stand again in their midst.

Erik grabbed his shield and sword from the side of the hut, without looking back. The men followed him along the track which led to the sea. He could see the raven sails billowing impatiently in the distance, and felt a sense of pride that this was where he belonged. Erik was Viking.

Chapter 6
October, 794AD

Abbot Faisal's Bell

The Monks reached the trees beyond the undergrowth, without anyone following them. Durstan had thought for a long time that Andrew was well beyond reason so far as the manuscripts were concerned, but he hadn't realised the extent of his feelings for Osfric. It wasn't uncommon on Iona for Monks to love one another. The Abbot turned a blind eye to these relationships, if it suited him. Everyone knew it encouraged those involved to stay at the Monastery. It was different with a woman. She would want to have the man to herself, and not share him with God. Andrew and Osfric were well recognised as an asset to Faisal, and the Monastery. The books they created were beautiful. There was little advantage to the Abbot in disturbing the arrangement. Osfric had been brought to Iona from Northumbria. He was a fourth son, too emaciated to be of much use on the land, but as Andrew's apprentice scribe he had blossomed into a gifted youth. The older Monk had given a shell to him, the one he used to hold ink. Durstan realised now that it must have been a love token.

The Monks slowed their pace when they reached the dense undergrowth. "Watch your step, Andrew. We'll be safe enough here." The tone in Durstan's voice carried little conviction, as he waited for his friend to crawl under the nearest bush before he followed him. They slid themselves and the manuscripts as far back as they could under the leaves, and Durstan pulled the foliage across the gap.

It was difficult to hear anyone approaching in the heavy rain, but a Viking came along after several minutes. He searched nearby, and carried on past their hiding place. Durstan held one of his hands over Andrew's mouth to stop him from crying out, and a knife in the other. His face was grim. He had killed animals for the pot, was well seasoned in the knuckle fights which broke out among the younger Monks, but he hadn't used his knife on a man or thought to do so. He was afraid, but instinct told him that he would know how to fight if need be in the spirit of the Ancestors. The Celts had not failed to defend their homes and families in troubled times. Andrew would no doubt rely on prayer, and hold his wooden cross in front of him for protection. He had laid as close to Durstan as the undergrowth would allow. The younger Monk didn't have any illusions. The responsibility for their lives would be his, if they were discovered.

"I don't understand why these books mean so much to you. They are only animal skins, inscribed with that fluid you call ink, and which some poor soul on Mull has taken the trouble to steal from the gall of an oak tree," he said, in frustration, with his mouth close to Andrew's ear. "None of us truly know, if those strange markings you make on them are good spells!"

"You don't understand, Durstan, because you can't read very well. I've asked you to learn so that you can see what I see. I could have taught you by now!" Andrew said, patiently. "These books can be passed onto other Monks, to learn from our writing. The world needs education, Durstan, and us as teachers. We have good memories, but can't remember it all. So much of our tradition is being lost as the years go by. People should be told about the Saints' lives, their miracles, and our Lord's Gospels. Don't you want everyone to know more about Saint Columba? I know you are keen on him. If the unbelievers don't learn the stories from our books and the bible, they won't understand how to follow Christ properly or our Church. As it is, their heads are full of tales about their own Gods. There's little room in most of them for our blessed Jesus. Like you they think there's magic in the manuscripts because of the intricacies of the pages, and lettering you call markings. All that does is help us persuade them to look further, and ultimately read. It takes a long time to make a book, and to my knowledge, not so many have yet been written. We have to carry on, Durstan. I am worried for the safety of these manuscripts. The Vikings won't appreciate them. I'm not so foolish that I don't realise they will simply tear them apart to get at the jewels on the coverings, and burn the writing in their ignorance."

"I didn't understand, Andrew. I'm sorry," Durstan said, feeling ashamed. "I always thought the books were beautiful, but the natural world more so. I've lived most of my life in the fields, now the Blacksmith's forge working with fire. I thought that I would only find God there, not in the strange markings you make. If we survive tonight I want you to tell me more about your letters. I'm beginning to see the magic in them." He squeezed Andrew's arm before looking out through the leaves. The rain had stopped. The track they had followed earlier was lit by moonlight. He turned back to his friend, and said, "there doesn't seem to be anyone else about. I'll walk to the Monastery to make certain that all of them have gone. I'll come back for you later." Andrew didn't reply. He followed

Durstan instead out of the undergrowth, with leaves and twigs in his robe and hair.

Durstan carried the books carefully, as Andrew slipped and slid across the muddy earth. They had gone further than the other Monks, and didn't see anyone else until they approached the vallum. Several of the huts were in flames. The Vikings could be heard in the distance, leaving in a state of merriment. Durstan had learned a few Norse words from travellers visiting the Monastery, and it seemed that they were intending to carry on along the coast, to look for another place to land at dawn. They weren't afraid to sail at night. They knew how to use the stars, to navigate a path across the sea.

"Durstan, I'm going to find Osfric, and give thanks that we're safe. We need to pray for those souls who have been taken," Andrew said, making the sign of the cross with his fingers, to protect them. Durstan's heart ached. He hadn't said a word about leaving Osfric behind once they had found a place to hide. He seemed to be clinging to the hope that he would somehow be reunited with the boy, but if Osfric was still on Iona Durstan was afraid of what Andrew might find.

"Pray for us both, Andrew. I'll return your manuscripts to their rightful place, and see to Osfric. There's no need for you to search. We both know you're better at praying than I am," he said, trying to smile.

Andrew joined the procession of men and boys who were walking into the enclosure. His eyes were darting in all directions, but he couldn't see Osfric. The bell was no longer pealing, and Durstan asked those who had hidden closer to the buildings if they knew what had happened. Vikings had taken the holy objects from the Church, some of the cattle, and two of the Monks as slaves. The boys had dawdled behind the others in a misguided attempt to get a closer look at the Norsemen. They had been easily seized. Another was hacked down from behind, and disemboweled. One of the Monks who was hiding closeby had stood up to vomit, and was pulled down quickly by those nearest to him. Durstan's face was grim. It would have been better if the boys who had been taken had died, despite the prayers the Monks would send to God for their souls. Vikings were not known to treat their prisoners well.

The air was filled with fumes from the fire. Some of the older Monks were coughing. Others were pushing and jostling to get into the Church. They had been told often enough by the Abbot that the house of God was a safe place. God would protect them when they were inside it. They seemed to have forgotten that wasn't the case earlier. The Church had not suffered any structural damage. A stone building was harder to destroy. Abbot Faisal stood next to the entrance, guiding the Monks and oblates between the carved oak columns which adorned it. "All is well now, Brothers. Be with our Lord in peace in His house, to give thanks that the intruders have left. Let us raise our voices as one, and pray to our Holy Father in Heaven. His Angels are listening. They bear witness to the miracle that has saved us tonight. God has watched over our Monastery once more and we are blessed, my Brothers, truly blessed. Deo gratias," Faisal said, also making the sign of the cross.

Andrew was asking in a loud voice if any of the Monks had seen Osfric. Aelfric the Saxon standing next to Faisal was watching him. It was well known that Aelfric hated men who loved each other. Durstan dropped the manuscripts onto the stones near the church. He pulled Andrew quickly away from the centre of the crowd, and held him tightly by the arm. "Osfric didn't make it. Gregor saw him being taken across the sand to the longship." Andrew paled, and collapsed against his friend's chest. "God is with him, Andrew. You have to believe it! The Abbot is watching. You'll only confirm his suspicions about Osfric and you, if you react too strongly. That'll be of no help. Go into the Church to pray, and grieve later. Faisal's waiting to start the sermon. He wants the glory of standing before the altar tonight. All you can do for Osfric is look after yourself, so that you will still be here when he comes back. Your prayers will be carried on the wind by the Holy Spirit. Osfric will take comfort from them."

When Andrew pulled away from Durstan, there was a different light in his eyes. The Abbot smiled at him as he walked past. "Hurry along, Andrew. We shall have to send to Lindisfarne for another apprentice. We seem sadly to have mislaid Osfric tonight." The hatred in Andrew's eyes was apparent. Indecision too, but the warning look he received from Aelfric was enough for him to stumble after the others crying quietly. Faisal's attention turned to Durstan who was about to follow Andrew into the Church, with two of the younger Monks. They were the last to go inside.

"No, Brother Durstan. Wait! Our prayers are the most important, but I think you must do what you can out here. Your Blacksmith's magic will be more potent outside under the stars. We shall need a safe place to rest our heads for the few hours of sleep we have left tonight. Brothers Aedman and Peter, as you're here too and your prayers are unlikely to be as useful as your older Brothers, you'll stay with Durstan. I've sent Roy the Blacksmith to see to the worst of the fires, with the craftsmen who weren't taken. Do what you can tonight, Brothers, while the rest of our holy community gives thanks for our safe delivery. I'm overjoyed to see that the Heavenly Father has saved our Church again, and the stone crosses which even the strength of the Heathen can't move." The Abbot looked around the paved area with pride. "I regret I shall need to replace some of the people we have lost. We can't allow our distinguished position in the Church to be diminished. We need their hands to make goods for trade, and those objects for which we are renowned."

Aelfric looked smug as he followed Faisal into the Church. Durstan wanted to comfort Andrew. Faisal and he knew that. The young Monk was tired to the bone. The Abbot's need to hold them all in tight control, with deed and word constantly focused on his desires and whims, was suffocating. Faisal had no remorse, but it wouldn't serve any rightful purpose to give him reason for recriminations. A part of Durstan wanted to tighten his hands around the man's throat for what he had done. There was little consolation in the thought that he might find an opportunity later, to balance the loss of Osfric's life. It was an unchristian thought which didn't involve love or forgiveness, but after today's violence, the Monk was beyond caring about the impact of any unspoken words.

Aedmon and Peter, both twelve years of age, were standing patiently beside him. They hadn't been at the Monastery for long, and preferred to be outside in the fields as Durstan did. Osfric was a few years older than them, and had quickly become their friend. Durstan spoke kindly to them. "Come on. Let's see what we can do." They returned Andrew's manuscripts to the hut which he used as a scriptorium, and followed Durstan as he walked around the enclosure. He went into each of the huts first. The oblates had seen enough already to give them nightmares, without adding more.

There were sixty huts used for sleeping, weaving, and crafting. The large hall too, and kitchen to look inside. Durstan found Roy in the fifth hut he went into. The Blacksmith clapped the centre of the Monk's back with a giant paw of a hand. "I'm glad to see you are safe, lad. Mighty glad. Our world is in chaos. It's beyond me to understand what's happened here." He shook his head, sadly. "My friend, the wheelwright, is dead. All from trying to defend his Wife from their dirty hands. She had gone back to their hut to look for a missing child, and chanced upon a Norseman instead. She's been taken, Durstan. Her children left motherless but we're to be thankful that Faisal, our Holy Father, is alright. The rat-faced bastard! He left us without protection in the huts outside the enclosure. No wall or vallum, not enough of us to fight, and only enough men to serve his needs without spending coin on too many bellies." Roy spat on the ground. "Not though it would have made any difference. Those Norsemen are savages, not like any other fighting men I've come across. They don't understand mercy and compassion. I'm not a Christian man, Durstan, but may any of the Gods who are listening help that poor woman tonight. She will be lying bound in the bottom of their longship, and a more kind and gentle soul you couldn't hope to find."

Durstan saw the distress in Roy's eyes. He pulled the older man to him for comfort, and they stood staring silently into the darkness. "I'll be alright, lad. Don't worry. I've seen things as bad as this before, and worse. They didn't torch the grain barn. Their fires have all but burnt themselves out in this drizzle. More's the pity the heavier rain didn't carry on pelting for longer. It would have saved us a lot of bother, but it looks as if we can still use some of the huts for sleeping tonight. The large one's alright too. We can do proper repairs in the morning. The thatch on the church roof hasn't fared so well. No doubt Faisal will want it done first, once he knows about it. I suppose we have to be thankful that none of the Kings, or Lords from Dalriada and beyond, were on Iona visiting our sainted Abbot and their Ancestors' graves. The Vikings would have enjoyed taking any one of them for a nice ransom. We would have been looking at a lot more carnage than this, if their men had rallied."

They turned around quickly. Aedman, who had been waiting outside the hut with Peter, was shouting. "Durstan, quickly, over here in the bushes. Brother Breac isn't moving. There's blood on his head."

As Durstan pushed Aedman away from the body, he felt the boy shivering. "Get away from him! Go with Peter, to see to the animals. They need a feed. They'll have been as frightened as the rest of us. Go now. Help them!" The ashen faced oblates turned aside, and when Peter put his arm around Aedman's shoulders, Durstan looked properly at Breac. The Monk had arrived on Iona not long after him. They had become friends. Bile hit the back of Durstan's throat. He spat it onto the ground. "God grant you peace, my Brother, and carry your soul safely to Heaven," he said, touching the wooden cross around his neck. Breac's skull had been beaten. It was missing in part from behind. No man could have lived after such a blow. The Death Angel would have come quickly for him. Durstan recited the only blessing he could remember, closed Breac's staring eyes, and turned aside to retch.

Roy touched the Monk's hand. "May the Gods speed

your journey, Breac, my friend. And carry you safely to the Otherworld."

Durstan's mind and body felt numb. He glanced at Roy before leaving the hut. Breac was the final piece in the riddle. He couldn't deny it any longer. Changes had to be made, but for now, he needed to be alone with his thoughts. He looked inside the rest of the huts by himself and found Eochaid, the traveller who had arrived two days ago from Ireland, to talk politics with Faisal. He appeared to have put up a fight when one or more of the Vikings had come inside the hut, but judging by the stench, he would have been far too intoxicated to cause much damage to anyone. He had been well under the influence of the Abbot's special ale from the south. The brew was reserved for esteemed visitors, and Faisal himself. Eochaid had fared little better than Breac. His face and chest were thickly covered in blood. Durstan held his ear to Eochaid's mouth, but the breath had gone from him. He closed Eochaid's eyelids and muttered a brief prayer for his soul before leaving the hut.

Durstan shook his head to clear his thoughts, and remove the horror from his sight. He wondered which one of the Gods, had been responsible for this.

Chapter 7

The Goddess Speaks To Durstan

The prayers were finished quickly, and Abbot Faisal led the Monks from the Church. He was fortunate that he could go straightaway to his hut to sleep since it had not been damaged. Roy showed the others which of the huts were safe to use. His eyes were filled with sadness when he said goodnight, before walking across the enclosure to his bed.

Durstan was sitting near the fire in the Hall. Andrew had fallen into a restless sleep next to several other Monks who were lying on sheepskins. The Abbot, in a rare gesture of kindness, had given permission for them to lie down where they chose for the rest of the night but Durstan couldn't sleep. His thoughts were filled with Norsemen. During the months around Beltane and Lughnasa they were known for trading, and welcomed in many places. They had treasures not seen before in this part of the world, including the golden stone from the Baltic called amber. A strange warmth had crept inside Durstan when he held a fragment. He dropped it quickly, fearful of the spirit which must be living within its facets. The traveller who had shown it to him laughed at his temerity. The man had picked up the stone and tossed it easily into the air, before returning it to his pack. He told Durstan that the only thing he had to be afraid of was not getting a good price from the buyer he had in mind, but the Monk had not been convinced. It was difficult to place trust in the unknown, especially spirits who might be dangerous.

A moon-faced Monk eased his portly frame into the space next to Durstan. His eyes seemed too large for his face, and he was rubbing his left ear distractedly. "Paul, you are worried. What's wrong? We are safe now." Durstan said, looking at the newcomer with concern. "You haven't mislaid Faisal's coins, or handed them over to a Viking girl by mistake, have you?"

"Don't speak of such things, Brother. You know how the Abbot is about his money chest." Paul looked around the hut, and said in a low voice. "For your information alone, Durstan, I have it buried in a safe place. Only Faisal and I know where that is, so don't ask me anymore. I can't tell you." Paul wiped his brow, but the sweat continued to accumulate.

"Everyone is asleep, Paul, except us. I was having blasphemous thoughts of my own."

"I warrant yours were not as bad as mine, Durstan. I feel as if I've come back from the dead. The gulls stopped screaming this morning, as if they knew then what God had put in the wyrd for us. I can't bear the sight of blood, but that seems to be all the heathens are about. These times are sent to test our faith. If only we could see the Christian God or touch his hand it would be easier, but all we have is what Faisal tells us. Like you, Durstan, I worshipped the Old Ones before Rome came to take over the protection of our souls. It's hard to completely abandon that path. I'll be honest with you, at times like this, I don't really understand what the new faith is all about. Maybe that's why we have the good Abbot to guide us, and Andrew's books for teaching if we can read their magic? Perhaps too, with Faisal leading our souls and concentrating on making money, that's why most of us here are so confused?" Paul looked at Durstan, and smiled. "But then is everything so bad? We are still alive tonight, you and I, before this wonderful fire. The Old Gods, or the Christian God, may yet be smiling on us."

Durstan sighed, heavily. "I don't know, Paul. I've been doing my utmost today in Christ's name to forgive the Norsemen for their sins, but I can't do it! Things don't seem any different now to how they were under the Old Gods, and yet Christianity is supposed to be better. The answer to all our prayers. What of the Abbot's promise of riches on earth and in Heaven, if we should be good and faithful servants of our Lord God? The only riches I've seen so far have gone to Faisal!" Durstan hesitated. "If I tell you something, you must swear on the Holy Gospels or one of the old oaths if you like, that you won't pass it on to another soul."

Paul nodded and touched his crucifix, to acknowledge that he accepted the oath. He liked to know other people's secrets, and even though this was Durstan, the information might be useful later. Passing on something which had been hidden had saved his skin from Aelfric the Saxon's lash on more than one occasion.

"The Goddess Brigid came to me in a dream, two nights ago, Paul. She told me in a voice as clear as the crystal water of the spring that I would leave Iona shortly, and I wouldn't find love in pursuing another man's God. She was beautiful, dressed in a gold and blue robe, with flowing white hair. I've never seen anything like it before. I think it must surely have been a portent. I could almost touch her in my dream. I'll not forget the scent of her skin. It was like the violet, the delicate flower you find beside the stream, at Beltane."

Paul was shocked. "I knew you had doubts about our faith, Brother. Who doesn't, given the way it is here? But I didn't realise it had gone so far. You say you have conversed with the Goddess?" He spoke, firmly. "Durstan, you must keep these dangerous thoughts to yourself. Faisal mustn't find out. He has spies everywhere who would sell your secret for an extra portion of meat. Life is hard enough without being punished for a few words said in the wrong way. Bones don't mend so quickly once they're broken. There are Monks here who, unlike Roy, enjoy those tasks when Faisal sets them. The Abbot said we should believe that today is part of God's plan. We should give thanks that the Father sent Jesus, his Son, to suffer for us. For your own sake, my friend, think instead about that lesson." Paul could see the confusion in Durstan's eyes. "If it's any comfort to you, Brother, I'm finding it hard myself to come to terms with the death and destruction today. Have you spoken to anyone else about these sacrilegious thoughts?"

"I've talked to my anam cara, Andrew. What I tell him won't be passed any further. I understand the need for caution, Paul. Even thought can be dangerous." Durstan stretched out his long legs towards the fire, searching for the warmth which was left in the embers. His Mother's face came to mind. He hadn't seen her since he was a boy, and he could still remember the day his Father brought him to the Monastery. She had pleaded and begged him not to take her son. Durstan felt a sharp pain in his chest which he knew from Athdar, the healing Monk, was the place where his heart lived. Athdar told him that this was where all of us feel emotion, most strongly, love and pain.

Durstan's heart ached even more when Ailan came to mind, and he struggled to find the words. "After I was brought here, Paul, I didn't see my Mother again. I was told by a fisherman a few years later that she had died. My Mother, late in life, had given my Father two more babes after me. Neither had lived long enough to take a breath. I've asked our Holy Father many times in prayer why that should have been the case. She was a kind, gentle, woman and He hasn't answered me in any way that I can understand. There's only confusion here, Paul. Not answers, and now, today's violence." Durstan paused.

"The Christian God hasn't spoken to me in the way the Goddess does in dreams, or when I feel the rain and sun on my face. I thought He might talk to me then, if as the bible says, He made all of creation. That's the place I expected to find Him, not inside our cold church, with incense and chanting. I've started to question whether being unable to believe in only one God might be connected to Faisal, and the way he administers religion. What we are taught here goes against nature in so many ways. What the Druids told our Ancestors they should believe. How can it be evil to speak kind words, smile, and love?"

Paul didn't reply. He hadn't realised that Durstan's doubts ran so deep within him. He had heard rumours of his friendship with Druid Brionach, but thought that was all they were. Perhaps he had been unwise in giving his oath, not to inform the Abbot of this confession? Durstan didn't notice how frightened the older Monk had become. Although Paul didn't care for Faisal, he was obliged to work closely with him as his Almoner. At more than fifty years of age, he didn't want to risk losing the softer privileges he had by condoning a blasphemy, if this should later come to light. Paul's heart was torn. He genuinely liked and respected the younger Monk, for his kindness and compassion, as did most of those on Iona.

Durstan stared at the flames, and shivered. His Mother had worshipped the Gods of earth, water, and sky. Sometimes in the half-light he caught a glimpse of how he imagined they might be. Once or twice he had felt a light touch on his face which might have been a spirit from the Otherworld. It could only be her. He wanted so much to believe that she was trying in the old way to watch over him, reach out to his soul. He hadn't told anyone else about this. He would be flogged close to death if the Abbot should hear a single word of it. Ailan was the only one in whom he could easily have confided, but she was gone. Andrew would be unlikely to understand, and might be scornful. He could be when he felt unsure about something. Durstan had been tempted recently to talk more to Roy. He sensed that he could trust the Blacksmith. He was having misgivings now about telling Paul his innermost thoughts. It had happened in a weaker moment, but what was done was done. He would have to trust the other Monk's integrity, not to divulge his private thoughts to others.

What was love anyway? A child's early memory, and the feelings he had for Ailan? His Mother might have felt love for his Father, whatever the man's faults might have been. It certainly wasn't the misnomered love stolen by some of the Monks from reluctant oblates, after nocturnes in the stillness of night. Durstan was angry when he saw the suffering in the boys' eyes. A hunger in the belly could be endured in a much different way, to the tearing apart of a boy's mind. All this was akin to looking at life through one of the dark stones in the grass. He knew so little about it. Andrew's relationship with Osfric must have come from love. He had seen them playing tag together on the sand, when no one else was there. They were laughing, and would often sit quietly together, at peace with their books. Andrew said that Osfric and he had stared upwards at the last full moon. The younger Monk insisted then that he had seen his fate. Andrew refused to believe him, and offered his cheek for a kiss instead of a lie. There was no going back now, to right the wrong.

Faisal said that God loved everyone, whatever their faults. People weren't perfect, but this served only as an excuse for the wrongdoing he condoned. Durstan hadn't been able to move beyond the look in the boys' eyes. Against Andrew's advice he had tried to persuade the Abbot to intervene. Faisal had turned a blind eye, and his favourite Monks continued with it. Durstan had noticed that the Abbot kept the men happy who were closest to him, and the oblates were not in a position to complain. As Andrew had feared, Durstan found his life more difficult in a number of ways, after he had tried to help them.

He looked up from the flames, with a start. His thoughts were wandering too far. "You have the most difficult job of all, Paul, as keeper of the Abbot's coins. It's often puzzled me why you accepted such an unholy job?"

"I thought I would have had many privileges when I took on Malcolm's role. As you can see, I'm fond of my stomach." Paul grinned. "Nothing else would have persuaded me to be in such close proximity to that man. I've been useful to him. I speak more languages than most, interpret conversations when visitors arrive, and because of it I've become a party to his political secrets." Paul lowered his voice, to barely a whisper. "I've discovered how Faisal manipulated his position in Rome, and succeeded in becoming a rich man. He wants canonisation too, as you've probably realised, and in his own mind he's already a Saint." He sighed. "I made a mistake, one day when I was at a low point. I talked openly to Malcolm. I thought the confidence between us wouldn't be betrayed. How was I to know that my oldest friend would unburden my words to Faisal himself, during his deathbed ramblings? My predecessor passed on more to me than keys, the night he took his last breath. I learned the hard way, Durstan, that there would be less privilege than I thought. Also, what I might expect if I stepped out of line again. Never forget that Faisal holds those nearest to him the closest. I'm taking a risk showing you this, but I trust you." Paul bent over, and lifted the hem of his robe. Both of his legs were streaked white with scars.

"I'm sorry, Durstan. I shouldn't have burdened you with this, but sometimes the evil here gets to me. I struggle when I see the ardent belief in younger men's eyes, or find someone like you who is trying to make sense of the upturned world in which we are living. Don't let what you have experienced on Iona cause you to give up! There are true followers of Christ. Saint John is to be trusted. He was speaking the truth, not Faisal's establishment apostles. Travellers say that the Church we have here from over the seas is about greed and wealth, that it's corrupt. The more I've seen, the more I can believe it. Some say that Faisal's plan is to become more powerful than any of the Lords of these islands. He inspires loyalty from fear and violence. He only has the Abbot's role through inheritance from his Father, not a religious conviction of love, kindness or compassion. He's little better than a Viking in that respect, albeit he can hide behind the Church with his wrongdoing." Paul dropped the robe onto his legs. "I would never have come here, Durstan, had I known the extent of it. Nevertheless I was fortunate, that the scars were all it was. It could have been much worse, and Faisal needs me, so I have survived. Some of our other non-conformist brothers have simply disappeared on spurious errands, and not returned. All this showed me without a doubt, the truth of the man we have leading our holy community. I've wanted with all my heart to get away from here. I've had lots of ideas over the years, but it always came back to where could I go? So in answer to your question, Durstan, my destiny is inextricably bound to the Abbot's. I pray daily to our Lord for protection, and if I don't think too much about it, life isn't so bad here when there's enough to eat."

Paul smiled, weakly. "As you can see, I'm the same as you. I do still have doubts. If our Christian God was so good and great, why did He let this happen to me? Why did He let such a Devil as Faisal be our Abbot? If what we are told is true, he's become the antithesis to Saint Columba, the difference between dark and light. We live in savage times, Durstan. I wonder if there will ever again be a season when we have the wind gently on our backs? I think it may not happen in my lifetime."

Chapter 8

After The Viking Raid

Durstan couldn't hide how shocked he felt. Paul was one of the gentlest Monks on Iona. His shorn, white, hair more tonsure than not was a common sight beside any troubled soul he could find. "Paul, if I wasn't already leaving here, this would have convinced me. You have no need to ask me this, Brother. I will keep your secret, even from Andrew if you wish me to. I understand now why you haven't washed with the rest of us in the stream or the sea, but looked for a private place." He embraced Paul. "I'm truly sorry, especially when I have been unexpectedly blessed. Faisal is talking of letting me go with Andrew, to the Monastery on Mull. He wants the heathen practises there stamped out. He's relying on the spiritual link between Andrew and I, strengthened as it is by the Blacksmith's magic he assumes I possess. We're to support each other, as missionaries."

Durstan's laugh was hollow. "My own view of the situation is a little different. It'll give the Abbot a convenient excuse to be rid of us both. I know that he's aware of my feelings about certain matters, and Andrew won't be able to continue much longer with the manuscripts. I'm afraid for him, Paul. He's becoming as much use to our Father as a dead fish in the sea. Faisal says Roy can easily train another to work alongside him as I do, but I am still to return here once Andrew's sight has gone. He seems to think that my anam cara should stay on Mull, but what he'll do there I don't know."

"I'll pray for you both, Durstan. Faith in the Christian God will help you. Andrew's belief is strong. Let him guide you on the mainland. Listen to his words. I'll pray too that your faith may in time be fully restored for the sake of your own soul. A man who doesn't have a focus is adrift in the ocean, without hope of sighting the horizon. I do have a few niggling doubts, but am reasonably certain that the Christ God is the true one. I can find peace here in how I feel when I'm inside the Church. Maybe this is your true destiny, Brother? Without your doubts you would still be too helpful to the Abbot at Roy's furnace, and not have reason to leave our beautiful island.

Durstan smiled. "I'll take your advice, Paul. Andrew will be the voice of my conscience, and I will pray for better days."

"Faisal has always been the same, Durstan. When I travelled from Ireland with him to Iona all those years ago, he insisted on bringing that damned bell. It's a useless piece of metal if ever I saw one. I remembered the sailors complaining about it before we left, and they were right. The bell was so heavy it nearly sank our ship, but the Abbot was adamant it couldn't be left behind. It was the prestige he wanted even then. We all knew what he was thinking. He would have the only Monastery in the islands which had its own bell. Look at how it's taken another life today! Some say the wildness of the bell's ring is a powerful magic, even a curse. I am afraid when I hear it. The Devil takes another life when it clangs. The unholy sound is a way of summoning evil. I don't fancy Osfric's chances with the Norsemen tonight. God help him. I hope his soul is spared." Paul made the sign of a cross, and spat superstitiously into the fire for good measure. "The boy will have gone already from the Abbot's thoughts. It won't be told in the tales around the fire that a young man lost his life, or was taken as a slave because he had to stay behind to pull Faisal's damned rope. He will have the glory!"

"Osfric may still survive, Paul. He has youth on his side, and will fetch a good price in the marketplace. His religious fervour isn't strong enough to deter the buyer of an attractive boy. As harsh as it is, there's nothing we can do to help him, except pray for his soul."

Paul smirked. "We must give thanks that the Abbot's money wasn't lost. We would surely have felt the pain of his sorrow in less food, with the excuse that extra fasting is good for our souls. I expect Rome will send him another altar cross and chalice so he's barely at a loss because of today's events. I've seen him frown sometimes at the Ancestors' cross in front of the church. Although I've never been one for shiny jewels, I love the craftsman's carving on the stone. I'm comforted by the solidity of a cross that's still standing after so many years. It was likely done by Columba's mason. It gives me hope that there may one day be better times than these. We're fortunate that the stone is too heavy for a Viking to put under his arm, or it would have gone the way of Osfric. I expect we can say the same of Faisal's bell." Paul yawned, and scratched his stomach.

"I'm sorry, Paul, I've kept you from your bed. There isn't many hours left of the night, but lie down now and try to get some sleep. There'll be plenty to do once it's light. Every moment with your eyes closed will count."

The Monk grinned mischievously, as his spirit rose proudly from old bones. "You know, Durstan, there's a time when the old don't sleep so much because we fear we may not wake up. When the eternal darkness does draw near, I'll be immersed in its power for a long time, but it isn't here yet. For now I don't need so much sleep, and I'm glad we've talked. I can see you are to be trusted, my young friend."

Durstan smiled. "Faisal was talking about Andrew and I leaving as soon as possible, but he'll probably expect me now to help Roy with the repairs before I go." He kissed Paul gently on his forehead." May God protect you, Brother, in these precarious times."

Paul's eyes glinted in the firelight. "Be careful, Durstan. Faisal has a long arm, and can reach out to you. Mull is not so far from here. He'll think you'll fill his coffers with more coins from Christian converts, and for that reason alone, will be interested in what you do. He will get to hear of your work whatever the outcome, so be wary. All will be well as long as Andrew and you are finding money for him. Loyalty to him travels between here, the mainland, and more distant Monasteries. The Monks there believe it's part of being a true Christian, to honour their Father Abbot in all he does and says, because he stands on earth as God's right hand. Faisal has become Lord to many that you may yet know nothing of. His power stretches far across the water. He expects all of his Christian converts to pay for the privilege of his approval, and which they happily do for the promise of salvation when they die." Paul spat again into the fire, causing the flames to rise.

"Faisal is desperate for sainthood, Durstan. He needs as many converts as he can get to plead a case to Rome. You'll help him with the gifts of money and goods along the way, but be vigilant, as there will be other dangers. The mainland is a lawless place. Outlaws hide in the forest, and the further south you go, men are fighting for land. Now the Vikings are here, we are all truly in God's hands. Thank the Lord the women didn't come to Iona today because of the heavy seas. If they had met the Norsemen on the beach, I don't want to think about what might have happened."

Paul paused. He had seen the light of happiness in Durstan, earlier in the year. "Your Ailan will be safe tonight. She's a good woman, that one. Maybe you'll talk again when you are on Mull?" Paul knew from Andrew that Durstan had shared Beltane with her. Durstan threw another log quickly onto the fire, and although Paul sensed his embarrassment, he was still curious. "I haven't seen Ailan for a while. I wondered why she hadn't been to Iona since Beltane?"

Durstan sighed. He had already told Paul his secret about the Goddess Brigid. There was no reason not to tell him the rest. "You know as much as I do about her not being here. I tried asking the other women but was met with stony faces, apart from one girl who laughed at me. These women look after their own in times of trouble so wouldn't tell me anything. I am ashamed to say that I was afraid of drawing attention to myself in being persistent. Faisal would have found out. Once Beltane is over we are expected to act as if it didn't happen and, in answer to your question, Mull may as well be as far away as Asia. I caught that surly woman, the one they call Oonagh, watching me. Her eyes were boring into my face, so I stopped the questions in mid-flow. It was simply hopeless. None of the Monks had any news, and the fishermen I asked denied knowledge of her. Faisal wouldn't have given me permission to go to Mull to search for myself, if I had asked. All that I could do was hope that Ailan would come back to explain, and now, that I may see her on the mainland."

Durstan rubbed his face, and said, sadly, "I've had many a sleepless night since I last saw her, Paul, but was forced to let her go. I've prayed every day to God, the Old Gods too, that she's safe. I guess you are going to tell me now that if the Christian God wanted me to know what had happened to her, I would have been given the answer."

"All I can tell you, Durstan, is what I believe. If God intends for you to see Ailan again, then you will." Paul squeezed his hand. "At least you'll be better fed away from here, and not need to fast on the pretext that starving helps us keep our faith. There'll be plenty of meat on the other side of the water. I hear the Lord's men hunt wild boar and deer in the forest." A glint appeared in Paul's eye at the mention of food. "I've not tasted meat like it since leaving Ireland." He patted his belly lovingly. "Faisal is truly a hard taskmaster in the way he keeps this Monastery. We're far away from Rome, and I suspect he doesn't always feel entirely safe. Not surprisingly, he has enemies. Some of them are powerful enough to challenge him. As for us poor Monks, in return for food and a place to live, we've had to bargain with the Gods and choose the Christian one as our protector. I'd bet a coin of anyone's money that Faisal believes our Lord God, and Rome, are the strongest of all so the ones to follow."

"I expect you're right, Paul, but it'll be good to see my sister again. I haven't seen Mora since I was a boy. I hear she has a son, Eoghan."

"That's excellent news, Durstan! I haven't seen anyone for years whom I could call family or friend from my youth. I don't know if any of them are still alive. I'm afraid my lot is linked to Faisal, and his confounded treasure chest. I have visions of dying with it lovingly in my arms, while a Norseman is chopping off my hands to get at the coins." He grinned. "What do you think, Durstan? Will they will come back again?"

"I fear the answer to your question is yes. Perhaps Faisal should consider exchanging the Monastery for the safety of Mull? We'd all be better placed under the protection of Lord Duncan's men. Apart from Aelfric the Saxon and a couple of others, our Monks don't know how to fight. They're mostly too young or old, and we only have a few craftsmen outside the enclosure who could take up arms. That prevented them from defending us today. If the Vikings should come later with more ships to the mainland, we would at least have an opportunity to move further inland, to get away from them. I'm afraid now that Faisal will think of giving us weapons to fight here on Iona."

"That might not be so foolish a thought, Durstan, but I doubt the Abbot will agree to cross the water to escape the intruders. He has too good a situation here to do that. There's not a large monastic community on Mull, and we wouldn't have enough huts if we were to go there. Don't forget too, that your plan would involve a delegation of the Abbot's power to Lord Duncan. Iona is Faisal's best chance of continuing to fill his coffers, also to stay in the running for canonisation. There are places where an Abbot will seek counsel from his Monks before making an important decision, and that does seem to me to be the better way, but we both know it won't happen here."

"More huts could soon be built. I've made a few, Paul. It's not such a difficult task. I still think that we would be much safer on Mull than living in isolation with an enclosure of non-fighting men, and Monastery boys who don't know how to defend themselves. The carpenters, wheelwrights, and other craftsmen are also peaceful men at heart."

"It's not me you have to persuade, Durstan. The problem is Faisal. He won't leave Iona. Self interest and arrogance will stop him. If he can continue as he has been doing he will rise further in importance within the Church. He wants that too badly. Our holy island is known far and wide for its Christian magic, and he loves being the Abbot." Paul pulled his cloak around his shoulders. An icy wind was blowing through a crack in the wall, and the peat fire had died down.

Durstan yawned. "I'm going to get some sleep, Paul. There'll be a lot to do in a couple of hours. Faisal will see to that." He moved wearily away from the fire to the nearest pile of skins, and laid down. The fur under his body warmed quickly. He dragged a pelt over himself for extra warmth, almost asleep as he did so. He stayed in the same position until Faisal's bell rang again.

Chapter 9

Roy The Blacksmith's Story

The sun was in their eyes as they mended the thatch on the kitchen hut, but neither Roy nor Durstan objected to it being there. It was pleasant to feel the warmth on their skin instead of trying to work in the rain. The enclosure was a bustle of activity. Monks hurried about their duties, while Faisal controlled what was happening from inside the Church. The damage caused by the storm and the raid had almost been rectified. Sweat ran in rivulets down Roy's cheeks. Despite the onset of autumn, a few marauding insects continued to be a nuisance in the midday heat. It was impossible to swat them and work at the same time.

Roy began to climb down the flimsy wooden ladder. He called across to Durstan who was standing nearby on another. "It's about time for ale and food, lad." He grinned. "At least there's some advantages, to working with me. You have the Abbot's dispensation to eat when you need to, not be told when you should be hungry, or have to join the starving souls in the refectory. That has to be worth all the coins in Faisal's coffers, and a few more besides." Roy threw a leather bucket of stream water over his head, letting the cool liquid run down him in rivulets. "That's better! I left the ale over there in the shade," he said, walking towards it.

Durstan was grateful to follow him. It had been a long morning after a short, and sleepless, night. His muscles ached for rest. He swallowed the first draught of ale with pleasure, and bit into the dry crust Roy had passed to him. The Blacksmith was cutting large pieces of meat from the haunch which he had covered with leaves. He wiped the animal fat from the knife at his belt when he had finished. "The carpenter's wife is a good cook. There's magic in her fingers when she works the meat on the fire. That man is well and truly blessed! I would marry her myself if she was free, if only to know I could always have this along with her nightly comforts. It's not nearly so tasty when one of the other women does it, but then no woman could ever match the alchemy of metal and fire. What do you say, Durstan? Therein lies the purity of love!"

Roy lapsed into silence while he chewed his meat, and Durstan let his curiosity get the better of him. He hadn't felt comfortable asking the older man before now, but today they were as equals. Men enjoying their food when they had worked hard for it. "I understand the craft, Roy. First and foremost, you follow the magic of the Blacksmith, but why didn't you marry away from here? I can see you with a wife and family in a different life." Roy's face darkened, and Durstan was afraid that he had overstepped the bounds of friendship. Men had their secrets which were not to be shared with others, except their conscience and the Gods.

Roy hesitated. "Perhaps you're right, Durstan? I know you well enough by now. I'll tell you more about me. My real name is Farnell." A sadness had entered his eyes. "I haven't said it for what must now be four years. It was my Father's name and Father's before him. I come from further south on the mainland." He stared at Durstan. "I was an outlaw."

Durstan looked at him in astonishment. "You, Roy!

Farnell! You are one of the most straight standing men I know. How could you have been outcast?"

Roy cleared his throat. "Thank you for your confidence, lad, but you may not feel the same when you hear my story. I was married, and accused of killing my wife. May Woden help me! I did love that woman. I thought my world had ended when she was taken." Durstan heard the pain in the depths of Roy's voice. "The Lord's favourite man murdered her when she refused him. It was easier to blame me, the husband, than lose a Lord's best man to trial by ordeal. I escaped before they could put me through it. I'd seen it done inside the Church. I knew my hand would blister in three days when they unwrapped the cloth. How could it not do that if I was made to grasp red hot iron, and walk with it for ten paces? Any magic I have is in my hands, Durstan. Although I know many believe in these trials, I had to protect it.

My family helped me leave. They had nothing to give me to live on, apart from a little food and ale. When that was gone, I had to make do as best as I could. After a time I came upon a woman in the forest, Merryn." Roy spoke softly. "I can see her now, a wisp of a girl. I thought her one of the fae to begin with. There was so little of her. She was an outlaw too, afraid of her own shadow. I had to fight her to begin with, to make her understand I wouldn't do her any harm." Roy laughed. "And for all the trouble I took she gave me a hefty whack with a tree branch across my head. The ache lasted for days and that was before she bit and scratched my arms and face to pieces."

He paused, as he remembered. "My poor, Merryn. She was frightened, always fearing the worst. She didn't have any protection from a wild animal or stray outlaw like me who would likely slit her throat to steal the clothes from her back, or so she thought. She had been wandering alone for days without food, and had been forced to leave her babe behind. It was all because the Lord's Lady said she had looked at her in a strange way. A curse was in her eyes. Merryn would have to go, to break the spell. He was mostly a good Lord and used to his wife's superstitions, so they didn't stone her for long. She still bore the bruises of those which hit their mark." Roy's voice turned to anger. "There was no good in what they did that day, Durstan. Merryn was a beautiful heart, and the Lord's Lady must have been jealous. I loved her then. I managed to forget my wife in the heat of our union. It didn't happen until she grew to trust me, and between us we were eking out an existence in a cave we had found deep inside the trees.

At least after that we had each other to hold onto at night, when memories and the sounds of the forest became too much to bear. She cried a lot at first for the child. I couldn't help her, only hold her close to me. It used to tear my heart when I heard her. We talked about going back to explain, even take the boy, but we both knew it was hopeless and eventually our thoughts turned to finding another Lord. There was only a slim chance of it happening, but we had to have some hope. I thought then that the feeling of helplessness was the worst that could happen, until I found her one afternoon on the floor of the cave almost outside her senses. She was lying on the pile of twigs she had been collecting. She could barely speak. Something had bitten her. One of those wretched river flies, no doubt. An engorged, purple swelling was on her hand. They were quick, those flies, and she had tried to be quicker. The poison needed to come out before it took hold. She whispered to me as I held her afterwards. Without a knife, as we only had the one, Merryn had sunk her teeth into the bite and spat the grey pus into the embers of the fire. She had fallen to her knees then onto her back, but some of it was still in her system. She hadn't been quick enough to stop the flow through her veins.

Merryn laid there waiting for me to return with the kill. Her hair was singed, and her other hand burned black from where she had fallen into the fire." Tears were streaming down Roy's face. "The fortunate ones in this life, Durstan, don't have to live as we did but we all have to eat. I had to leave her sometimes to hunt further afield. I was always back as soon as I could be, and we needed the water too, so one of us had to go to the river. It was the only place we could drink. Our stomachs were rumbling for food all the time. That Devil fly must have been more virulent than the others. My Merryn wasn't strong enough to fight it. She lasted the rest of the day, and at the edge of the night, the Goddess came for her.

I asked Brigid over and over again to take me too. I was stunned, shocked I suppose, to be left alone again. I remember staring at the deer I had killed. Its glazed eyes stared back into mine. I went at it in a frenzy. I threw the carcass onto the earth floor before sinking my knife into its soft underbelly to skin the flesh, and damn me, if the animal hadn't been with calf. I had killed another Mother. I had a second death on my bloodied hands. I remember pushing Merryn roughly away from the fire with my foot. I was too tired to lift her. There was nothing I could do to help her. I thought to take the body outside once the fire had rekindled, and the meat was baking on the stones. I knew I had to eat before I did anything else. Both of us had been without food for a few days. It didn't matter anyway. The wolves would have Merryn before morning."

Roy paused. "Truth be told, lad, I felt suffocated being

near her. My nostrils were choked, but there was nowhere else to go. It was freezing outside. It would have been a certain death if I had ventured out. Nights are always colder when you are alone and hungry. I sat on the floor after I had taken a few bites of meat, looking for what comfort I could find in her proximity, but she was long cold. I had wild thoughts of searching the forest for a replacement. It's bleak at night in a dank cave without a woman, or anyone's words to warm you. I could still remember the gnawing in my gut before Merryn came along. I knew her bracelets would fetch a good price at market but I couldn't take them from her. They belonged to her Husband, and were all she had in exchange for the son she had left behind."

A solitary tear trickled down Roy's face and he let it run down to his chin. "Life without a Lord, Durstan. Who would have it? It's hopeless. There's not often any way back once you are there. No one will risk helping you. Even the new Christian Church with all its promises turns its back on the outcasts. Huh! Unless of course you can hold yourself up as a proper hermit. Someone who leaves this sorry world voluntarily, to seek God in the wild. How many of those exist in truth, other than how circumstance has made them? Not so many, I'll be bound. Most of them are insane men sent further into madness by how they are forced, or have chosen to live.

I left the cave at first light. I couldn't bear to be there without her, and I wandered aimlessly. One of your lot, a kindly Monk, sent me away when I came across him at the edge of the forest asking for food and drink. I can still hear his shouts as he came at me with a stick. Merryn was right to stay with what she knew! She didn't have time for your Christian God. She used to say that the Old Gods had been with us all our lives, so why change direction? I can see now that it's people like Faisal, and the Church, who are causing all the trouble in the world. You only have to look at how things are here. The Old Ones would bring food to our hearths when we treated them properly, made an offering. It's the natural order of things. The Lady who took against Merryn had joined with your Christ, and look at the good which came from that!

It's funny though how life turns about. It was another Monk, Lyall, who found me three summers ago wandering on Mull. This one called me Roy when I couldn't speak properly because of a fever, but the change didn't matter. My soul knows who I am. I hadn't eaten or drank for as long as I could remember, and Lyall half carried me to a cave by the water where he was living. He fed and washed me in the tradition of Celtic hospitality. He said later that I slept for days until my mind cleared, but it was then that the questions began. I didn't tell him everything. I didn't see the need. Eventually, it came to Faisal's attention that I was a Blacksmith, in good health by this time, and without a Lord. He seized the opportunity and I, in my black mood, agreed to come to Iona to serve him. I had nowhere else to go. It was a chance to work again with the flames, use the spells in my hands. How I had missed that! Once you've found your own true magic, Durstan, there's no turning away from it for the world to be right. One master is much the same as another, but when I'm working as a Blacksmith, I'm set free in another place to this.

Faisal did his best at the beginning to convert me to Christ, before he realized that I was too unlikely a follower. I thought we had reached an uneasy peace when he saw I could make a wealth of goods for him to trade, but you know Faisal. He doesn't give up. And now… I hate him.

I can't abide his interference. He insists my tools have to be blessed in church every season. There's no need for it, but the weasel is adamant that if I want to live behind the enclosure with the craftsmen, I have to accept his ruling. He says that Iona is his island. I detest him but a man needs a master for protection, even though I believe these Vikings may be beyond even his powerful hands. I will never accept his God as mine. It's enough that he's trying to control the magic I have in my hands on the assumption that his is the stronger."

Roy leaned over the leaves to cut another wedge of meat from the bone. "On a good day I can accept that it's the best compromise we will reach, and the blessing is I'm more comfortable being with the craftsmen than living as a Monk. They are the best people for me, Durstan. Craftsmen celebrating life in all its seasons. It's better than being outlaw but I still miss her, my Merryn. How it is between a man and a woman who love.

Life can trick and trap us, Durstan. I'm convinced that the Gods play games with our lives despite the wyrd, but I'm fortunate that Woden gave me the Blacksmith's magic. It's been my real protection. Faisal knows that life here and the size of his coin chest would be very different without that skill, and the other craftsmen living outside his enclosure!"

Roy looked, into the Monk's eyes. "All that aside, I'm glad to have found you in my life, Durstan. If you need help when you leave here, send word and I'll come to you, Faisal or not. We are family now. Woden has also given the Blacksmith's magic to you. You've heard my tale. Now what's yours, with that girl I've heard mentioned connected to you at Beltane? Ailan isn't it? It isn't any good to keep difficult things inside. I'm not one of the others who preaches holiness beyond reason. I've felt love from a woman." He looked searchingly at Durstan. "It could be I might understand how you are feeling."

Durstan said, quietly, "I don't mind sharing it with you, Roy. It'll be a relief to tell you, although if it gets to Faisal's ears that I've spoken of it, I expect it'll be a flogging for both of us. But what's new about that?" He glanced across at Roy. "It did begin at Beltane, no before. Ailan and I became friends. We agreed to celebrate in the old way, neither of us knowing what we were doing, and even though I would be breaking a vow albeit with the Abbot's consent. I couldn't help it, Roy. I had to do it." Roy put his hand on Durstan's shoulder. "She stayed behind that night, after the other women had gone back to Mull. I learned then that Druid Brionach would be celebrating with us. I thought he would stay on Mull at Duncan's enclosure, but Ailan told me about the sacred place we have here at the far end of the island. It's next to the sea and used to belong to Brigid's Priestess until Columba came with his men. They killed her, and the Druids who were still here."

Roy's eyes widened, in shock. "I was horrified too. I've not spoken of it to anyone else. I don't doubt the love in our blessed Saint's miracles, but there's so much we don't know about how the Church took over Iona. Faisal hasn't told us, and it was over two hundred years ago. Most of the story will like as not have gone from people's memories. It was agreed afterwards that one of the Druids who had escaped should be allowed to keep the flame alight in the Priestess' hut, to honour the Gods. The tradition has continued quietly since then, but the way things are I'm not sure how long the old ways will last." Durstan paused, to take a mouthful of ale. "Ailan said that Faisal has tried hard to get rid of Brionach, but hasn't been able to because the Druid has the Lord's support. You'll have heard the rumours about Duncan being afraid of upsetting anyone, most of all the Gods, and the old Priestess' hut is on the edge of Iona so left alone by the Abbot.

It was only this year that Brionach decided to celebrate Beltane there, and not in the fields behind the Monastery. He brought a slave girl with him. Ailan didn't know her name, but she was beautiful and a virgin. I swear she could have been the Goddess herself, Roy, with milk-white skin. I knew that Faisal would turn a blind eye to me not being in the Church that night, along with the others who joined in the ritual. It seemed right at the time what we did, but now I'm not so sure. There's a part of me that wishes it hadn't happened. That night was like nothing I had experienced before. The drumming and smell of herbs burning on the fire under the stars. The Druid had draped a stag's skin across his back. He was chanting an invocation to the Gods, as we stood in a circle around him. When he led the girl to the stone slab in front of the Priestess' hut, the sea was shimmering bright in the moonlight. She walked towards him wearing only a thin, white, shift. When he pulled it down her naked body he picked her up, and laid her on the slab, all the while wearing the animal pelt. When he was done he cried out that she had been taken by the Old Gods, and her blood stained the stone.

The night became frenzied. Ailan and I ran down to the shore. I could tell she was overcome by it all, and so was I. It was nothing like I had expected. We were lightheaded. The Druid had given us a potion to drink beforehand. He cast a love spell on us, Roy. Afterwards I was certain that she had taken my heart. I thought she felt the same."

Durstan sighed heavily, and rubbed his eyes. "I don't know where the Druid and the girl went, or for that matter any of the others. It was as if everyone else in our normal world had disappeared. I took Ailan's hand in mine. I held it as we walked back to her coracle on the other side of the island. I kissed her again. We whispered promises before she left." Durstan paused, and Roy looked at him expectantly. "I never saw her again, and I still don't have any idea what happened to her."

Durstan's voice was raised in anguish. "God help me, Roy. I don't know what to do. Ailan haunts my dreams, and every waking breath. I will never forget that night. When Faisal talks of magic I was part of it. I found it. The magic in love, and it's still there between us. I can feel it, Roy. I wish I knew why she didn't come back. If she was afraid, surely we could have talked about it? I tried to think of every possible reason which might have prevented her, and there is none."

The Monk stared into the distance and said, quietly, "I pray that God will let me see her again, on Mull."

CHAPTER 10
Three Days Later
Mull

Faisal held his arms upwards to Heaven, and said a blessing for Andrew and Durstan, under the pale sun which lit the early morning sky. "In nomine patris filius sanctus," the Abbot intoned. The Monks were assembled in front of the stone cross dedicated to Saint Columba, enjoying the rare privilege of standing outside to pray, instead of being interred in the island's dark church. A gentle breeze rustled their tonsured scalps. Tearlach, the incense bearer, waved the censor wearily across them. Heavy smoke drifted along the sand and spiraled upwards. Its musky scent permeated the Monks' unwashed robes and skin. A few of the older men coughed when he moved too close, and the fumes hit their lungs.

"We are gathered this morning to wish our Brothers well on their journey. I believe that with God's help they will save many heathen souls on Mull from the torments of Hell," the Abbot said, gazing at the Monks with impassioned eyes. "Brothers Andrew and Durstan leave us now in the light which shines from our sacred shore. They are part of the precious flame which Iona has become in an evil, unchristian world. They will be an example of our piety to those who have yet to believe."

"Well said, Father!" Brother Ignacious, one of the Abbot's

favourite Monks, shouted the words as encouragement to those who were more reluctant to voice their support.

Durstan's thoughts had wandered to the coracles which were waiting at the water's edge. He had checked earlier that there weren't any holes or tears in the skins which covered them. He realised with a start that the Abbot's hard eyes were upon him. "You will do well, my son, to mind the Lord's ways when you are on the mainland. Sin encircles us, Brother Durstan, and makes mockery of God's work." He pointed a scrawny finger. "Don't forget my words because you will surely stand before God for judgment, at the final reckoning. In the meantime, as our holy Father's representative on earth, I shall also hear of any misdemeanors on your part."

The sun was directly above Durstan, and he felt the warmth of its rays on his face. "Thank you, Father, for guiding me. I shall ask God in my prayers, to show me His path." Durstan glanced at Andrew before pushing the nearest coracle into the water. He clambered swiftly in, and reached down into the boat for the oars when the coracle was caught by the current. He breathed deeply in the pure air.

Faisal clasped Andrew to his chest in a conspicuous embrace. The heavy folds of the Abbot's robe draped around them. "May the Holy Spirit walk with you in these troubled times, my Brother." Faisal dropped his arms when he felt the proximity of Andrew's bones beneath his skin. He turned away to disguise his distaste. The smell of food cooking on the fire had reached him, and he began to walk towards it.

A few of the Monks stayed on the shore, to watch Andrew and Durstan leave. They shouted messages of goodwill until the waves carried their brothers too far away for them to hear. Durstan's arms acclimatized easily to the task of rowing, but he slowed his pace to wait for Andrew who was in danger of losing control of the small boat. Durstan could see that he was holding the oars tightly with clenched knuckles, not concentrating on what he was doing.

Andrew's thoughts were in a turmoil. He was experiencing serious misgivings about whether he would be able to safeguard Durstan's soul, and Osfric had left behind too many memories to forget. Life on the island had quickly resumed its monotony, and he had learned a long time ago that it was best to try to be thankful for what he had. It didn't serve any purpose to complain. He broke the silence. "We are fortunate, Durstan, to be leaving Iona. Paul has wanted for many years to return to Ireland, but Faisal refused. Old age prevents him now from travelling. That isn't right. I can say it freely out here. Paul didn't deserve such a life. He's been a loyal servant to the Church."

Durstan shouted across the distance between the coracles, in an attempt to lighten Andrew's mood. "You know as well as I do that Paul relinquished his right to leave Iona once he took charge of Faisal's coins. He became the most important Monk at the Monastery!"

"I've also been thinking about Ailan," Andrew said, irritably. "If you see her on Mull, you mustn't forget that we are travelling under the Abbot's direction. Beltane has gone! There'll be a bed and Church waiting for us at the Monastery. Our brothers will fear the worst if we don't arrive. Mark my words, Durstan, any other news will soon reach the Abbot's ears." Andrew glanced at him. Durstan's face was expressionless. He sighed, heavily. An image of Osfric had come to mind, causing him to relent. "After we have seen the Monks, perhaps you can walk to the Hall? Faisal told me to speak to the younger men and boys at the Monastery, to find out who would be capable of writing a manuscript. They'll travel to Lindisfarne, and be taught the ways of pen and ink, as Osfric was." Andrew's voice quivered. Grief was making him feel exhausted. "The Abbot is under the impression that my eyes will prevent me from teaching them. Once they are done at Lindisfarne, they will be sent to Iona to create new manuscripts."

Andrew's words caught in his throat, as he tried to stay calm. He couldn't row with tears in his eyes, and he didn't want to be left behind. There could be another Viking raid at any time. The other Monks had assured him that they wouldn't be back this year, but their word wasn't a guarantee. "Faisal also said that we should send regular reports with the fishermen, or travellers who might be going to Iona. You can see now, Durstan, that we aren't quite so free as you might have thought."

A red flush spread across the young Monk's face. He had been thinking again of Ailan's body beneath his own. He said, angrily, "I'm looking forward to seeing my sister and her family, Andrew. I'm not prepared to risk that privilege, so there's no need for you to worry. I'm fully aware that if Faisal heard something he didn't like, I could easily be called back to Iona, and I don't want to talk any more about Ailan. I promise you, in Christ's name, that any feelings I may still have for her won't stop me from spreading our beliefs as I have been told to do." A large wave was getting closer, and Durstan watched with concern while Andrew struggled to turn his coracle around, so that it was again facing Mull.

After a few minutes of calm sea the young Monk said, wearily, "perhaps I shall be able to persuade my kinsman to follow Christ? It's common knowledge that the Abbot has been trying to convert Duncan for a long time. He is obviously hoping that I shall be more fortunate. I've been told that there's a Christian church inside his enclosure for prayers on the Lord's day, but Druid Brionach also frequently visits Mull with Duncan's blessing. I don't know how often the church is used, Andrew. Apparently Duncan doesn't prevent his people from believing in the Old Gods, and I expect Brionach will have influenced that decision." Durstan frowned. "Faisal is adamant that Christianity is to be the only religion from now on. He said that I'm to cut down as many of the oak trees as I can, to stop people from worshiping under them, and because they are venerated so highly by the few Druids who are left on these shores."

A pained expression crossed his face. The trees were a beautiful part of God's creation, and not causing any harm. If this carried on, the Abbot would soon be removing the carvings of the Green Men and Maidens from the churches. Everyone believed that they were only there to persuade the non-believers to come inside, and because the Christians had stolen the Druids' sacred places on which to build their houses of God. No wonder the world was in turmoil, and belief confused. Durstan often found himself drawn quite naturally into the Green Man's eyes, through the foliage in front of his face. The carved wood was beautiful, and the powerful depiction of the Old God staring at the Monks inside Iona's church, made it difficult to look away. He felt sometimes that the Old Ones were trying to make him listen to them, but it was a blasphemous thought and fanciful. It couldn't be any more than that.

The Monks rowed steadily, and when they were halfway across the sound, the sea became turbulent. It was difficult, to carry on a conversation. Andrew was satisfied with

Durstan's assurance that he would obey the Abbot, but he wasn't aware that the younger Monk's thoughts had returned to Beltane. Durstan felt guilty. He had started to believe that Ailan was his true anam cara, not Andrew. It felt unnatural for them to be apart, and Durstan knew he wouldn't miss Andrew as much, if he didn't see him for several solstices. He was feeling now so unlike himself that it was as if some ungodly hand had reached in to twist his entrails. He felt as if he had been cursed, whilst knowing that he couldn't have been. Athdar had told him that these black thoughts were the reason he was suffering from so many minor ailments, and his heart ached every day. *Why was life so hard under this new God?* Durstan ran a hand across his eyes. It was easy to see how much Andrew missed Osfric from the pain etched on his face, and the flattened tone in his voice. Durstan knew without a doubt that he was still in love with Ailan. He ached, for her.

The ebb and flow of the waves pulled the coracles against the sand as they approached the shoreline. Durstan jumped into the teeming sea, and struggled to drag his coracle onto the beach before turning back to help Andrew. It was heavy work, but the second boat was landed safely in a few minutes. A fisherman was walking towards them. Durstan hauled himself from the sand onto his feet. He could still feel the icy coldness of the water through his sandals, and on his bare legs.

"Brothers, welcome! I hope all is well with you. The coracle is a marvel. Is it not? But also a risky way to travel, if you aren't used to the ways of the sea."

Durstan clasped the fisherman's outstretched arm which was thickly muscled for a man in his middle forties. He was grinning at the Monks. He had lost several teeth, and some of the others were blackened. "You're right, my friend.

Rowing isn't for everyone, but God was with us on our journey," Durstan said, smiling. "Brother Andrew and I are visiting the Monastery here. I'm Durstan. I have a sister, Mora, on Mull. She's married to my kinsman, Duncan."

The fisherman's swarthy face creased into an even wider grin. "I'm Cormac, one of Duncan's men. Your sister's husband shares his table readily with strangers. They'll take you warmly into their hall, kin or not. I also know that the Lord is sympathetic to your Christianity."

Cormac looked carefully at the Monks. "Will you share my breakfast, Brothers? I can only offer you fish, but it was freshly caught at dawn. There's a morsel of bread, to wash down with good ale. It's on the weak side for my liking, but you'll soon be set right again after such a feast. I guarantee it. Brother Andrew, if I'm not mistaken, you're looking queasy from the crossing." Cormac hit Andrew kindly at the centre of his back. "You need food, to line your stomach. I usually have a bite myself before I walk through the forest to the Hall. It's a peaceful time away from the women's mouths, and my Branach, a lazier son no man would want! I expect you'll be used to better fare at the Monastery, but the fish will be tasty from the fragrant twigs I've laid on the fire. You did say that you came from Iona? Sometimes we see men of your religion from other places which are much further away." Cormac turned his bloodshot eyes towards the fire where the fish was cooking.

An enticing aroma filled the air, and Durstan felt his mouth watering. "Thank you for your generosity," he said. "We'd be glad to eat with you, Cormac."

"If you pull the coracles further up the sand, Durstan, you'll be able to hide them in the undergrowth over there. You won't have to carry them later, if you do that. It's a safe enough place, and I'll see to our breakfast. There's a flat rock over there, if you fancy a rest, Brother Andrew."

Durstan watched the fisherman's broad back and strong legs as he strode across the sand, to the rocks where he had left his belongings. Andrew followed him. Although short in stature, Cormac had the look of a man well used to hard, physical work. Durstan surmised that he would fish, to fulfil his duty to feed the Lord and his men, then his own family. He hid the coracles in the undergrowth as Cormac had suggested, and joined Andrew and him next to the fire. A light breeze was blowing from the sea which made it pleasant to sit, and watch the mid-morning light skimming the waves.

Cormac patted his large stomach appreciatively, and smiled at his guests. He handed the fish and bread to them on flat stones. "You'll find good wooden bowls at the Hall, but I make do with nature's plates when I'm out here alone. A stone and fingers are all you need for food. I'm glad that you're here, Brothers, to share this with me. I fish this stretch of water alone. There are other fishermen at the enclosure, but each of us has our own part of the sea to work. Lord Duncan hopes we will catch more that way, but my view is we are all at the mercy of the Gods wherever we put our boats."

Andrew took the food from Cormac. The smell of burnt wood and cooked fish mingled with the scent of the sea, and Durstan's stomach churned in anticipation. Neither of the Monks had thought to bring food or ale for the journey, nor had anyone else made the suggestion. The crossing had taken longer than expected since the wind was blowing against them. Andrew lived in faith that God would provide as He had done here, but Durstan's belief wasn't quite the same. Although the means might be given to him, it usually involved an effort on his part to achieve the result. As the younger Monk ate he realised that neither of them could rely now on food being available, even the tiny portions they received at the Monastery on the day after a fast. Durstan wondered if Duncan was trying to find a way to optimise the fishing, because of the famine a couple of years ago when the crops had failed. It was the same famine which took Ailan's Mother. Faisal had told the Monks at the time that they should be grateful to be on Iona. Many of them hadn't believed him, but there was enough shellfish to eat and grain in the Monastery barn. The Abbot reminded them often that the Church would always provide for its faithful.

Steam rose invitingly from the white flesh of the fish, and Andrew spoke a hasty blessing before he took his first mouthful. Cormac had served the food clumsily in his enthusiasm, but that made little difference to the men's hunger. They savoured the taste in silence. The fisherman finished first. He wiped his mouth with the back of a greasy hand, and sucked each one of his fingers in turn until he was sufficiently satisfied. He laid back against a tall rock with a contented smile, and stared at Durstan. "It's not often I get to share my meal with two holy men. I'm surrounded by women at my hut, and my son who's not much better than a girl. Tell me your story, Brother."

Durstan would have been happier, to have slept for an hour. Andrew's eyes were half-closed. Their sleep had been interrupted as usual last night by the bell, and the rowing had been hard. The Abbot had also given him extra work to do before he left, but Andrew and he owed a debt of gratitude to this man for his hospitality. He realised that he would have to become used now to speaking about life on Iona, and Christianity. Andrew and he would be faced with many questions. Durstan told Cormac about how he had arrived on Iona, and their lives at the Monastery. The fisherman listened intently, then belched. The foulness of his breath stained the air. "What of your situation, fisherman?" Durstan said, dutifully. "I'm eager now to hear more of your world, and learn if you are Christian, or not."

Cormac stretched his limbs across the rock, and used his hands to shade his eyes from the sun. "I live inside your kinsman's enclosure, less than a quarter of an hour's walk from here. Oonagh is my wife, and Branach, the son I mentioned.. We share a hut with the girl to whom he's handfasted. I had another son, Edgar, but the Gods took him. I'm praying hard that they'll decide soon to take my Wife, and her vicious tongue!" Cormac began to laugh until he noticed the look of displeasure on Andrew's face. "I'm sorry, my friends. I forgot myself. You are men of the Christ religion, and may be offended by what I say. I'll be honest with you. If Oonagh dies then I have been thinking of taking a younger Wife to have more sons with her, and not leave it to Branach. The fault with Edgar and Branach lies with Oonagh. Nevertheless she's holding firmly onto her mortality, and my every day."

Andrew said, sternly, "don't you love your Wife, as you should in the sight of God? You speak as if you've been with her for many years. Christian or not, it's your duty as her Husband!"

Cormac rubbed the black stubble on his chin. "The marriage was a handfasting, done in the old ways before the Ancestors' standing stone, so is only for as long as love lasts. As the Gods will bear witness, I did love her for a long time but she has changed. I'll still be true to Oonagh for now, even though I have my eye on the young, widowed slave." He grinned. "She has a child already, given to her by a Husband who has gone to the Otherworld. She can easily bear me more. I've wanted her body warming my bed at night for a long time. I can tell you!" He rubbed a hand across his eyes. "If I should cast Oonagh out from our hut, it wouldn't be without a son for her protection, albeit it's only Branach. He's still a man which is better security than none. The trouble is, knowing Oonagh, she'll ask Lord Duncan for help if I do that. Branach and his new Wife may well get a hut of their own in time, but she'll have nowhere else to go if it's not with them. May the Gods help us! The Lord won't give her a hut to herself, and the other women hate the sight of her miserable face. Her looks went long ago, so her only chance will be if Branach gives her a home. There isn't any guarantee that he'll do that. He would have to give up the opportunity of spending more time alone with that scrawny wife of his. He can't seem to leave her alone, if you know what I mean, Brothers." Cormac laughed, lasciviously. "It all comes back to the sexual act in the end, my friends, but don't take offence at my words. It's only nature, and I can't tell you how it is with me in any other way."

Durstan was startled. Cormac was talking about the woman with the severe face who used to come to Iona every day with Ailan, and she still did. She was the one who, God forgive him, he didn't like. Oonagh, with the vicious tongue and a snake's bite for a mouth. He had heard her use it on Ailan more than once, and felt angry that she could be so spiteful. Even in Christian charity it was hard to forgive, especially when Durstan saw the hurt look in Ailan's eyes. "I'm sorry for both of you, Cormac," he said. "Love belongs to everyone. It'll stay a lifetime if it's cherished, but it can also easily be taken away from choice, or God's will." Durstan looked thoughtfully at the fisherman. Oonagh would have endured much at the hands of such a Husband.

Andrew said, sharply, "we'll pray for you, Cormac, for the best outcome to your troubles."

The fisherman stood up. "Thank you, Brothers. I shall have to go to the Hall, or the fish won't be worth having. My family will make you welcome, and Durstan, you'll be able to talk with Lady Mora. If you want to walk to the Monastery later, you can go from the Lord's enclosure. It's further inland, but when you know the way, quicker than walking from where we are now. Branach or one of the slaves will show you the path through the forest."

Andrew nodded, reluctantly. It would be poor manners to refuse so kind an offer, and he had seen the light of hope in Durstan's eyes. Cormac bundled the fish together in leaves stripped from the first line of trees. He grumbled to himself as he collected them, and his meagre belongings. "By Woden, Branach should be here helping me! Can you believe it? A grown man who says that he's afraid of the sea. He complains that it'll have him one day, and the other men have taken against him for his surliness. He gets that from Oonagh. They carry charms to protect themselves when the Lord tells him to go with them into the fields to plough. Duncan will have had enough of him soon. If Branach isn't careful, the Lord will find an excuse to make him an outcast. I've warned the fool about it 'til I'm without breath to speak. A son has a duty to obey his father in the natural order, not refuse to listen, but even when he did come with me he tangled the nets. It was obvious that the Gods didn't like him being in a coracle, and there's talk now of him being cursed. All of them believe that he'll poison the fish, if he touches them. What can I do?"

Cormac stopped speaking when a different thought came to mind, causing him to regain his good humour. "I wouldn't mind being on the sea alone with the lovely Saille," he said. "She could certainly help me, even though fishing isn't a woman's work if you understand my meaning." His raucous laugh startled Durstan, and even more so, when the Monk recognized the name and Saille's connection to Ailan.

Chapter 11

Cormac The Fisherman

The Monks followed Cormac along the narrow path which wound through the trees. The sound of the sea was faint in the distance, and a dank smell filled the air. Andrew began to lag behind. He said, to Durstan in a low voice, "God took the snakes from Iona when our blessed Columba landed there, but that's not the case on Mull. Shouldn't we walk more carefully? I'm afraid of Woden's creatures!"

Cormac laughed, heartily. "Brother, whether you are speaking of your God or mine, the mighty Woden can send a snake to you at any time. A snake is a snake is a snake, and will be more afraid of you than the other way around. If you keep to the track and walk only in my footsteps, no harm will come to you. You have my oath. I make this journey every single day, without mishap."

The fisherman walked confidently through the dappled half-light, even in those places where the path twisted and turned until it became little more than a track made by the deer. Andrew followed behind warily, while Durstan seemed to be in a trance. He was carrying half of the day's fish, and wasn't used to being in so great a forest or hearing the cries of birds speaking in a different language. Ailan would have said they came with messages from the Gods of the forest, and were taking care of the trees so that no harm befell them. Durstan frowned. *Why did everything always come back to her?* Even in this strange place, Ailan owned his thoughts. The Monk turned his attention to the oak trees which were reaching out to touch the Christian God's heaven. He could understand the fascination which they held for the Druids. A doe crossed their path, and looked at them nervously before she darted out of sight. Her fur glistened in the half-light. Durstan saw Andrew make the sign of a cross, to ward away evil. He shook his head sadly. The animal was one of God's creatures, not a Devil.

As the trees began to thin, the men walked easily through the undergrowth. The light was strong again, making it easier to see the way ahead. A wooden palisade surrounded by a wide ditch appeared in front of them as if by magical intention. A great Hall dominated the landscape from its vantage point on a low hill. Cormac quickened his steps, and began to climb the bank. Sweat trickled down his face. He was breathless from the exertion. The Monks followed at a slower pace. Andrew's footsteps faltered on the rougher ground. Cormac was speaking to a lanky limbed man who had opened the wooden gate. A tunic and hose hung loosely on his torso. "Norvel, these men are travelling with their Christian God. Don't try to interfere with them." He looked back at the Monks so that they could share in the banter. "Brother Durstan here is kin to the Lord, so let us pass without any of your daft questions! There'll be no more for you to learn by asking them."

Norvel looked curiously at the Monks before he stood to one side, to let them into the enclosure. Durstan caught the stench of his body, as he hurried through the gap. The Lord's man closed the gate securely behind them. Durstan looked around in surprise at how similar the layout of the enclosure was to the Monastery, apart from the stream which was running here. The water flowed into the ditch around the fence. This gave the settlement additional protection from intruders who might try to enter forcibly. The enclosure seemed huge at first glance. It could easily be home to more than two hundred people, and the Lord's animals.

A large, wooden, building with a thatched roof stood at its centre. Durstan assumed that this was the Hall. The oak door at the front was guarded by ornately carved pillars. It was surrounded by smaller huts in a field of mud. Rain, animal and human waste, had made the ground akin to a bog. The smell was overwhelming. Andrew had pulled the top of his robe across his mouth. His face was puce.

A small, stone, church was on the right hand side. Durstan pointed to it so that Andrew could see the beautifully carved cross near the entrance. The craftsman had engraved ancient serpents and Celtic patterns on the stone. Their secrets were waiting to be deciphered. Faisal had told Durstan that the church was an important step towards the mass conversion which he was seeking. It was a sign that the Christian God was at Mull, and with the Monks on their journey. Andrew did look happier since he had seen it.

The aroma of meat cooking on the fire filled the air, and helped to overcome the unpleasant smell inside the enclosure. Cormac turned to the Monks. "The fish we had earlier, Brothers, was a good morsel but this meat goads my stomach. You'll be well looked after tonight, my friends. The Lord's table is the fullest, Durstan. That's more often than not thanks to your nephew. There's little doubt that Eoghan has the wildness of the forest in him, but he's an impressive shot with an arrow. Duncan's men are happy to follow him when there's a hunt. There's never a shortage of game for the pot when Eoghan's home." The fisherman slapped Durstan's back. "Your nephew is a likeable enough fellow, but we have to be careful with our women when he's about, although I have no need to worry. My Oonagh is safe enough!" Cormac laughed. He failed on this occasion to notice Andrew's disapproval.

"Let's get the fish sorted out. It's weighing heavy on my arms, then I'll take you to the Hall. My hut is over there," Cormac said, pointing at a shabbily, thatched building.

The enclosure was bustling with activity. Children and animals ran between the huts, and Andrew stood quietly at Durstan's side. He looked as if he had forgotten places like this existed. Durstan punched his arm playfully, and Andrew gave him a weak smile before they followed Cormac along one of the mud tracks. The fisherman pointed to the kitchen on the other side of the enclosure from where the smell of cooking was coming. He laughed and joked with several other men as they walked past them. He mentioned the Christian God, and how he was hoping now for a better life because of helping His Monks. People ceased what they were doing to stare. A group of rowdy children had started to follow Durstan and Andrew. An old man said that the other fishermen had come back from the sea hours ago, and it was as well Cormac's fish didn't take so long to cook on the fire as a haunch. The fisherman replied with a ribald gesture, much to the amusement of those nearby.

A woman's voice could be overheard from inside Cormac's hut. "He'll be here soon, Mother. There's no need to worry."

"Tsk! The sun is high now, even for him. He'll no doubt have fallen asleep in his ale, and be dreaming of large breasts belonging to a Goddess. It's no matter to Cormac that we're hungry, or the fish needs to be on the fire. The Lord won't feed any of us tonight if my idle husband hasn't worked for it, but he won't suffer. He'll have eaten his fill on the shore, as the Lord says he can after he has caught the fish. Duncan is too generous at times." She was still complaining as she left the hut, followed by the other woman.

Sunlight sparkled momentarily in Durstan's eyes, and his heart leapt. He hadn't thought to come across her so soon if at all, certainly not here in the fisherman's hut. The Monk looked at Ailan with shocked realisation then concern. Her hair was a tangled mess. The tunic she wore was too small for her frame. It was stretched tightly across her belly. Her body looked ready to break free from the confines of the cloth. Ailan was heavily pregnant. Durstan stared at her in disbelief. He averted his eyes when she caught him looking. A man whom Durstan hadn't noticed earlier stretched up, and grasped her wrist. He glanced furtively at the Monks, but turned to Oonagh as soon as she began to speak.

"My Husband! Where have you been this time, Cormac? There's talk of a bear roaming the forest. A deer was killed near the enclosure. I thought at first that its death cry might be yours, and you know how much we need you to survive." She stopped, in surprise. "Oh, but you have two holy men with you! Brothers Durstan and Andrew, if I'm not mistaken." She attempted to alter the tone in her voice, to sound more respectful.

"Hush, Oonagh," Cormac said, quietly. "I'm here now." He turned to the younger man who still hadn't moved. "Get off your backside, Branach. Take word to Lord Duncan that I'm here with two holy men. If you take the fish too, we'll all be able to eat today. Remember your responsibility. Ailan and the whelp need feeding, not just your Mother. Don't shame me any more today. I rue the hour you grew to be a stronger man than I because, son or not, all this would by now be a different story."

Cormac spat a large globule of phlegm in the direction of his son, and thrust the fish at him. Branach moved reluctantly away from Ailan. He stepped closer to his Father as he walked past him, and snatched the fish from Durstan's hands. "Don't threaten me, old man, or you know who'll be the worse for it!" He said, angrily. Cormac moved quickly out of his way. The Monks were also obliged to step aside when Branach pushed past them. He called over his shoulder, to Ailan. "Mind you don't do anything I wouldn't like, woman, while I'm gone!"

Durstan's anger surged through his veins when he saw the look of fear on Ailan's face, and Cormac tried to ease the tension. "I'm sorry, Brothers, for my son's behavior. He shames our family. There's little I can do to help it. I had hoped he would be good mannered in your company." He turned to Oonagh. "I fed our guests before we walked back from the sea. That's what took me longer, my Wife."

Durstan looked in consternation at the ground. His thoughts and stomach were churning. He had a reason now which explained why Ailan hadn't come back to Iona after Beltane, but surely it couldn't be because of this Branach? And there was obviously a child! Durstan's heart plummeted. *Maybe he had been wrong about her from the outset?* Branach had always been her husband, whether married or handfasted. No one, least of all her, had thought to tell him. *Perhaps all of them had believed it was a fine jest at his expense?* Despair clung to him like sodden fur. He knew nothing of the ways of women or their magic, but he had heard gossip. These were undoubtedly women's wiles. The more worldly Monks on Iona called them that, but Durstan would never have believed it of Ailan, and a child too! Exhaustion ran through him, as pain seeped into his bones.

He was grateful to Andrew when he moved closer, whilst he tried desperately to control his emotions and act as if he was unconcerned. It was possible that not everyone here knew about the Beltane ritual on Iona. They had celebrated their own on Mull. Durstan felt instinctively that it would be wise to be wary of Oonagh. He caught her eye. She was watching him, with undisguised interest. If he wasn't careful, there might be unpleasant repercussions for Ailan. Whatever she had done, he certainly didn't wish her any harm, and the situation here didn't seem right. His heart was aching so much that it felt as if he was being torn in half. Perhaps he still didn't know everything about love, but he could feel it? His heart ached even more when he thought of who might have fathered Ailan's child. She had only been with him once at Beltane so it couldn't be his. His child wouldn't have taken. He knew that much at least. He had kissed her gently afterwards and whispered into the soft skin on her neck, that nothing else mattered except their love for each other.

But he had been wrong. This is what came of playing the Devil's games! Abbot Faisal had been speaking the truth about mortal sin, and Durstan had his punishment. His eyes flooded with sadness. There was nothing now he could do apart from remember who he was, a Monk. It was his sacred duty to put his personal feelings aside. He needed to help this family if he could, by making them Christian, since the Old Gods must surely be at the root of this. Durstan looked at Oonagh, and thought of Cormac's words. She hadn't aged well. Her short, grey hair was streaked with white. It had the look of an old, animal pelt. Lines of unhappiness were etched on a face which the sun had worn as hard as leather. It wasn't difficult to see that the handfasting had reached a natural ending when she stood next to her Husband. It couldn't have been helped by the other woman Cormac had mentioned. A heart could easily be stolen from such a stale marriage.

Oonagh and the fisherman were still arguing. A young boy sat silently at the side of the hut listening to their bitter words. Andrew put a hand on Durstan's arm, turning him towards the child. He said, loudly, "who is this, Cormac? We'd like to know all of your family. You didn't mention any children." Ailan pushed past them, and stood next to the boy trying to shield him with her body. Durstan had recognised Tam. His heart softened. Despite her lies, she had spoken the truth about her brother.

"The boy is my daughter's brother so of no concern," Cormac said. "Let me take you to the Hall, Durstan."

Ailan held Tam close to her, as the men walked away. The boy was watching an insect crawling on a nearby bush. Her face said that her heart was breaking, while pride and confusion prevented Durstan from looking over his shoulder. Ailan couldn't stop staring at his back until Oonagh spoke sharply to her. "Stop it, girl, with that boy! You have work to finish. Get to it! I'll soon find something to keep his little hands occupied." Oonagh grabbed Tam's ear, and used it to pull him away from his sister. The boy didn't make a sound when she pushed him in front of her, to follow Ailan inside the hut.

Chapter 12

Beth

Durstan couldn't stop thinking about Ailan, as he followed Cormac and Andrew across the enclosure. He barely heard Andrew's whisper when he turned his head. "What sort of Devil is she, to have done this to you? We need to pray now for help and guidance. God will have the answer to this, if we seek forgiveness for Ailan's sins. I've been praying for the souls of those evil men who took Osfric. You'll find strength in your faith, Durstan."

"I know you aren't looking forward to seeing Duncan and my sister, Andrew, but they are my family," Durstan said, angrily. "I'll gladly pray with you later, but we can't use their church before we've spoken to them. I've waited years for this moment. Ailan or not, I desperately want to see Mora again."

"I know that, Durstan, but we mustn't forget God's place in our lives or that He takes precedence. I met your kinsman when he came to Iona to visit his Ancestors' graves. You were in the fields at the time. I told you then that your sister had married well, so you have no cause for concern. The coins and gold Duncan gave to the Abbot were a hefty price for what he received. You won't be disappointed, Durstan. Duncan is a good man. He admired the manuscripts Osfric and I were working on, and said he understood their importance when I explained it to him."

Cormac had stopped in front of the door to the Hall, and the Monks stared at it in admiration. The wood was painted red, yellow, and blue from plant dyes. Celtic knot work and serpents entwined themselves around the pillars, to protect all who entered there. Andrew said, grudgingly, "This is as good a piece of art as I've seen in any Christian church. I can't help but feel that the best should be offered to God. Richness like this outside our holy church is one of the reasons Abbot Faisal has sent us here. This is the Devil's work!" Durstan's frown was enough to stop Andrew from saying any more. A giant of a man was standing behind the half-open door. He was a swarthy skinned slave who would not listen kindly to words which insulted his Lord.

Cormac answered the man's abrupt greeting. "Gar, we've come to speak to Duncan. The Monk here is Durstan, Lady Mora's brother, and the other holy man is Andrew from the Iona monastery. They don't carry weapons except for Brother Durstan's hunting knife."

The slave held out a gnarled hand for the knife, and stepped aside so that the Monks could enter the Hall. "Wait there," he said, pointing at the wooden benches on either side of the fire which was burning at the centre of the floor. He crossed to the opposite end of the Hall where richly woven hangings created a private area behind the cloth. He spoke through the gap in one of them. It was immediately flung aside by a large man. Lord Duncan's black hair and beard were cleanly trimmed. He was wearing a dark coloured tunic which enhanced his distinguished demeanor.

A tall woman followed him eagerly into the main part of the Hall. Durstan knew immediately that she was his sister. Mora looked like their Mother. Her eyes met his in recognition, and she pushed past Duncan to run into Durstan's open arms. Andrew averted his eyes, in embarrassment.

The Lord's voice was deep, and authoritative. "Faisal told me when I went to Iona last that you would be coming to us, but I didn't know when." He watched his Wife and Durstan embracing. "I'm pleased you are here. I've been telling the Abbot for years that you are a part of this family, but Faisal has repeatedly refused my request for you to join us. His excuse was that you were doing the Christian God's work, so you couldn't leave the shelter of His monastery. I've questioned him at length over his right to argue with me, his Lord, and he dared to tell me that he served only the Church in Rome!"

Duncan continued, angrily, "that man has exceeded his authority far too many times. He believes that he is a law unto himself, hiding behind that damned crucifix he wears. More's the pity the chain didn't strangle his scrawny neck. I have authority over Iona. This Rome he talks of is far across the sea. It's a place most of us haven't seen, and I'm not so sure he has the protection from there that he says he does. The Romans left these shores centuries ago. They've shown little inclination to return. I've given the Abbot gold and jewels for you, Durstan. All to no avail. His promises have been empty until now. You have my apologies, kinsman, for the delay. I have let you down badly. It was my duty as head of this family to have brought you here sooner, even if that meant by force."

Duncan crossed the Hall, and placed a manicured hand on the Monk's shoulder. "There'll be a time when I can redress this wrong, and I shall do so. Now, I'm curious. What has made the Abbot change his mind?"

"We are here, my Lord, to help our Father Abbot convert non-believers to the Christian faith, with your permission of course," Andrew said, unable to hide the annoyance in his voice.

Duncan smiled at him, and chuckled. "You have my blessing, Brother, to speak to anyone here. I'm afraid that you'll find they are set in the ways of their Ancestors, but you may try."

Durstan still had his arms around his sister. He was overwhelmed by the richness of her tunic, the bronze necklace she wore, and the softness of the blue woollen cloak around her shoulders fastened with a filigree pin. She was beautiful and age, nearly forty summers, had caused this transformation from the skinny girl he had last seen. Mora was similarly scrutinising Andrew from across Durstan's shoulder. Her thoughts were coming quick and fast in the sheer delight of seeing Durstan again. Her brother was the same except for the years he now carried. His skin was clearly in need of water, and fresh robes wouldn't be amiss. One of the slaves could clean both their sandals and shave their beards before tonight's feast. So much facial hair was suitable only for an outcast, certainly not a brother, but that too could come later. Mora wanted to hold onto Durstan for as long as she could.

"You are our Father's son, from the line of your face. It's the same as our Grandfather's, and your eyes belong to Mother. They're kind and gentle, as hers used to be." Mora traced Durstan's features with a slim finger. "We've heard so many tales of what goes on at that Monastery. I can't tell you how relieved I am, to see that you are well. There'll be no need now for you to go back. You are free!" Mora said, oblivious to the frown on Andrew's face.

"I had some news of you when Duncan visited Iona, but

it seemed as if that awful Abbot was holding you prisoner. If only Father hadn't taken you there when he was full of ale. You may not know this, but you were meant to be fostered with our neighbours in exchange for their son. Father could have the dark Gods in him sometimes! Mother didn't recover from it. They had been arguing over a trivial matter, and he punished her by taking you." Mora kissed Durstan's cheek softly. "Duncan thought that Faisal was waiting until he could get the best price he could for your freedom. He's an evil man, that one. Ask Duncan! I wanted so many times to go to Iona, to have it out with him and tell him what I thought, but my husband wasn't happy for me to do that." Mora looked at Duncan from the corner of her eye, knowing that he wouldn't chastise her in front of their guests.

She noticed that Andrew was watching her. "We can talk more of this later," she said. "All I'm concerned with now is your comfort. Forgive me, Brother Andrew, but you both look in need of a wash in the stream and fresh robes scented with herbs. We are fortunate to have clean water from the spring running across the enclosure, although it's not the case when the Gods take up residence there during a storm. It's a struggle to keep the stream from flooding the Hall and our huts, when that happens."

Duncan grinned. "You can see that my Wife likes to preserve standards within our home. Thankfully, it's your turn now, Brothers!"

"Hush, my Lord. I know that you also like having a good home. I'll ask one of the slaves to attend to your needs, my two Brothers." She smiled brightly at Andrew. "You'll look well then, to sit at our table tonight. There'll be more than a few curious glances come your way. I expect you'll want to represent your God in the best possible light."

Durstan squeezed Mora tightly in an embrace, and she wriggled with laughter. He felt the crushing ache return to his heart. At the same moment as he thought Ailan would never again leave him alone, two young women burst into the Hall in an explosion of colour and light. The Monk was drawn instinctively to the red haired woman, with tinkling laughter and startling eyes. They were as green as the fields in summer. The second woman was shouting, as she ran. "I let you win this time, Beth. You know it. Don't you go boasting that you are quicker than me."

Mora frowned, and moved reluctantly away from Durstan. "Beth, Alys, you are here in time to meet my brother. Durstan has traveled with Brother Andrew from Iona. Come closer to the fire. There's a cold wind today, creeping through the gaps between the timber."

Alys glanced guiltily at Beth. "I'm sorry, Lady Mora! We had no idea you were here or that you had visitors," she said, looking keenly at the men. "We were hungry, and searching for something to eat." Beth's eyelashes fluttered, hiding her beautiful eyes. Durstan watched with undisguised interest. She brushed past him, and he caught the scent of her skin before she joined Alys on the bench opposite Andrew. Durstan felt his heart quiver. He hadn't previously seen anyone as exotic as she was. He was fascinated. His eyes followed her every movement. Andrew was in the meantime looking at the women in distaste, whilst Alys grinned cheekily at him.

Mora clapped her hands twice at a child on the other side of the Hall. The young slave was replacing the dried grass underfoot. She told the girl to bring food quickly, before she turned again to Beth. "It's good to see you in such high spirits, my Lady. I hope you found the guests' hut comfortable after your journey. I looked in on your

Mother earlier. She was still asleep, resting before the feast tonight. For as long as I have known Kate, she will stay in her bed if she can!"

Duncan coughed, uncomfortably. "I'll see you tonight, Durstan, and Brother Andrew." His eyes didn't quite reach Mora's when he said, "wear the amber necklace I bought for you, Wife, from the Baltic trader. Its richness compliments your beauty." Mora blushed as she watched her Husband stride from the Hall.

The slave brought a thick, vegetable, pottage and morsels of chicken from the kitchen. She served Beth and Alys first, then the Monks who took only a little. "When you arrived last night, Beth, we didn't have an opportunity to talk. I could see that both of you were exhausted. My Husband hasn't said a lot, but it was a surprise that you had come. What happened?"

Beth drank from the pottery cup the slave had set down beside her. "I found out that my Mother was staying with you, Mora. I have to see her before she's taken to Ireland. Once inside the nunnery, I have little hope of being able to speak to her again. Uncle told me a few days ago when he was full of wine, that the men he sent to escort her had died of a fever, and she was here. I thought she had long gone. He's planning to send more men soon so that Mother can finish the journey. I've decided to ask Lord Duncan to offer us both sanctuary, and Alys too," Beth said, confidently. "She's been my companion since we were children. She would fare badly, if she had to return to my Uncle without me." Beth kissed her friend, prettily on the cheek.

Durstan saw the look of alarm which crossed Mora's face. "I understand that you don't want to lose your Mother, Beth, but surely your Uncle is your natural protector as a kinsman?" He said, curiously. "Shouldn't you turn to him, if you are unhappy? The risk of a blood feud with your Uncle is the last thing I suspect Lord Duncan will want."

A look of annoyance crossed Beth's face. The Monk sitting opposite her was attractive. It was easy to see his interest in her, but she couldn't understand why he was arguing against her proposal. She wasn't used to being challenged. Perhaps this Christian magic was powerful? Beth bent her head slightly, so that he wouldn't be able to see into her eyes. "We had a couple of slaves with us, and one horse. It was all we could take, to get away quickly. Alys bribed one of Uncle's men to let us have it. I had ridden him before. He's a friendly spirit so came willingly. Alys and I laid on the ground next to the animal on the first night beside the fire we had lit. We were travelling through the forest, and had sought the protection of the Gods who were there. None of us slept a great deal, but the Goddess Brigid answered our prayers. She let us feel the warmth of the fire all night long under an invisible cloak of darkness, so we were safe." Alys took her hand, and Beth smiled at her.

"The Goddess protected us for two more nights, but the day after that was awful." She paused. "Uncle's men found us. Alys and I were a little distance away from the others. We were collecting berries. The horse was loose, and had wandered after us. I'd noticed the berries before we stopped for a few minutes to rest." She faltered. "There was nothing we could do against so many armed men. They slaughtered the slaves who had belonged to my Father for years. All because they refused to say where I was. Alys and I managed to get away, but we could hear the men for a long time afterwards searching for us. We were terrified of being discovered."

Beth looked up, to meet Durstan's eyes. "It's not a pretty tale. We could smell the blood on their knives that day." She lowered her eyes again. "We walked along the old paths after that, listening to the wolves. They kept their distance and the horse was swift. I had my dagger too," she said, touching the jeweled weapon which hung from her belt. "We carried on like that for another night, and we came across the stream yesterday morning. It refreshed us. We thought that if we followed its course we would eventually reach the sea, and we could find your enclosure more easily from there. We didn't want to spend another night alone in the forest."

Beth's eyes sought Durstan's again. "In answer to your question, Monk, I can tell you now that my Uncle is Aodh. You'll have heard of him on Iona. He's been there many times, and is Lord of the lands adjoining Duncan's. They stretch far into Dalraida and beyond to the edge of King Offa's Mercia."

Andrew nodded, thoughtfully. "I've met your Uncle when he came to visit Abbot Faisal, but I know nothing more of him. It's unlikely Durstan will have spoken to him. Your kinsman isn't our concern."

Beth scowled at him. "Uncle controls all of the family land and property, since he is our only living, male relative. If Mother or I should marry it would be instead under the control of a Husband. My Father was Mercian, so the King also has a right to be involved in our affairs. Some of our land lies within the boundaries of his middle kingdom. By King Offa's law, we should be able to say something of how our marriages are done. Uncle laughed at me when I argued with him. He said quite categorically that we are too far away from Offa's court to enforce the right. He clearly wishes to benefit from this situation by disposing of Mother, so that she can't bear a son despite her age, or marry again." Beth began to cry softly. "Uncle wants to handfast me to a neighbour for their mutual benefit, but whose three previous wives have died at his hands. I can't expect to fare any better once Odhran is tired of me. He is an old man, and they want me to bear a son which would unite their lands. I can't do it, Mora." Her eyes pleaded with the older woman for support. "I don't know if Mother has told you any of this, or if she knows it all. I couldn't speak to her last night. I don't love Odhran, and he certainly doesn't love me. I would be the receptacle for his child, that's all. There's evil in that. My son should be born to the right Father."

Beth wiped her eyes, and looked shyly at Durstan. "I know it from dreams, and the signs which the Gods have given to me. My son will one day be a great man in his own right. I know too that it can't happen from such a beginning with Odhran. Lord Duncan is powerful. That's why I'm here. If he refuses to help me, I don't know what I shall do. I also don't know what my Mother intends, if anything. Father was killed in a raid by outlaws when he was away from our enclosure. Uncle Aodh took us in out of duty, as my Father's brother. Mother has been his prisoner for years. He has been waiting for the right time, to make a marriage agreement for me before ridding himself of us both. Even if I didn't hate Odhran so much and survived a handfasting, or Christian marriage if that is what he chose, he could still treat our child as he wanted to. My son or daughter would be brought up by a manipulative, cruel, man which I truly couldn't bear."

Beth paused for breath. "The marriage to Odhran is imminent. I've already been considered by him, as a woman. He's eager for the union. He's been pressing Uncle to proceed with it."

Durstan was looking at Beth, with concern. "No one should be forced to go through a marriage or handfasting if it's against their wishes," Andrew said, firmly. "Our Christian God doesn't allow it. He will help you, if you ask Him in your prayers. Brother Durstan and I will also pray for you both, and the souls of your dead slaves. The holy bible shows us that the faithful walk safely at the centre of the path. God will be there for you when you are ready, if you are Christian."

Beth said, cautiously, "Thank you for offering us the protection of your God, Brother Andrew. I'm willing to learn more about Him. Perhaps He can offer us the safety we are seeking, if Lord Duncan can't?" She gazed into Durstan's eyes, and his face came alive with pleasure.

Mora spoke severely. "Enough! We are sorry for your troubles, Beth. I will ask my Husband what he can do, if anything, but none of us here can make promises to you. The world we live in is an uncertain place, even with trust in the Gods we have chosen to follow."

Chapter 13

Eoghan

Kate picked her way delicately through the mud, and was closely followed by Beth. "I swear, Mother, those huts have ears. The walls are so thin. Everyone seems to know everything in this place. If Uncle Aodh wasn't so awful, I'd go back to him. I didn't ruin my shoes when I was there. He might be old and miserable, but he's had sense enough to use stones underfoot in the main parts of his enclosure for the storms when they come." Beth looked ruefully at the soiled leather on her shoes. "These are only fit now for a slave on a bad day!"

"An enclosure is a small place, Beth. At least we are safe here for the time being." Kate said, linking arms with her daughter as they walked between the huts. Although it was almost dark, there was still enough light coming from the occupied huts for the women to see where they were walking. A group of men had gathered in the Hall to drink ale while they waited for the food to be served. The kitchen was bustling with activity amid the preparations for the feast.

"I'm still tired from the journey here, Ma. Let's sit outside the Church. Those stones in front of it are high enough for us to pull up our feet away from the dirt."

The women made their way over to them, and Kate said, "it'd be nice to go inside out of the cold, but Brothers Durstan and Andrew will be in there."

"I heard the Monks talking after we had left them. They were arguing. I don't like the old one, Andrew. He wanted to go straightaway to the Monastery and not stay for the feast, but Durstan didn't. He was desperate to spend some time with his family. Andrew was being horrible to him. Durstan stood his ground, so he had to give in. Andrew said he would walk to the Monastery with someone called Branach provided Durstan joined him in a couple of days. I expect that he's gone by now and with good riddance, so there may only be Durstan inside. I'm not sure, Ma, that the candlelight coming through the window slit will be for his Christian God. There's a Pagan altar next to their table in the Church. Don't forget, it's Samhain tonight. Alys and I saw the altar earlier when we were looking around. It was so pretty. It had been decorated with leaves and berries, and looked much nicer than the Christian one, with its white cloth and battered wooden cross. I think that the Old Gods should have first call on our prayers tonight. Lord Duncan must surely agree. We shouldn't run the risk of offending them, but come on, Ma. We're alone now. What are you planning? You can't be content to go the nunnery, as you promised Uncle you would?"

"No, of course not! I've been trying my best to think of a way out, but you know how it is. Both of us need a Husband, or be seen to obey your Father's brother. If not, the punishment will be unbearable, and Aodh hasn't liked me since the time I stood up to his Mother." Kate smiled. "She cursed the day I was born. I sent the magic back to her. She died not long afterwards. I heard Aodh insisting that your Father denounce me because he had proof that I had an evil eye, but you knew your Father, Beth. He refused to hold with superstition, and told his brother to desist. Besides, I could always twist him around my fingers."

"And… what are you going to do? This isn't like you, Ma. To give up, without a fight," Beth said, anxiously.

Kate's smile widened. "Ahh! You haven't met Duncan's younger brother, Eideard. Have you? You'll like him. Once I got rid of my two escorts with a draught of poisoned ale apiece, and had a little time to play with here, I tried to interest Duncan himself. I wouldn't have hesitated to be his concubine or even a second wife, given that he isn't a strict Christian, but Mora has a vixen's eyes and jealousy to match the deepest emerald. It fell flat, so Eideard became the next best thing. Admittedly, he's not quite as attractive as his older brother, but it wouldn't be a bother being in his bed."

"Ma, you are quite dreadful at times!" Beth said, clearly shocked.

"Hush, child. Both of us will need to be skilful, to survive what the Gods have thrown at us this time. Every woman wants to make the most of herself, and have a happy life. May the Goddess smile on us, since we can't do it without the right man. Beth, my sweet, you only have to look at Mora's furs and jewels to see it. She's done well enough to change from the young girl who took Duncan's fancy to become his Lady. A love match that one, but there are still no guarantees that it'll last. Those of us less fortunate in life have learned to sharpen our skills for when opportunity arises again. We can rattle the threads of the wyrd as well as any woman." Kate's voice hardened. "Pah! I have no illusions. Mora would do the same to survive. There's no difference in any woman beneath it all. You've seen her cling to him, and everything she has. You'll have to begin soon, Beth, to use your womanly charms. There's magic in love, and sexuality. Virginity is the highest prize of all. Once taken by a man, it's irretrievable unless there's trickery. A virgin's blood is always the most potent for a spell. Why do you think the Druids prefer a pure, young, girl for sacrifice instead of a Wife? It's the way of the world, daughter, our world. We must needs live it."

She kissed Beth's cheek gently. "You did well to run from Aodh, and Odhran. It's given you another chance. Those men know how to play games a little too well, and are dangerous. They kill what they can't have, or for pleasure if the mood takes them. I've been busy too. I've cast a spell to charm Eideard, but it hasn't yet taken. I didn't have fresh blood to use, only a little which had dried on a cloth I found outside the kitchen. It would have been from some animal or another, and too old to be of much use. Nevertheless I had to try. I haven't been able to go into the forest. I still don't have my freedom here but the Goddess will find a way for both of us, if the amount of charms I've made has anything to do with it. My guess is that Alys has already pointed you in the Monk's direction in case Duncan is unwilling to help. You can trust her. Alys' interests are bound to yours. I'm sure that if it could have the desired effect, she would be happy to take on the Christian for you."

Kate laughed. "All frivolity aside, Durstan's God is a powerful one. I heard Mora say that his Church has protection from those across the sea. Rome is mighty, Beth. I believe it's stronger than Aodh, and any of his following. That could suit our purpose."

Beth felt uncomfortable. She began to fidget. "I'm not sure that I can do this, Ma. Durstan is nice, but I don't feel the fire in my blood when I look at him. I have thought about kissing him. I'm not certain that I want to."

Kate looked worried. "Beth! Don't forget our Ancestors. You and I are descendants of the Celtic fae. You must use the magic they have given to you, to get closer to him. I'm pleased that the older Monk has gone. He would have become an obstruction, given half the chance. I can help you too with charms, and the right herbs. You must take it into your heart that the Monk may well be your only option. It's the same as Eideard is mine, unless a miracle should come through for us. Quickly now, go into the Church. You can make a start before you have any more time to think about it. I'll wait here for you. You'll be safe enough."

Beth's eyes, darkened with fear. "Alys has been telling me the same thing, but I can't do it. Not yet, please, Ma..."

Kate sighed. "There's no need to be afraid, child. The Monk won't harm you. He doesn't have it in him, but if it bothers you so much then leave it be for now. We don't have Duncan's decision as yet and, unlikely as it may be, the Lord may still help us. I've certainly prayed enough times to Brigid for that to happen."

Beth squeezed Kate's hand, and said, "Ma, who's that?" A man was riding swiftly towards them on a large, black, horse. He spoke before Kate had the opportunity to reply.

"Two beautiful ladies gracing my Father's enclosure at dusk! I think Lord Duncan is doing rather better for himself these days, and I've only been gone overnight. Kate, I trust you are well," he said, alighting from the horse. He stared at Beth transfixed. "Who is this? A girl with red hair that sets the darkness aflame, and who has the look of you. Brigid can't have sent two from such a mould, to bewitch a mere man."

"Eoghan, this is my daughter, Beth," Kate said, with contempt in her voice.

The young man grasped Beth's hand, and brought it sensuously to his lips. "Good evening, my Lady." His eyes travelled the length of her body before he fixed them firmly on hers. Beth shivered within the depths of his voice, and because Eoghan was still holding her hand.

Kate saw her daughter's reaction. She said, hurriedly, "Mora was worried about you last night, Eoghan. We thought you might have been in trouble."

His laugh rang across the enclosure. "Mother should tend more to her weaving! My men and I are more than capable of fending for ourselves. She knows that. We had ridden too far when out hunting. It was late so we made camp for the night, and threw the animal we had caught onto the fire. It made a good meal." He dropped Beth's hand, and rubbed the dark stubble on his chin. "I would though have to agree with Mora that bathing shouldn't go amiss before tonight's celebration. I wouldn't wish to offend the Gods, or the ladies. Besides Samhain is my second favourite feast in the turn of the wheel. A New Year is the best time for a new beginning. What do you say, Beth? Given that Beltane is such a long way off."

His eyes stayed with Beth as he slapped the mare on her hindquarters. "Come on, girl. We have much to do before we can enjoy ourselves. I'll see you again tonight, my Lady, at my Mother's table." Eoghan threw himself carelessly up into the saddle, and cantered across the enclosure to the barn.

Kate could see that Beth was confused. Her eyes were saying it. If only she was more like Alys. She was too beautiful to be so naive. It would be her downfall. Eoghan didn't have sufficient power, to help them survive Aodh's tricks. Kate had learned as much from Mora. His Father despised him for the time he wasted, but it was a pity.

Beth and Eoghan were twin souls even though they didn't fully realize it. Their spirits had folded lovingly into each other when they were close. Kate didn't blame Beth in the slightest for her reaction to him.

As if reading her Mother's thoughts Beth said, quietly, "perhaps we could petition the King, if Lord Duncan doesn't help us?"

"We are women, Beth. Despite our looks, do you really think that even if we could get to see so important a man as Offa, that he would waste time listening to us? There'll be many around him who have a similar tale to ours, of whom he can have his pick. One of his men would laugh in our faces, and send us back to Aodh without further ado." Kate looked sadly at her daughter. "I'm very much afraid that we have been on our own since your Father died. I've been trying to tell you that we have to do the best we can for ourselves."

She hesitated. "I saw the light in your eyes when you looked at Eoghan, but don't be tempted. My guess is Duncan won't become involved in our trouble. It'll be Durstan then who can help us both. Listen to me, Beth. You could be our only chance, if Eidard sides with his brother against me. Get Durstan to take you to his Monastery on Iona, and speak to the Abbot. You've seen with your own eyes that he's an important man. The great wooden cross he carries with the gold on the front. Don't forget too, he's close kin to Duncan. I've heard tell of the Monks' Christian charity. They won't turn us away. They can't. It's against their faith to do so. From the little I know, they offer sanctuary. Why not, to us?"

Kate stared across the dark enclosure, with fear in her eyes and a churning heart.

Chapter 14
1st November, 794 AD

Lora's Story

Last night's smoke from the fire, and grease from the meat fat, filled the cold morning air. Lora's face felt grimy as she took the leftover scraps outside to feed the dogs. The poor creatures were half-starved. There was usually only a little left for them to eat after the men and women at the Hall had fed themselves like animals from the forest. Lora tried to make sure that her favourite, a grey wolfhound she had called Aelf, took the best of the scraps but she had to be careful. If she fed him first the others would set upon the dog, snarling and biting. Lora had prayed to the Goddess last night that there would be enough for all of them this morning, and her prayer had been answered. She was sweeping the dirt floor under the Lord and Lady's table when she noticed several large pieces of meat. Mora must have dropped them. May the Goddess bless her! Aelf would be well fed today.

Lora was fifteen years old. She tried to hide behind her long, dark, hair whenever she could. It framed an oval face and brown eyes. She loved to listen to the tales which the travellers told when they stayed at the Hall, but not the old hermit who came sometimes. The Gods had sent him mad. She was afraid when he was there. Those who spoke of faraway lands told the best stories. There was a great world beyond the Hall, across the sea, and within the Heavens. No one she knew had reached the stars, unless Brionach the Druid had been there. Her heart ached to leave Mull, to see the amazing sights of which the travellers had spoken.

Lora's Father had died six years ago, and her Mother had a hut of her own for the two years she lived after him. She hadn't been told to sleep in the Hall with the others next to the fire. They were the ones who didn't have a place, and were only one step away from being outcast. There was no dignity in that. Thankfully, Lord Duncan had thought well of her Father. Lora dreamed of being a lady. She had been watching the stranger, the one they called Beth. The way she walked, dressed, and her manners. It wasn't right how she taunted the Monk, flaunting herself at him with sweet words. Brother Durstan was a kindly man, and no match for that one with her dark arts. Lora had heard her talking to her companion, Alys, about the magic she could do. The Gods alone knew what she was seeking from Brother Durstan.

Lora blushed to think of it. She wasn't too afraid of Brionach, and his magic. She loved to listen to him. He could enchant her for hours in the way he talked, and laughed with a soul-filled light in his eyes. She teased him about this faraway look. He must visit places in the Otherworld and, although Lora hadn't said so, she longed to be able to go with him. She had seen him considering her, but it couldn't come to anything. He was Druid, an exalted one. Whilst here she was sweeping up around these stinking, snoring, bodies. They would want their breakfast soon, more ale no doubt, and the kitchen fire was still too low. It was taking a long time this morning to catch because of the cold, but nothing changed. It was the same last year, and every other that had passed. Once Samhain night was done, the Holly King began his preparations to fight the Oak King again, at Yule. The wheel turned, and turned. It was Nature's way.

Lora looked inside the wooden shelter where the tree branches were stored, to keep them dry. She chose a smaller one to drag into the Hall. As she pushed it onto the fire, a large splinter cut the palm of her hand, and the flames rose around the new wood. A drop of her blood fell into the fire, and was devoured by the brightest spark. She shivered. The Gods must be angry with her this morning. She touched the blue stone which was hanging from a leather thong around her neck. It had belonged to her Mother. Lora prayed that the magic within it would be strong enough to protect her, that Mother was with Father and the Ancestors, and all of them were watching over her.

"Hey, Girl! Watch what you're doing. You dragged that over my foot." Kennan farted loudly, and tried to grab Lora's waist when she hurried past him. The ale was still in the man. "Come here!" He shouted, slurring his words.

Lora escaped outside. She would have to move quickly. Kennan would come after her to urinate once he was fully awake. She didn't want to be nearby when he did. Eoghan was another one to avoid at all cost in the early morning, and late at night. Lora shuddered when an image of the Lord's son came to mind. No one was behind the enclosure gate. She slipped easily through one of the slender gaps in the fence, to follow the narrow path into the forest. It took her into an enchanted world of frosted tree branches which had created a canopy of snowflakes. A lone robin flew alongside her as she walked, hopping from tree to tree. Lora loved the peace she found here, but knew that she couldn't stray too far from the enclosure. The wolves would be hungry, and looking to pick off a single prey. She was startled when she felt a wet nose touch her hand. She had forgotten about the dogs, and Aelf had followed her. Lora sighed in relief. She felt safer with the animal at her side. His spirit was a faithful friend.

A low whistle caught her attention. The Druid was hidden from sight in his white robe and stillness. Sometimes it was as if he wasn't there at all, but would appear then right before her eyes. Lora was afraid of him when he did this. She was comfortable with the Old Gods whom she had known all her life, but Brionach remained a mystery. He was neither young nor old, and had depths which it was impossible to see into. His magic was powerful. Lora found sometimes that she couldn't avert her eyes from him, but he wouldn't harm her.

"Why are you out so early, Lora, and alone except for your dog? This isn't a safe place for either of you to walk. Let's go back to the Hall. If you have another destination in mind, it would be better to wait for others to be about, and the wolves sleeping."

Lora tried to lower her eyes from the intense blue of his. Brionach was playing with her. She sensed that he already knew why she had run away this morning. "I'm on my way to the shrine, to make an offering to the Goddess. I slip away when I can, often while everyone is asleep. I'm not usually missed, if I go early enough. Isn't the forest also a dangerous place for you, Druid?"

He smiled, at her feistiness. "I have nothing to fear, my Lady. My cloak is warm, and I have a staff for protection. Danger keeps its distance whenever I have it with me." The Druid looked down at the oaken stick he was holding. He felt the power of the runes which had been carved into the wood travel through his veins. "I'll walk with you to the shrine, Lora. I've been waiting for dawn. I'd like to thank the Goddess Brigid for the blessing of light."

Lora followed Brionach along the path through the trees until they began to thin, and the sound of a waterfall filled the air. She ran in front of the Druid, anxious to be at her destination. The copse was beautiful. Droplets from the waterfall and underground river fell onto the moss-covered rocks below. The snow had melted where the screen of trees protected the shrine. Lora knew that the pool under the fall was dark and murky because the Goddess hid there from mortal view. This place was a sanctuary between the world of the Old Gods, and men.

The Druid put Lora's thoughts into words. "The Goddess has chosen a beautiful place to rest, and from where she can bless the earth with abundance." He dipped his hands reverently into the stream, cupped the water, and drank deeply. It revived him. He had spent the night under the protection of the oak, and feasted with an ancient King in his dream of a past life. When the King had drank too much ale and lay in a deep sleep Brionach met him in the sacred place where past, present, and future become one. The Druid was tired, and concerned for the young girl who had crossed his path. He could see that she was troubled. He held his hand out to her. "Come here, next to me, and try the water. Its purity will refresh you."

Lora shook her head with a smile, and turned to face the stone shrine set between two of the oldest trees. She stared at the altar, with its strangely carved figurine in the recess. "Thank you, Druid. I've come to see the Lady. It's so lovely here. In summer when the shrine is covered in flowers, daisies from the fields, and the offerings. At Yule there are holly berries, and mistletoe. Look now! The Priestess has left leaves, to celebrate the season. They are beautiful, in a different way."

"Hear my prayer, Lady Brigid," she said, quietly to the Goddess. Grant me your protection." Lora began to shake uncontrollably, and Brionach saw her tears falling.

He could see in his mind's eye why she was seeking help from the Goddess, but he would have to ask her to tell him, so that she wouldn't be afraid to talk about it. "You shouldn't be like this, child. Why are you frightened?"

Lora stared at the effigy of Brigid. "Please don't ask me, Brionach," she said, sadly. I can't tell you, even though I know you only want to help me."

"Has someone hurt you?" The Druid said, gazing deeply into her eyes. Lora nodded. "Who was it? Tell me! I can't help you, if I don't know who is to blame."

"It was someone who is close to Lord Duncan and Lady Mora, so please don't ask me any more. I'm too afraid, to talk about it."

Brionach unraveled her words, as they tumbled over each other. "Duncan and Mora, so you must mean the boy, Eoghan? He is pursuing Beth!"

"Yes, but she hasn't listened to him," Lora said, stammering. "I don't know if I am going to have his child."

Brionach sat down on the edge of the pool where Lora was kneeling, despite the iciness of the earth. He pulled her gently to his chest until her face was resting against his shoulder. Her tears seeped through his robe, and his heart burned with the intensity of love. When she was ready to stand again, he helped her to her feet.

"I shouldn't have told you, Brionach. You must promise not to tell them. Beth is the one for Eoghan, not me. I've heard that she uses dark arts in her woman's magic, and I want none of it. The older women know which herbs to use in getting rid of a child, if it's not wanted, so I'll be alright if it does happen. I know that I need to keep away from him, in the meantime."

"Don't blame yourself, Lora. You mustn't do that! You still have your life before you. It'll be a beautiful one, if you wish it so. I'll give you a potion, if that's what you think you'll need." Brionach considered his words carefully. "But I don't see you as a Mother, Lora, not yet. It's too soon. I'll also give you an amulet, to protect you. We can ask the Goddess to bless the charm, to keep you safe. You must have it with you at all times, and make sure that you don't do anything to attract Eoghan's attention. Let one of the other women clean his sleeping place, preferably one of the crones. Let her see to his food too. Beth is his match, not you. I can see that there won't be another in this lifetime after her. Eoghan has no right to hurt you, Lora, or anyone else. Once Beth accepts him, it'll be over."

Lora smiled at Brionach when an image formed in her mind, of Eoghan with one of the old women at the Hall! He smiled too. It was also in his thoughts. "I will be more careful, Brionach, but what about Brother Durstan? Beth is tantalising him!"

"Men and women make many mistakes in the dance of love, Lora. It can easily hurt them. The Monk's soul is young. He hasn't yet realised what the Gods are saying to him, or how the threads of his wyrd are woven. If his thoughts weren't full of this new religion, he would understand. It's there for any of us to see. Durstan has also been confused by the darkness in Beth. The balance between dark and light does come right in the end, so don't be afraid for the Monk or yourself. Good and bad happens in all our lives."

Lora leaned towards the Druid, and kissed his cheek.

"Thank you, Brionach. I'm grateful for your kindness. Mora won't hear a word said against that son of hers, even though she must know what he's about, and Duncan wouldn't be interested. He would simply see it as Eoghan's right with the women, not that we have any feelings. He wouldn't take it seriously, but he also wouldn't want a child from this. Eoghan and I are obviously not handfasted or married in the Christian way. There wouldn't be a rightful place for a baby at the Hall, Brionach. I'm sickened by it! I want to forget him. It wasn't how I imagined it would be, with the man I loved. I had hoped to celebrate next Beltane with a good man, to handfast to him afterwards. That may not happen now because of Eoghan's selfishness. I don't have a Father or other man living who will stand beside me, and Lord Duncan won't." She sighed, sadly. "If I had been someone like Beth, with land or status to interest him, it may well have been a different story but my position is hopeless. I think sometimes that Mora would have made a much better Lord. She came from a poor background like mine. She understands how it is, to be a woman in these times."

Brionach saw the stricken look in Lora's eyes, and he held her again as she carried on speaking. "Machara died from her husband's hand last year, when you weren't here, Druid. He's yet to be tried by Duncan at his court, and it won't happen. We all know that. Our lives don't count for much unless the Lord is truly interested in us. A woman is most likely to die in birthing. If she does survive to a greater age, but can't spin or weave because of infirmity and has no family left to share their food with her, she may still be cast out to die in the forest. There's not much of a chance if you're a woman, and don't have the love of a good man to care for you."

Brionach held Lora tightly against his chest. Every bone in his body wanted to show her that she could have the safety she sought. "The life you want will still happen, Lora, despite Eoghan. You have to believe it! The dreams we have for the future can come true, if we hold onto them." He kissed her forehead gently. "Let's go back to the Hall. It's cold here, and you're shivering. I'll give you the herbs I promised, even though I don't believe you'll need them. Hide them well. You'll have to take to your bed for a few hours, if you do have them. Tell them it's the moon time, so you won't be questioned closely, and you'll be fine afterwards.

Come with me now, my Lady! It'll snow again soon, and we shall both be thought missing. They'll assume the wolves have had us for breakfast. Duncan will send men into the forest to search, and neither of us wants that to happen."

Brionach held Lora's cold hand inside his own, as she fell further into the depths of his eyes. She thought that she would drown in their blueness. This was the man she should have been with last night, and the Druid knew it too.

Chapter 15
17th December, 794 AD
The Threads Of The Wyrd

It was early afternoon, and almost dark. Durstan and Beth were sitting next to the fire, enjoying its warmth. They were alone except for several men who were talking on the far side of the Hall. The wall hangings glowed in the flickering light, but the torches lit by the slaves and hung from the timbers did little to lighten the shadows. Beth was captivated by the flames, while gazing into them had hurt Durstan's eyes. He felt as if he was looking into the biblical Hell Faisal enjoyed talking about, so he stared instead at the shadows.

Beth leaned closer to him, to touch his arm and draw him back. He could smell the herbs she had used to scent her hair. It seemed strange to have the delicate hint of spring at this time of year. It was undoubtedly part of a woman's magic. Abbot Faisal had warned the Monks to be wary of it. "You don't seem happy, Durstan," she said, softly. "What's wrong? You've been miserable since you left Brother Andrew at the Monastery yesterday. Do you need cheering up?" Beth wriggled, and realised that she was enjoying herself. This was much easier than she imagined it would be. She had been trying to remember everything Alys had said she needed to do. Now that it was happening and she was sitting next to a man, Beth was acting instinctively. The Monk was kind, and much to her surprise, she was finding him increasingly attractive despite Eoghan's interference.

The Lord's son disturbed her, especially at night when he entered her dreams with his smouldering eyes. They bored into her soul, so that the only way she could find peace was to throw off the fur coverlet, to cool her inflamed skin. There didn't seem to be a way of escaping him, or for that matter, Kate and Alys. Beth longed to be free, to follow her own path, but winter was always the same. Everyone had so little to do except feast, drink too much ale or wine, and generally get in each other's way. She assumed that this was the reason she missed the richness of Aodh's Hall so much. The hangings there were more luxurious, the pots beautiful, and the magical reflection in his glass had warmed many a cold heart. She sighed, heavily. "Durstan, I felt hurt when you left so soon after Samhain. I want to get to know you, Christian and Monk. That intrigues me. I've not met the like before."

A smile played on Beth's lips, and he blushed when she looked deeply into his eyes. The afternoon was taking on a surreal quality. Durstan recalled the oath he had sworn yesterday to Andrew, in a genuine attempt to protect the vows he had made to God as a boy. He tried desperately to clear his mind, but Beth's presence was intoxicating. She had filled his exhausted spirit with joy, and it was a relief to talk to someone other than Andrew with his stern face.

"I'm sorry, Beth, I haven't been ignoring you. I don't really know what's wrong." The lie slipped from his tongue and he coughed nervously, being unused to falsity. "I wanted to come back here, as soon as I could… to see my family." Beth pouted, "…and you too, of course. Andrew agreed to me coming back, on condition that I begin converting others to Christianity. We've almost reached our Christian Lord's birthday, and he's anxious to have good news to send to Iona." He frowned. "I'm worried that I won't have an opportunity of persuading many people, since it's the Yule feast. A time for the Old Gods, and for everyone to enjoy themselves, not to think about taking on a new deity.

Andrew finds all this much easier than I do. He's in his element at the Monastery. A couple of the young Monks seem as interested as he is in writing manuscripts. Andrew can talk about that all day every day. You may already have gathered that writing isn't for me, and my soul has managed to tie itself in knots during the last few months," Durstan said, sadly. Ailan had sprang to mind again, and her obvious betrayal. He changed the subject quickly. "When I was walking back to the Hall, I thought at one point I would have to turn around. The drifts were high in places, but I had promised my sister that I would be with her at Yule. I felt foolish at times, walking through the snow with a processional cross, especially when I didn't meet anyone else in the forest. Nevertheless I believe that having God's protection helped me travel here in safety."

"The snow doesn't seem so bad inside the enclosure, but your journey sounds awful, Durstan. Weren't your fingers and toes bitten by the ice? " Beth said, with concern.

"No, the cold weather doesn't bother me too much," he said, with a half-smile. "I'm used to being out in the fields with the sheep. I've struggled often enough with them to survive the winter, but the thing is…" Durstan paused. He felt uncomfortable, and was unsure of the words to use. "There's someone here I knew before… Ailan. You may have met her. We were friends…" Durstan hesitated, and found that he couldn't say any more.

Beth's back had straightened, in annoyance. "Yes, I know who you mean. I've seen her a few times, and heard about her from Alys. She's unpleasantly big. She's having a child. Her husband is a pig of a man, and his Mother is little better. She must have you under her spell, Durstan, if you are thinking about her so much." Beth's skin colour had changed to a deep pink. "That woman is nothing but a Devil!" She spat the words from her lips.

Durstan's heart sank when he realized his mistake in mentioning Ailan. "We can't be talking about the same person, Beth. The Ailan I know is a harmless soul whom God hasn't always smiled on kindly. That's all." He looked sadly at the beautiful woman by his side. He didn't understand why she was behaving like this. Beth was obviously used to being given everything she needed to live a comfortable life, including the silver armbands she wore, and the large emerald ring which matched her eyes.

Her red hair swung magnificently across her face. "It sounds as if you would be the best one to know all about that."

"I don't understand. I only mentioned that we had been friends. If this is jealousy, Beth, it's a sin. There's no need for it."

"Me, jealous of an ugly woman! Whoever she is, she can't compete with me." Beth pulled the emerald ring from her middle finger, and threw it into the heart of the fire. The flames rose rapidly before dying against the stone which sparkled in a prism of coloured light. "Ask me anything you want to know, Monk, and the Goddess Brigid will answer you because that is my intention."

Durstan was starting to be afraid. He didn't know Beth well, or how powerful she could be. He shook his head. "Can't you see what you're doing? You are the one who plays with magic, not Ailan. Please leave the darkness alone. It isn't right. I am Christian, not pagan like you, and magic isn't a toy. You may be able to see things in the fire which I can't. That still doesn't make it right for me to listen. Take lessons from the Druid, if you must, but stop playing with it. I know there's a lot do in this world with its superstition and charms, but I thought you were different." His hand had crept to the wooden crucifix around his neck. "You only need to have faith in the Christian God, and He will protect you too, if you pray. The Lord our God cares for all those who believe in Him." Durstan bent over the fire, and retrieved the ring with the help of a stick. He pushed it onto the hearth stones to cool.

Beth's eyes flashed triumphantly. Durstan was talking about giving her the protection of his Church. Duncan still hadn't answered her request, and she was becoming increasingly afraid that Aodh would send men for them despite the bad weather. Kate had also stressed again the importance of obtaining the Monk's help. She said that getting a decision from Duncan and his brother was proving akin to pushing the wind.

Beth felt that it couldn't do any harm if she tried a little harder now, to persuade the Monk to agree to her every wish. "I can tell, Durstan, that you're attracted to me." She grabbed his hand and placed it on her left breast, leaning towards him expecting a kiss. The Monk pulled away from her quickly. He felt as if his hand had been put in the fire.

"No! Stop it, Beth. I can't. It's not right. Whatever you might think I'm a Monk, and we… aren't married in the Christian way, or even handfasted. Besides…" He couldn't continue. Ailan was with him again.

Beth was elated. She felt powerful, but realised that she may have gone a little too far, too soon. She attempted to look shamefaced, and lowered her eyes to her hands which she had clasped on her lap. "I'm sorry, Durstan. I thought you wanted me to do that. I did see something in the flames this afternoon which has worried me." She paused, as if not wishing to continue.

"You may as well tell me all of it, Beth," he said, irritably. "What we've done is bad enough, and this has to be the end of it. My vows prevent me from being involved in devilry."

Her eyes blazed. "The Gods are getting ready for you to return to them. They want you back. You've wasted opportunities you have been given. That has angered them." Durstan saw the flames from the fire dart in every direction. He tried desperately to remember his conversation with Brionach at Litha, when they had sat through the night on the machair, and the Druid told him that he would see Ailan again. But Beth's voice was drawing him closer to her. "I'm repeating the words which the Gods said to me, Durstan. I know you want me, handfasted or not, Monk or not." She fondled the charm which Kate had sewn into the edge of her tunic.

Durstan stared at her mesmerised. He was finding it difficult to understand what was happening. She was a vibrant woman, full of life, and this afternoon had been far beyond his experience. It was true that he was tempted by her touch. He knew now that he should have kept his distance from her. He wondered fleetingly why she was interested in him when she could have the choice of any man, but the thought was soon gone. She was beautiful, and he had touched her intimately. "Will Alys leave us alone, Beth? If we go to your hut."

"Yes," she whispered, as her lips grazed his. He knew then that he was lost until she said, "but we can't. Not yet. I want to get to know you better first." She looked around the Hall. "There's no one here that matters except us, so kiss me properly." Beth looked down demurely at her hands. Durstan pulled her roughly to his chest, unable to withstand his frustration any longer. He pressed his lips hard against hers. She tasted of the forest, the sky and Sun, an enchanted night. The kiss deepened at his insistence. She didn't struggle but managed to whisper, breathlessly, "not yet, Durstan. When it's Yule!"

Eoghan, who had been watching them from the shadows near the door, strode angrily into the snow which covered his Father's enclosure.

Thirty miles further south beyond the forest, two men were also sitting next to a blazing Hall fire. Aodh's voice betrayed his excitement. His eyes were alight with greed. He was the eldest by a few years, nearing fifty summers. The leanness in his face was turning to fat from indulging in excessive feasting, and wine.

Odhran looked haggard. He had been riding with one hundred of his men for the last four days. His straggled, black, hair and unkempt beard were dirty. The skin on his face was pockmarked from a childhood illness, and had the appearance of misshapen pebbles on a track. His dark eyes bored into Aodh, willing him to accept the proposal. "It's a difficult journey for the Monks to make in this weather but, as usual, they are misplacing trust in the Christian God to protect them. I'm told too that the Saint's bones need to be in Durham for Yule on their Lord's Day. The Abbot there sent a message weeks ago, that this was to be done. They delayed, arguing that Aldin's remains should stay in Whitby, where they have been for the last fifty years. Pilgrims give coins to see the bones, and more to touch them. Quite understandably, they are anxious to keep them for as long as possible. Durham is, however, the greater Church. Their Abbot has the Northumberland King's ear, so is not to be disobeyed. He no doubt wants to add these to the collection which he has already amassed. My guess is, he will pay handsomely to have them returned to him, if they should be stolen on the journey to Durham. The casket is valuable too. It's covered in precious stones from across the seas, and is well known to house Aldin's bones. Their validity wouldn't be questioned, if we had both."

Odhran smiled. "This is where you come into it my friend, Aodh. A respectable Lord who can act as go-between. If I try to sell the casket and its contents to the Abbot, the King's men will surely come after me, given how I have angered him in the past. You on the other hand are independent, simply the person who has learned of the whereabouts of Saint Aldin. You can say that there's a trail of men who need to be bribed to get them back, and once agreed, we can share the Abbot's coins between us. The King trusts you. I need money to pay my men, Aodh. I also haven't forgotten about the girl and her fortune, not to mention my bed." Odhran's eyes filled with lust.

"Are you sure the bones and their casket won't be well guarded? The Abbot will surely send men to travel with the Monks, if they are as important to him as you say?"

Odhran smirked. "We are talking about a small group of holy men who think that no one would dare interfere with them, or their God. My source at the Monastery tells me there will only be a handful of riders, travelling through the forest. They will be an easy target to ambush. Now, Aodh, what of the girl? I hear she ran off while I've been away on other business. She has spirit. I'll give her that!" His laugh resonated through the Hall.

Aodh was anxious to please him. They had been friends for several years, and he was well aware of the younger man's mercurial temper. He also wanted Beth off his hands, as soon as possible. Kate, the mother, had been troublesome enough. Aodh didn't want Odhran to change his mind at this late stage, or to run the risk of losing his share in Beth's inheritance. So, despite his reluctance to become involved in Odhran's latest plan, he decided to help him. "She has gone to Duncan's enclosure to find her Mother, and thinks to escape us. She is safe enough there for the time being. Don't worry! Beth is still yours for the taking, Odhran, once we have dealt with this latest problem. It would help me too if you could see your way clear to sending a couple of trustworthy men with the Mother. Kate is to be taken safely, or unsafely as I would prefer to say, to the nunnery in Ireland."

Odhran grasped Aodh's hand in his, to signify their agreement. He pulled the older man to his chest in a hearty embrace, and said, "you mentioned a new wine that has been sent to you. I would like to try a glass before the night is over."

Aodh smiled with relief, and shouted for a slave to bring glasses. All the loose ends of the wyrd would soon be woven together again.

Chapter 16
17th December, 794 AD

A Shell Necklace

Ailan walked to the beach in the falling snow. She had slipped out of the hut, to be by herself for a short time. Durstan and Beth! She couldn't bear to think of it. How could he have done this? She had seen them in the Hall with their heads bent, laughing and sharing a jest. They might as well have been kissing. Monk or not, he was like all other men even Branach, and what did she have? A Husband who was roughness itself, and a necklace taken from the sea. She stroked the shell with cold fingers, and gasped as the sharp edge cut her finger. The taste of blood when she brought the wound to her lips made her feel even more angry, then tearful.

When Duncan told her to handfast with Branach, she had tried to be happy. They lit the red candles together, used them to fire the white one, before extinguishing it as a symbol of their love. That proved the most difficult, to say that she loved Branach. It was impossible now to lie, and she deeply regretted taking part in the ritual. The better option would have been to risk being outcast for disobeying the Lord. Durstan would have searched for her in the forest, if that had happened, and there could have been a different ending than this. All of it was her own fault. She was being rewarded for insulting the Goddess, in the way she had used the love Brigid gave to everyone.

Vomit rose into her throat from the baby. She had cried so much on the way here, that her head was thumping in time to Thor's hammer. She had come with the half-thought of walking into the sea and letting the waves take her, but that meant Tam would be left alone. An angry serpent writhed uncomfortably in her chest. Women like Beth had simply to snap their fingers, and the world fell at their feet the right way up. Her hand tightened around the shell. Much good it did keeping this trinket. They had found it whilst walking on the beach at dawn. It was the day after Beltane. Ailan could have sworn that she had seen love in Durstan's eyes when he picked it up, to give to her. She sobbed.

The Old Gods had smiled on them, and now she had offended the Christian one. Of course this was her punishment. She clutched the shell tightly, ignoring the sharp edge. Beneath its smooth surface, it held the essence of the sea as she had held Durstan. Tsk! He had probably given Beth those silver armbands she wore, and jeweled brooches for her fine cloak. His sister would have been happy to delve into her own jewellery casket for him. It was obvious that Mora wanted to please Durstan, as every other woman did. Ailan pulled hard at the shell, and the leather thong holding it in place broke free of her neck. She refused to wear his amulet any longer.

Warm tears stung her cold cheeks, and her knees sank into the wet sand when she fell forward. She was exhausted. Her heart was beating too hard. She could feel the child moving anxiously within her, and realised that she needed somehow to cope with the loss. Durstan was gone. The Gods had taken him from her, and she had become a

Mother instead. Her son had the right to everything she could give him. Tam needed her too. Ailan felt a sharp pang of guilt. She should have been thinking of them, and caring for her brother. Oonagh was evil. Ailan had often heard her curse others. She may well have placed Tam in danger by running away.

She hauled herself upwards, surprised by the weight of her wet hair and clothes. Her eyes were red and sore, but she had reached a decision. She had to talk to Durstan. She had felt ugly, and turned away when he seemed to want to speak to her. What a fool she had been. It would be difficult to approach him now. He was constantly with Beth or Mora when he wasn't inside his Church. Ailan couldn't go in there. The Christian God would be angry if she went inside His sacred place. If Oonagh or Branach saw her, she would be in even worse trouble. No! A message would be the best option. Saille couldn't take it to him. Mora would have something to say, if she saw a slave speaking to Brother Durstan, a holy man from Iona. The Goddess whispered in her ear. "Tam!" He was the only one who could slip unnoticed into the Hall. Ailan's heart began to race. She could tell the boy to repeat the message to Durstan. He loved learning riddles, and despite being so young, Ailan was sure he would be able to remember four words. "The baby is ours." She couldn't tell him how much she hated Branach and Edgar. That would come later. The pain in her arm was a constant reminder of what had happened.

Ailan turned around, with renewed purpose. She would go back to the enclosure. It was important Durstan was told that she hadn't betrayed him, and wouldn't have done in any circumstances. The Gods alone knew what he must have thought, seeing her with Branach. She could also say with certainty, that the child wasn't his. The Goddess Brigid had told her so in a dream. The baby was Durstan's. Ailan walked carefully, so as not to leave deep footprints and run the risk of annoying the Gods any further. After taking a few cautious steps away from the sea, she ran back to pick up the necklace. It was still beautiful, despite the cord being broken. She held it tightly in her hand next to her heart, and without almost daring to breathe, the thought came. Maybe Durstan would come back, one day?

Ailan hurried through the trees to the enclosure, and stumbled fearfully into Cormac's hut. She knew that she had been gone too long when Oonagh looked up from the fire. Her grey hair shone greasily in the half-light. "Where have you been this time, girl? I shouldn't have to look after your whelp of a brother, and my son, now that you're here. It's your duty, not mine. Have you forgotten that Branach needs a winter cloak for when the snows are at their worst? He won't have it, if you don't sit and weave. I need a new shawl too. This one is threadbare." She banged the wooden table with her fist. "You need to look to your tasks, girl, and see the state of you!" She smiled, with pleasure at Ailan's disheveled appearance.

Ailan mumbled an apology, with her eyes downcast. Branach looked at her, and tried to ignore the baby's bulge. He wished they had a hut of their own. He thought that his Mother listened to their lovemaking at night. He had taken to hitting Ailan to please Oonagh, but felt ashamed afterwards, especially when Ailan no longer looked into his face.

Oonagh had been watching Branach from the corner of her eye. Her face reddened with anger. He wouldn't hear a word said against the girl. The Goddess was her witness that she had tried enough times. Surely he could see what was happening immediately in front of him? It was Ailan's fault that Edgar was dead. Her favourite boy who hadn't known what he was doing. The girl had set her evil eye on him, to see how it would feel to lie with a man like Edgar. Ailan should have been punished instead of him. Oonagh silently cursed her. Branach had always been a fool. He was his Father's son, of that there wasn't any doubt. Her useless Husband was never here. Cormac preferred of late to sit with anyone who would welcome him, and drink too much ale instead of being in front of his own fire.

Tam was asleep, rolled in a wolf skin near the wall. When Oonagh hit the table, it didn't disturb him. The boy was odd. He had the look of the Druid about him at times. It was plain to see that Ailan doted on him, more than she did her Husband, and Branach was her man! Even though he was rough with her, they were bound in the old way. The boy had lived six summers too long. Oonagh smiled, and cleared her mind of angry thoughts. She had known for days what she would have to do, to get her son back. It was simple. She had to kill the boy. He was a part of Edgar's death, as much as his sister. Let them both pay. Ailan wouldn't survive long without him, if the baby didn't see an end to her. Oonagh would find a way, and soon. The Gods would let Edgar come back, if they had the boy instead. She hummed happily to herself when she thought of how the girl's pretty face would appear tomorrow. Her cheek would be wearing another bruise.

Ailan was looking at her Husband, with fear in her eyes. He seemed puzzled by her withdrawal from him, as if he was expecting more. She thought that he might want love but she couldn't give it to him, not the way he was. And there was Durstan. A rush of love warmed her skin momentarily before it was gone. It was as if Branach didn't realise what he was doing when he hit her. She feared constantly for the baby. He had only punched her abdomen once, when she had cursed him in anger at the way he dealt with her. A trickle of blood had run down her legs. He shrugged his shoulders when he saw it, and thank the Goddess, the bleeding had stopped by morning. It was obvious that she was being punished for his Mother's benefit. They would often whisper together, and draw apart when she came across them.

Ailan thought again of Durstan's gentleness, and the laughter they had shared. Branach didn't look at her lovingly or put his arm around her shoulders for comfort. He hardly spoke to her. She cringed from the earthy smell which permeated his skin. Durstan's was infused with incense from a wondrous place, the Otherworld, and the Gods. Ailan sighed. Was it a surprise that she had fallen in love with him? ...She had to send the message.

It had crossed her mind recently, that Branach's eye could easily stray to another. He might abandon her on one lie or another. It would be done, with Oonagh's encouragement. She had to begin thinking clearly again. She couldn't allow Tam and the baby, to be at the mercy of the forest. She didn't have any illusions that however ill-treated she considered herself, none of them would last long outside the enclosure.

If only Branach had been stronger, they might have had a chance. He had tried in his own way at first. He had even let Tam ride on his back to please her when they walked by the sea, but that ceased almost immediately. Oonagh was unhappy about it. She said that Branach should save his strength for fishing, men's pursuits to feed and clothe them, not take part in a child's game. Ailan remembered when Durstan had played with Tam on Iona. She had watched them, and he had looked around with a smile, to catch her eye. She could tell that he was enjoying himself.

Branach noticed the faraway look in his Wife's eyes. It infuriated him. *No wonder Mother said that she was evil.* Although he hadn't liked his brother, you only had to look at the harm which had befallen Edgar, to see that Oonagh was right. He would be better off without Ailan. Mother had said that once they were rid of her, he could have another. One of the new slave girls was pretty. She would do. Lord Duncan should not have told him to handfast with a she-devil. Ailan must have used her magic on him. She should have been stoned instead of handfast, and thrown from the enclosure like Oonagh said.

Branach stared at Ailan, and frowned. He knew in his heart that he would find it difficult, to let her go.

Chapter 17

The Yule Feast

It was snowing heavily, and the Yule feast was in progress. Everyone at the enclosure had left their own hearth to celebrate the solstice with Lord Duncan. A huge log had been brought in yesterday from the forest by ten men. It was burning in the fire pit at the centre of the Hall, and the flames cast a cheerful glow all around.

Mora felt a sense of pride when she saw the number of people at the gathering, but this was quickly followed by disgust at how badly some of her Husband's people were behaving. Kisses and more were being exchanged freely. It was the fault of little else to do in winter, and too much feasting. After this there would soon be Beltane, when the Gods allowed them again to be with anyone they chose. No wonder handfasting didn't last long. Mora stroked the fine cloth on the sleeve of her tunic. She was fortunate to be married to the Lord. Women like her weren't often discarded unless for political reasons. As the Mother of Duncan's son, she represented the stability within his household. She had celebrated Beltane with the others only once since her marriage. Duncan said afterwards that it was not for her, as the Lord's Lady. It gave too many men the opportunity of getting closer to him so he forbade it. Her heart died a little every year when he went with the women into the forest, to celebrate the fertility of the earth. It had been harder to bear at the beginning until she had learned to accept it quietly, and occupy herself. It wasn't wise to rouse Duncan's anger. A few of the men who remained unaware of his decision continued to ask for her hand at Beltane, only to be refused.

The Lord's Lady did take part in the celebration at some enclosures if her Husband was less concerned, or perhaps the woman had a wanton eye? Mora wondered if she had joined the others, whether it would have made Duncan's actions easier to bear. How she felt afterwards, looking at the woman he had taken, but she wouldn't think of that now. She was safe for the time being. There wasn't any risk of a concubine replacing her or a second Wife. Duncan was sitting next to her tonight, and he would be snoring happily at her side when he had taken his fill of food and wine.

Eoghan was safe too on her left. He had arrived late, and had already drank too much if his demeanor was the measure of it. Mora sighed. The boy had become used to drinking heavily. He seemed to have something on his mind. It was unlike him not to have a girl beside him or on his lap. His mood would likely be about Beth. She was beautiful enough but another one to avoid as the plague, being cast from the same mould as her Mother. Eidard was certainly a match for Kate, but not the daughter for Eoghan. Mora couldn't help but think of him still, as the boy who had sat on his Mother's knee and put his head next to her heart.

She sipped her wine appreciatively, and looked around the Hall again. The women had tried their best to look festive for the feast. A few had saved new tunics made during the summer weaving. They had dyed them burnt gold, and leaf green. The Hall looked beautiful, with half the forest seemingly brought in by the men in branches of fragrant pine and holly. The Druid, who was seated on the other side of Duncan, had been out with a sickle knife to cut the sacred mistletoe. It was hanging from the beams, and candlelight danced at every turn. Lora was standing behind Brionach's chair. Mora noticed that she was wearing the copper bracelet she had given to her earlier in celebration of the solstice. It was one she had tired of, and good enough for a slave. She had also considered whether to give Lora one of her old tunics, even though the girl was smaller and would have found it necessary to tie a leather thong around her waist, but she had decided not to at the last minute. The cloth was pretty. It could be turned into a shawl to wear at Imbolc, if the season was warm enough. Mora was proud to have the finest clothes at the enclosure. She was wearing her favourite jewels tonight. They were more than good enough to rival Kate's necklace, and Beth's arm bracelets.

The Druid would play his harp soon. Mora intended to ask him to play again tomorrow when the Hall was quiet. The people tonight had drowned the scop's words, as they left his lips. Although Roan looked as if he didn't object, Mora knew that he did at heart. It took him weeks to compose the multitude of riddles and poems he was expected to tell at a feast. Naturally he wanted people to listen, to enjoy his words about the Lord's greatness in battle, the magic he could do. Duncan had laughed heartily, when he had seen the colourful rags the scop was wearing to entertain them. At least he had pleased the Lord sufficiently for him to be well fed tonight.

Brionach refused to gossip, but Roan was another matter. Mora was enthralled by his tales of other Halls.

He would describe in detail what the ladies were wearing, the jewels, and beautiful cloth. If there were any unusual tradings from over the sea, or people not seen before, he would tell tales about them. Duncan laughed when Mora tried to repeat his words. The Lord had seen much more of the world when he fought in Northumberland, and further south. He even knew some of the men who were called Vikings. Those who killed, and had terrified the Monks. Duncan liked the scop to travel, to spread news of his greatness, so that none would risk trifling with such a powerful Lord. Scops were well known for concocting outrageous tales, but Duncan had made Roan swear an oath to the Gods that he would only speak in his favour. Mora had chuckled tonight when the new bells he was wearing on a leather strap across his body jangled as he ran. He had jumped across the Hall, to the sound of the men shouting after him. It was a piece of foolishness which had delighted them all.

She had grown up with the people here, but they still made her despair at times. They missed so much when the ale was in their blood. A few years ago, she had tried to get them to reduce the amount they drank, and Duncan had come back to a surly reception. He ordered an immediate feast despite it not being a solstice. It was the only occasion when Mora feared that he might beat her. His belt was ready, but once she began to cry, he relented. She was forced instead to sit next to him at the feast, smiling in acknowledgement that she had been wrong. Her Husband was there to restore order to the chaos she had created. Mora hadn't forgiven Duncan for the humiliation she endured that night. Her heart couldn't accept that he was right. The world was in a turmoil. Most seemed confused or afraid, and too much ale didn't help.

She glanced along the table. Kate was sitting with her head close to Eidard's shoulder. Her hand had crept into his. She was whispering provocatively into his ear while her breasts strained to break free of her tunic. Eidard was smiling, and holding her hand for all to see. Duncan grinned at his brother. He raised his glass to him in blessing, and Beth was with Durstan again. The girl was next to her Mother. The pair of them were no doubt conniving more trouble. The food on the wooden platters in front of them lay untouched.

Durstan was also feeling distracted. It was impossible to keep his thoughts on God, although he had been trying to pray silently. They continued to drift in other directions. How his fingers had brushed against Beth's when they walked into the Hall. How he had felt when he kissed her, a few days ago. She had looked up at him tonight with her startling green eyes, making him feel again that the Ancestors' blood was coursing through his veins. He had seen Eoghan look her way more than once from where he was sitting at the other end of the table. Odhran was also pursuing her. Yet here she was with him, an ordinary Monk, apparently enjoying herself. He was mesmerized. A warm glow spread across his face when he realised that Beth was watching him. Whether or not she was aware of the effect she was having, there was nothing he could do. She had enchanted him. May God help him! He grasped the wooden cross hanging from his neck in an attempt to escape from his thoughts, at the same time as Beth decided to lean closer to him. She raised her voice to cut through the noise of the Hall, the laughter, and raucous shouting. It was the feast everyone had been waiting for, a time of plenty at mid-winter. "I hope that it's me who is filling your thoughts," she said, assuming that it would be.

"I can't seem to think of anything else," he said, immediately. He hadn't meant to tell her this. Alcohol formed the words. Durstan had grown accustomed to weak ale, as part of the daily diet on Iona. Although the wine which the slaves were serving tonight had a pleasant taste, it was much stronger.

Beth laughed in delight. "I was right. You do like me. I wasn't entirely certain that you did. You are a Monk, whatever that means. I've heard a little about the vows you make to your Christian God. It's much easier being pagan, and definitely a lot more fun."

Durstan was confused. He wasn't used to playing games with words, and was finding it difficult to talk to Beth. This wasn't the same as having a conversation with Ailan. He could tell her anything, but the man within him began to rise to the challenge. He pushed Ailan from his mind. Truth had to be the best defence. "I feel overwhelmed by you, Beth. So much so that there isn't a gap left in my thoughts for anything else. I'm sorry, if you assumed it was any different."

Beth reached across the table, to put her soft fingers inside his large hand. Durstan felt powerless to retract his clumsy bones. He had lost his soul. He was thankful that Alys wasn't sitting near them, but across the other side of the Hall. He didn't feel sufficiently confident to cope with her lewd remarks. She had her arms around Rae, one of Eoghan's men. Durstan had noticed him earlier push his fingers down Alys' tunic. She had thrown her head back and laughed, then kissed him hard on the lips. Durstan wished he dared do the same with Beth. The wine had made him feel relaxed, and he couldn't take his eyes from her.

Beth had also seen Eoghan, watching them from further

along the table. He had glared at her when she caught his eye. It was easy to see that he was angry, even from a distance. She shivered. Durstan seemed oblivious to him. She was trying to ignore the confusion she felt when Eoghan rose unsteadily to his feet. He staggered towards them, and held onto their table with both hands. "I missed you, kinsman, when you arrived. You left with the other holy man." Eoghan seemed to be in difficulty finding his words. "My Mother is glad to see you. Perhaps some of the others too?" Eoghan's eyes raked Beth's skin lasciviously. Her heart missed a beat. She couldn't hold his gaze. "I will speak with you later, and you, my Lady." Eoghan bowed to Beth in an exaggerated manner before he staggered across the Hall to join several of his men.

Beth's blood pounded through her veins from the physical attraction she felt for Eoghan. She sensed that Kate was trying to catch her attention, and she turned dutifully to Durstan. He had dropped her hand when Eoghan approached them. "Are you afraid that your God will punish you for holding my hand?" She said, with her thoughts elsewhere. "Perhaps send a thunderbolt to strike you down?" She paused, to breathe deeply. "Instead of trying to convert me to your faith, Durstan, why don't you follow the Old Gods? They prefer us to behave as nature intended." She grabbed his hand, and Durstan pulled it quickly away. He felt as if he had been bitten by a serpent.

"I am Christian, Beth, and my Father Abbot wouldn't agree with what's happening here tonight," he said, in a voice unlike his own. "God is in all of creation, including the love we feel for each other. I can't see that by holding your hand I've committed so grave a sin, but I know others would disagree so we had better stop doing it."

Beth hadn't considered that this might be the Monk's

reaction, and she felt irritated. She hadn't met anyone else like Durstan. The challenge he presented was starting to interest her. She had felt the power of earth and sky flow from his fingers into hers when he held her hand earlier. It wasn't an unpleasant feeling. He was strong. He didn't seem to realise it, but she would find a way through the barrier he was creating between them to protect himself. She smiled warmly, at him. "Let's be peaceful for a while, Durstan. I want to hear more of your God. I'll tell you about Brigid and the Old Gods I follow, if you'd like me to. It would be good to know more about each other."

Durstan flinched when he saw Branach come into the Hall followed by Ailan. They found places at a table next to Oonagh. When she realised that Durstan was staring at her, Ailan averted her eyes. If only she had been able to get a message to him, to tell him the truth. Tam hadn't grasped what she wanted him to do, and there wasn't anyone else she could ask.

Durstan was confused. If only he hadn't drank so much wine. Something wasn't right. If Ailan still loved him she would have sent a message, and she hadn't done. His heart sank. Beth's fingers were pulling the sleeve of his robe. "What's wrong now, Durstan? If it's the Old Gods, I promise that I won't speak of them again tonight."

Ailan was with her husband. He was sitting next to a beautiful woman. That was all he needed to think, and Durstan turned his attention to Beth. "Everything is fine. I'm sorry. I can tell you stories about Jesus, if you would like to hear them. They are good tales. Our world is changing fast, Beth. Christianity will unite everyone in time. Kings, and Lords, will all be in agreement if there is only one God. Abbot Faisal says that our Church in Rome will send mercenaries to protect us. God sent His only son to save men, and Rome will follow this example with a Christian army. My heart also tells me that it can't carry on being the way it is now at the Monastery. If you believe in my God, you follow the light of love."

Beth stroked Durstan's hand with her fingertips. "I was listening when you told the children a story about the Nativity. Was that Jesus' birthday you were talking about? I liked the tale of the Kings travelling far with gifts for the baby. Tell me more, Durstan. I love stories."

He squeezed Beth's hand, relieved that they seemed to be having a normal conversation, albeit shouted into one another's ears. "It's written in our bible, the book which teaches us about the Christian God. I've heard that powerful men in Rome are arguing because the stories inside it are open to different interpretation. They can't agree on which version is the true one. I suppose it's the same as when the scop tells his tales. We have to decide what we believe to be true, and the parts of the story he has fabricated."

Beth nodded, slowly. "It sounds much like the conflict which exists between the Old Gods and Goddesses. Our stories are from the Ancestors' memories, and the Druids' runes." She hesitated, but only for a second. It was the right time to ask. Durstan was gazing longingly at her. "When you leave the Hall to join Brother Andrew, will you take me with you to Iona, and speak to your Abbot for me? I need your protection, Durstan, sanctuary. Duncan won't agree to me staying here. Mora said that she can't persuade him to intervene. You were right. He's too afraid of starting a blood feud, with my Uncle Aodh, and Odhran. Duncan doesn't have enough men of his own to defend the Hall, and fight off an onslaught if they take offence. There have been reports of Odhran's men searching closeby. It's only a matter of time, Durstan, before he finds me. Duncan intends to hand me over to him. I know he does." A solitary tear stole down her cheek. "Please help me. Don't condemn me to a loveless marriage with Odhran. I can't bear the thought of it."

Against his better judgment, Durstan squeezed Beth's hand. He hadn't forgotten about Ailan, or that it was unwise to become involved in this situation. Faisal would undoubtedly be against it. He would be blamed, yet he didn't know how to refuse. Beth obviously needed help, and God had placed her in his path. Durstan felt confused. *Perhaps this was what the Abbot meant by Christian duty?* "We shall have to see what God intends for us, Beth. I'm only a simple Monk. I don't know if the Abbot will take you in. I've seen him turn others away when, like Duncan, he didn't want men taking arms against him. What about Eoghan as a protector? He is obviously interested in you."

"No, Durstan! Eoghan frightens me, in a different way to Odhran. He searches me out, and talks so intensely. I don't know what to say to him. My words become jumbled when I speak, and he's a bad person. I can feel it. The Goddess has sent warning signs to me. Please help me, Durstan. I feel safe, only when I'm with you."

Beth looked down at their clasped hands, and Durstan's heart melted.

Chapter 18

Matters Of The Heart

All was softly white in the forest beyond the enclosure. It was still snowing, as the winter moon hung low in the sky. Durstan had his back against the cold, damp, timbers at the side of the Hall. Beth was kissing him. He pushed her away gently. "Let's go back to the feast. We shouldn't be doing this!" Her eyes searched his for a way to continue. When she found the look of defeat within them, she laughed. She grabbed his hand, and pulled him along behind her through the snow.

Alys picked up her cloak when they burst into the hut. She smiled slyly at Beth, and left. Her friend had clearly stolen the Monk's heart, at least for tonight. She wondered if Beth had cast a spell to make this happen. She had talked of it, but Alys was sceptical. Every woman has her natural magic. Love is a powerful ingredient, but the darker arts are another matter. Despite Beth's father being Druid, it didn't mean that she would be able to follow him on that path. She hadn't undergone the Druid's lengthy training. It was strange too that she hadn't turned to the powerful magic they used for protection when escaping from Aodh's Hall, if she was able to use it. Perhaps she was more afraid of entering the Otherworld than being found by Aodh? What did any of it matter? Let tonight be as it was going to be. The Old Gods and Eoghan were still the best. He was a real man! Alys' heart turned a somersault when she heard his voice. She walked across the enclosure as if in a dream, to gossip with the women in one of their huts.

Beth stood with her back to Durstan as she removed her clothes, and laid under the fur on the pallet. She felt nervous, but equally elated. She had won the protection of the Church for Kate, Alys, and herself. Durstan was trying not to stare at her as she undressed, but was finding it impossible. Beth didn't look the same as Ailan. He felt a pang of guilt. He had to forget her. He was no longer part of Ailan's life. She had betrayed him, and he still couldn't understand why Faisal thought that lovemaking was a sin. The Monks who celebrated Beltane had the Abbot's tacit agreement to be on the shore that night so as not to offend the Old Gods. This surely wasn't any different? Durstan remembered how his heart had soared when he was with Ailan, teasing her about the honeyed cake, but enough of that! It was all for nothing, and made the hurt inside him gnaw harder. This wasn't the place for misgivings, and he didn't love Beth.

Durstan's hands touched her skin, and he murmured, "you are beautiful." Beth's smile was radiant, but he didn't see the tears which escaped from her eyes during the night. When they found each other again in the half-light of the dying fire, they talked awkwardly of how it might feel to be in love, until they fell into a dreamless sleep.

Beth could hear Alys' voice in the distance, asking her if she was awake. Her friend had crept into the hut when she saw through a crack in the wall that Durstan was no longer there. The slaves were making a noise in the kitchen, and she had decided to leave the pallet she was sharing with one of the women in her hut. "Beth, wake up! Tell me everything. I can't wait any longer to know how it was with the Monk."

Beth stretched out her hand for Durstan, but he was gone. Her heart sank. She didn't want to share this secret so soon with Alys. Nevertheless she knew that she would have to say something, or not hear the end of it. She felt a softness when she thought of Durstan. "I will never forget last night," she said, in a hoarse voice, while pointing to a nearby pot. "I need some water." Alys handed it to her, and sat on the edge of the pallet.

Beth drank deeply. She dropped the pot onto the floor once it was empty, and laid down again. Sleep was still in her eyes. "I don't want him to be a Monk, Alys, or a servant to this Christian God. He should be with me now," she said, quietly. "I'm afraid sometimes when I see the future. I know he's in danger. The Goddess warned me that he must be careful." Beth paused. "I was so afraid of what his reaction would be when I tried to persuade him last night, but it turned out exactly as you thought because of Ailan. I don't know him properly, Alys, but I think that I could love him in time."

Beth stared across Alys' shoulder into the distance. "The Gods haven't let me see how this will turn out. I'm frightened." She searched for her friend's hand, and held it tightly inside her own. "Some of the Monks on Iona have fathered children, if the gossip is to be believed. I'm not sure whether Durstan would be happy to do that, or if I can persuade him to leave his holy island, but I can't be with him while he's a Monk. I know I can't. He said that he was going to the Church as soon as it was light, and I want to make an offering to the Goddess once his prayers are done. Mother gave me a potion to take last night so there won't be a child, but I need to ask Brigid to tell me more."

Alys looked at Beth, in despair. "May the Gods protect us from men, and virgins! Beth, don't you remember our plan? You need Durstan to be Christian. You were only meant to seduce him until we gained the protection of his Church, and the Christian God. We can't fight as men do, so have to use our womanly skills. It's the reason the Goddess gave them to us. Your Mother believes that Aodh and Odhran won't dare defy the Christians, and Duncan has refused to help us. Whatever you are feeling now will pass. Just think of it, Beth. If you are unmarried on your twenty first birthday, your Father's land in Mercia and coin chests will be yours. King Offa will return them to you. There's no reason to believe that he won't keep his promise. More's the pity Aodh became your guardian when your Father died, and had any say in this. He's evil, that one, but you know how much I hate him after what he did to me last year. Think of it again, Beth. A comfortable life of your own to manage. There won't be any more running, or chance of being bedded with a man like Odhran."

Alys was fully aware that her own safety lay in Beth's hands. Aodh wouldn't take kindly to her having escaped with his niece. "There isn't any need for you to be bound to Durstan and his Church for the rest of your life. You are different to me, Beth. You'll have your own land and money, if you can only get beyond this. You'll be able to choose which man should stand by your side, and life changes constantly. Enjoy it, as it is now. Do as I do. I have my eye on one of the men here. I know you, my Lady. You wouldn't be happy without your jewels and furs, or the status. I can't see you as a Monk's woman, dressed in coarse cloth." Alys giggled. "And there are too many good, skilful, men out there for you to stay with your first lover. It's simply not fair on the others." She grinned, mischievously. "I didn't stay with the women, all of last night. I changed my mind once I started thinking about Rae, Eoghan's friend. I'd been trying to decide whether or not to go to him, or let him wait. I had my answer when you turned up with the Monk."

"Alys, you didn't! I thought you loved Hearn at Uncle Aodh's enclosure, and planned to handfast with him," Beth said, sounding dismayed.

"I do, but why waste an opportunity with a good man? I won't be this beautiful forever." She frowned. "Rae was full of ale last night by the time I got to him. He told me things in the throes of falling from there into loving me. He said that Eoghan thinks you have bewitched him, and doesn't care that you have. He won't rest until he has you next to him at night, whatever it might take. Rae laughed because the men are teasing Eoghan about his obsession for you. It's stronger than any feeling he has had previously for a woman."

The happiness in Beth's face infuriated Alys. "I told him that it wouldn't happen, but Rae was adamant. Eoghan is not a man to be trifled with. He's done some terrible things, Beth. You must be careful of him." Alys' eyes were full of malice. "Do you remember Ailan?"

"How could I forget that woman? Her name seems to be on everyone's lips, especially Durstan's! What about her?" Beth said, irritably.

"You'll never guess what happened to her?" Alys lowered her voice, confidentially. She told Beth about Edgar, and Ailan's handfasting to Branach. "Rae told me what Eoghan did to the Addle-Head when he found him. I can't tell you how bad it was." Alys paused, to catch her breath. Beth wouldn't have Eoghan, if she wasn't able to. "Edgar didn't know what he was doing when he attacked Ailan, and what Eoghan did was evil. Keep out of his way, as much as you can. The Monk's magic may not be powerful enough, to protect you from someone like him."

Beth blushed. Alys wasn't aware that Eoghan had been seeking her out at every opportunity, and she had sensed that there was more between them to come. She didn't want to discuss it. Alys had been acting strangely. Something was bothering her. It was unlike her not to say what it was. Despite their feelings, the two women put their arms around each other as they had done since childhood, and listened to the sounds crossing the enclosure from the kitchen. Beth could smell wild boar cooking on the fire. It was drifting through the loose timbers in the hut and making her feel hungry. She pulled away from Alys, intending to get dressed. Her friend handed the clothes to her one by one, smiling when she saw how hastily they had been discarded.

"I thought Durstan might have kissed me this morning, Alys, before he left. He did tell me last night, how guilty he was feeling. I suppose that was the reason he didn't. If only he believed in the Goddess, and here I am wondering if I could be in love with a man who has a different God. I didn't think that would happen. It's too incredible."

Beth laughed. "If I wasn't talking about Durstan, I believe I would be afraid of him, and his strange stories. His prayers sound very much like spells to me. I hope that this Christian God doesn't take offence, that I've managed to steal a Monk's heart from His Church," she said, trying to make light of it, then silently repeating the words of a charm for her own protection.

Chapter 19

Love Is The Answer

Durstan was walking between the darkened huts. It was bitterly cold. He had left Beth as soon as his eyes opened. He felt ashamed, and desperately wanted his life to change. He quickened his footsteps. It was too quiet here. The sooner he was inside the Church the better he would feel, even though God had been far from his thoughts last night. A grey figure appeared around the corner of the nearest hut, and hurried towards him. Durstan stopped. He didn't yet know the enclosure's ways, unlike the Monastery where the Monks were awake during the night.

"Uncle! I thought it might be you. You were much too busy last night with Beth for us to speak." The jealousy Eoghan felt had turned to hatred, and he couldn't pretend otherwise. His eyes retraced the Monk's footsteps in the snow, to the door of Beth's hut. "Aah, I can see that your evening didn't end in the Hall." His voice seethed with anger. He knew that he could kill the Monk, with one slash of the knife at his belt. Eoghan's fingers tightened around its hilt in anticipation, but it wasn't the right time. People had started to leave the huts. Eoghan's hand moved reluctantly away from the knife while Beth's shadow on his uncle's face continued to taunt him.

Durstan sensed the violence within the man standing

opposite. He realised that the situation would have to be handled carefully. Eoghan belonged to Woden. "Nephew, it's good to see you out so early. You were too far into your wine last night for us to talk, but your Mother has told me a lot about you. May the Lord bless you, and keep you from harm!" Durstan made the sign of the cross in the air between them.

"Mother is pleased to see you after so many years," Eoghan said, moving closer to the Monk's face. "You are safe here because of her, and my Father. No one will breach the hospitality given to a Lord's guest. On the other hand, step outside their world, and things will be very different." He smirked. "So, kinsman, when do you plan on leaving us?"

"I'll be leaving here as soon as I do, and not before I am ready," Durstan said, sharply. "I'm to join my Brother Andrew at the Monastery, and may be sent to some of the more distant islands before we return to Iona."

Eoghan prodded the centre of Durstan's chest with such force that the Monk was pushed backwards. "Let's hope that doesn't take you too long," he said, in a low voice. "Last night with her was enough, too much in fact. I would hate to see Lady Beth bothered again by your attentions, if you take my meaning." Eoghan half-turned to spit on the ground, before he walked away whistling to Woden.

Durstan shook his head sadly, and carried on in the direction of the church. He glanced through the half-open door of the Hall as he was passing it. Several men and women were sleeping beside the dying embers of the fires. He blessed them quietly in an effort to recall his holy duties. These were the poor, lost, souls who called the Hall fire their home because they didn't have another. They were fortunate not to have been outcast, as they may well have been with a different Lord. Durstan noticed Lora watching him, and he put a finger to his lips. He didn't want to be drawn into conversation. She stared at his back as he walked away. She knew that he had been with Beth last night, as did the rest of the enclosure. It had caused a lot of gossip, especially among the women. The Monk was not the man for a she-devil like her.

Durstan felt that he didn't have the right to object to the cold air inside the Church. He walked past the table dedicated to the Old Gods. The three candles on the Christian altar were burning low, and a fire hadn't yet been lit to warm the stones or dried grass underfoot. Durstan couldn't see the opulence of the jewels on the golden crucifix, only a confused image of Beth and Ailan, a woman's limbs tangled with his. He groaned, loudly. He couldn't remember having such a strong feeling of evil within him after Beltane. His soul still belonged to God. Perhaps Faisal's teachings were no longer relevant, and that was the problem? They were based on an ancient doctrine when opinions had been different. Durstan's head ached, as these thoughts niggled deeper inside his mind. He was startled to feel a soft touch on his arm.

"Why are you here so early, Brother?" His heart sank. The last thing he wanted to do was discuss Beth with Mora, especially when he hadn't had time to consider how he felt. His sister was another who didn't seem overjoyed last night, by Beth's relationship with him. May God help him deal with this! He needed to pray, to find out what he should do.

Nevertheless Durstan leaned dutifully towards his sister, to kiss her cheek.

"I could ask you too why you're outside before dawn in

the middle of winter, instead of with Duncan in a warm bed?" He said, gently.

Mora managed a half-smile. "You have yet to learn, Durstan, that my marriage sometimes causes me pain. When that happens I go to the shrine or, if I can't get there, come here to speak to Brigid." Mora gestured in the direction of the Goddess' altar. "I think it's a little colder outside than in here but, you're right, there isn't much difference. Our breath would be better spent in prayer, instead of misting our faces in frost. Is that why you haven't answered my question?" Mora said, rubbing her hands together vigorously to warm them.

Durstan could see the unhappiness in his sister's eyes. He led her by the arm to an oak bench where they could sit huddled together, and he held her hands inside his own. He breathed, deeply. "I feel lost, sister. I don't know where God's path is taking me. There's precious little love at the Monastery. Our Father Abbot seems to preach against it, whilst my heart tells me that it's the most important part of creation, a joy which God made for us."

Mora felt something snap inside her. "So, it's true. You were with that girl last night. Did she make you happy, Durstan?"

"No. Yes. I don't know, Mora! Except that I'm wrong to have bound her to me, when I don't love her. Beth still thinks that I can help her. She says that Duncan won't agree to have them here for much longer, and as I am now her man, I should find a way to protect her. I'm not sure she is right about our involvement or that I can do what she wants. I'm a Monk who has feelings like any other man, and I make mistakes. I suppose the best option will be to take her to Iona for sanctuary, even though I don't want to go back there, and the Abbot may not grant it.

Faisal is unpredictable at the best of times. I expect that he'll look for payment in coins which I assume Beth doesn't have. This Odhran will pursue me if he finds out I insulted his name last night, and if as Beth says, she is promised to him. Both he, and the Abbot, will want to see me punished for my sins! Let's not forget too that I've been questioning my belief in the Christian God because of all this, or your son who has now threatened me."

"Eoghan, again!" Mora said, angrily. "I'm so sorry that you are unhappy, Durstan. I can understand why something like this has happened. Faisal, with all his talk about a new God, has caused such an upheaval in people's lives. You've only to look at us sitting in front of two altars, to see that. The Old Gods have been with us for longer than we remember. Why does the Abbot think we need another? I don't suppose there's much I can do about him, but don't mind Eoghan. I'll see to it that he's the least of your worries. Duncan will deal with his wildness, and this fascination he has for Beth. The boy is used to having anything he wants. He's taking it badly that she has preferred you to him. I think that the most pressing problem is what's to be done with her. How we can break the spell she has cast on you."

Durstan smiled, weakly. "You don't know the whole story, Mora. There's Ailan too." He paused, feeling his face redden. "She and I celebrated Beltane in the old way. It was only a short time ago that I thought I wouldn't be able to live without her. I'm so confused, Mora. I think I still love her."

"Ailan, the woman who is handfasted to Branach?" She said, trying to keep the surprise from her voice.

"Yes, that Ailan," Durstan said. Her name tugged at his heart, as it left his lips. "She's carrying Branach's child.

We met when Andrew and I had coracled across the water from Iona. I saw her with him again, last night."

"And that's why you were with Beth." Mora frowned. "It sounds to me as if you need to hear the rest of the story, Durstan." She told him then what had happened to Ailan, the day after Beltane. How Edgar Addle-Head had pursued her, and Duncan said to Branach afterwards that they must handfast. "Ailan would have been outcast with a child had Duncan not stepped in, but I'm so afraid she has been given an intolerable life, Durstan. The Mother is a vindictive woman. She doted on Edgar, despite his disability, and Eoghan enjoyed himself far too much in the way he dealt with him. I'm sorry to say it was my son's dogs who caused his death, but I rather suspect Oonagh lays the blame for it at Ailan's door. I had no idea you were a part of this," Mora said, sadly.

"I don't understand. I didn't know for certain, but I thought Ailan may have somehow managed to stop coming to Iona because I was a Monk. We couldn't have a future together." He began to stammer. "...and now, from what you've said the child may be Edgar's, not Branach's."

"Or yours, Durstan. Possibly only the Gods know the truth of it? It needs once, a single seed, for a child to take if it's the right time."

Durstan's eyes were fixed on the altar, and crucifix. "What have I done, Mora?" He said, in a low voice. "How could I have treated Ailan so badly? Beth too? May God forgive me. Everything has turned out badly when I had hoped things would change for the better. If Faisal is to be believed, I am reaping the rewards of sin." The Monk's eyes were filled with passion. "I do believe in the Christian God, Mora, but I can't bear being without Ailan any longer."

She stroked his hair, in an attempt to comfort him. She

could see the pain in his eyes. "I was thinking about all this before I met Beth. The Church has changed, Mora. It's trying to fit in more easily with our Ancestors' beliefs. A lot of the Monks don't know what to believe or which God or Gods to follow. A number have broken their vow of chastity. Some even have children, despite them not being recognised by Faisal. That's wrong too. The children aren't at fault, but the Abbot won't agree to it. He thinks only to continue allowing the Beltane celebrations, as a means of pleasing the Old Gods. It's an unnatural way to live, Mora, without love. I can't do it any longer. There has to be a better meeting than this, of the old and new." Durstan wiped his eyes, to rid them of emotion. "I'm sorry to have burdened you with my troubles, Mora. Andrew is my anam cara, but I can't talk as openly to him."

"Durstan, search your heart! If it's truly Ailan you love, then there is your answer, not last night's episode with Beth who is nothing more than a conniving cat. Perhaps the faith you have in your Christian God has protected you, from falling in love with her? I don't think she is meant to be your future, even if your threads of the wyrd have become tangled with hers. You need to act quickly to help Ailan." Mora kissed his cheek. "Perhaps your God, or our Old Gods, had their reasons for putting you on this path with Beth? We may not otherwise have spoken this morning, and you wouldn't have known what happened to Ailan. Love is the answer, Durstan. It's the reason why I stay with Duncan, my wayward Husband. I like to think it's still there between us whichever woman interferes for a time, and however much it breaks my heart when she does. I accepted a long time ago that Duncan would always be swayed by a pretty face, or smile. He can't help himself. Some men are like that. Yet in the end, love is what we're all searching for. I don't think that it would be there for me with another man, but I could be wrong. If I am, the Gods have so far not shown me otherwise. When things get too bad, I come to the Church, to speak to Brigid. The Goddess helps me feel better again. This can be a beautiful place to sit, and dream."

He stood up, wearily. "I am pleased that we have spoken, Mora, but I must pray." He kissed her forehead, and she put her arms around him briefly before she left the Church.

Durstan knelt in front of the Christian altar, and stayed there until his stomach began to rumble several hours later. He had reached a decision. He would follow the Christian God, and his heart's truth. If that was Ailan, then so be it.

Chapter 20

A Marriage Proposal

"Have you thought about it yet?" Eoghan said, trying not to sound too interested in his Father's reply. Duncan was sitting on the other side of the table, pulling meat from the haunch which a slave had placed in front of them. The men stopped from time to time to take mouthfuls of ale, and eat a morsel of bread.

Duncan spoke with his mouth full. "If you mean the girl, Beth, then yes I have. The answer is still no! Your Mother wouldn't hear of it, and neither will I. In any case, she has eyes only for the Monk whom I would remind you is a kinsman." Eoghan opened his mouth to protest, and Duncan said, firmly, "you may as well not say anything. I am not prepared to let you have your own way this time. Take another girl often enough, and you'll soon forget her!"

Eoghan crashed his fist onto the thick wood of the table, in anger and disbelief. "You would choose the Monk over me? I doubt he's even a man beneath his maiden's robe, given all that meekness, and bless you nonsense he goes about saying to all he meets. Father, I am your close flesh and blood, a true kinsman. I want this woman above all else, and you're telling me to find someone else." He wiped a hand across his face in despair. "I can't get her out of my thoughts. I want to marry her in the Christian way, so it'll be for the rest of our lives. I seriously believe a handfasting won't be long enough to purge Beth from my soul." Eoghan stared at Duncan, willing him to agree. It was a tactic which had been successful in the past, but the Lord ignored him and carried on eating. "You surely haven't forgotten what it is to lust after a woman, not be able to slake that thirst or hunger, whatever you might do otherwise to cure it. You, a man above all others, my Father. I thought you would understand." He said, slyly, "I remember that girl a couple of years ago whom you couldn't seem to get enough of, 'til Mother noticed too much, and..."

"Enough!" Duncan shouted, and threw his cup against the wall. It shattered into a thousand shards. "I won't talk about that with you, a spoilt brat who is barely a man, and cries because he has for once been denied what he craves. Eoghan, you have to understand that you can't have everything you ask for. Children are taught that. It's the will of the Gods who we have in our lives. They speak through me as your Lord, and the threads of the wyrd." Duncan sighed, heavily. "You don't have any cause to complain. There hasn't been a need in your life which hasn't been met. You've ridden the best horses, have the finest clothes, dagger and sword that we can give. You've bedded more women in your short life, than most men will do in all of theirs. Nevertheless, on the matter of Beth, be silent now! I will hear no more of it."

Eoghan glared at his father, and left the hut in a rage. He pushed the slave girl roughly out of his way, knocking her to the ground. His face was crimson as he walked briskly across the enclosure, to put as much distance between Duncan and himself as he could. The rhythm of his steps began to calm his mind, and he slowed his pace. A solitary figure was entering the Church, a woman. It would be quiet inside, and he changed direction to follow her, intending to take his Father's advice.

Eoghan was surprised when he saw that it was Beth. He wanted more than anything to take her in his arms, but she had so far spurned his every advance. Durstan flashed through his mind. He shook his head angrily, trying to remove the image of the Monk from his thoughts. How could that man be his kinsman? It was ludicrous. Duncan had made the wrong decision. Eoghan looked around quickly to make certain that they were alone, before he pulled the wooden bar across the door. No one could enter or leave the Church now, without his permission. "Beth, why are you here alone?" He said, softly. "Is Alys, or your Monk, hiding behind one of the altars?"

She blushed when she saw who it was. " Eoghan, cousin. I wanted to make an offering at your Mother's shrine by the river but the snow was too deep, even with the slaves walking in front to clear the way." Beth looked up into his eyes, and was alarmed by the darkness within them.

"Why do you need Brigid's love when you have mine for the taking?" He said, holding her arm. Beth tried to pull away, without success.

"Please, Eoghan. I don't want any trouble, and you're hurting me. Let go of my arm. We can sit together in the Hall, and talk," she said, trying not to sound as frightened as she felt.

Eoghan laughed when she began to struggle. He pulled her to him, and kissed her deeply. They toppled backwards onto the ground. Their fall was broken by a bed of dry grass in front of the altar which had been dedicated to the Old Gods. "I won't hurt you, Beth," he said, gently. "I want you as my Wife. Say yes!"

Beth lay completely still. She was shocked. Her lips

had responded to Eoghan's, and he had said he wanted to marry her. *No wonder the Gods hadn't shown her this.* The air around them shimmered with natural magic. Kissing Eoghan surely couldn't have been an act of love? She had promised Kate that she wouldn't forget Durstan. He was going to protect them, when Aodh's men came to Mull. Beth struggled to her feet, as soon as Eoghan stood up. He watched her from the other side of the altar. He seemed wary of her reaction. When he took a step forward, Beth warned him that she would use the jeweled dagger she was holding in her hand if he came any nearer. "Eoghan, I am not yours to take. I haven't given you any reason to believe that I am. I came here to speak to the Goddess. I belong to Durstan. You are wrong about there being love between you and I. As for me being your Wife, that's definitely not going to happen. I'm meant for someone else," Beth said, looking at him in confusion and despair while her eyes told him the truth.

Eoghan raised his hands, to show her that he wouldn't come any closer. "If you mean the Monk, Beth, it's you who is wrong. You and I are well matched. We both know it. You can see as well as I, that love is following close behind. It's right between us," he said, persuasively.

"No, Eoghan! You have to keep away from me. This will never happen again, as long as I can hold this dagger in my hand. Do you understand me?"

"I won't let you go, Beth," he said, passionately. "I can't."

As she pulled her cloak tightly around her body, her eyes didn't leave his face. She walked quickly to the Church door, praying silently to the Goddess for protection.

"Don't be afraid of me, Beth. I wouldn't hurt you. I have told you the truth. I do love you. I've not admitted that to any woman before today. Here, let me. I'll take the wood from the door so you can leave. I won't follow you. I promise, but tell me what you mean to do. I'm in enough trouble already with my Father because of Edgar."

Beth paused, as an image of Ailan came to mind. The other woman's experience with Edgar couldn't have been anything like what had happened here today with Eoghan. "If you mean shall I tell anyone about this then I think I should, but another part of me says not to. We have so much trouble in our lives already, Eoghan. Don't forget that apart from Durstan, my Uncle Aodh has betrothed me to Odhran who will stop at nothing to have me. He wants my land and money. Durstan is going to ask his Church to protect us, Mother and I."

"If you accuse me, Beth, you'll be doing it falsely," Eoghan said, desperately. "You want me, as much as I want you. I know enough about women to see that. I'll deny anything took place here today. If it's not believed, I'll say in my defence that you encouraged me, and cast a spell for my heart. People will believe me. I don't need to do this. You are becoming known as an enchantress, and need to be careful of that."

Beth's emerald eyes flashed dangerously. "No one would believe you, Eoghan, but you'll have nothing to fear from me if you keep your distance. I don't want any trouble with you, or anyone else." Beth pushed her way past him, and through the unbarred door. She didn't look back even though her senses were screaming at her, as the threads of the wyrd became more tangled. She knew instinctively that she should turn around, and run into his arms.

Eoghan called after her. "I'll go away for a while, Beth, to give you time to think. The Gods have blessed us, allowing us to meet. We've been given something which shouldn't be cast aside." She turned around then. She thought that she had heard the beginning of love in his voice, and he walked towards her. "I'm sorry. I would never hurt you. Please believe me. I've not felt like this in the past, with such a madness running through my blood." He smiled, feeling more confident. "I want to look after you, Beth. Neither the Monk nor Odhran will get in my way, but I'll go into the forest for a few days to hunt. Duncan is already angry enough with me. It'll be better if I'm not here until his temper has cooled."

Eoghan was relieved when he saw the softness return to Beth's eyes. She didn't seem to be afraid of him any longer. He kissed her lips gently before he walked away.

Beth was overwhelmed. Eoghan had changed everything. She didn't know how she could hide the way she was feeling. It would be impossible now, to be close to Durstan again. Her heart began to race. Could she really love Eoghan enough to marry him? He was right. She wanted him more than anything else she could think of. If only Kate had listened. Maybe she could talk to her again? Durstan would be distraught, especially if he discovered they had kissed next to the Christ altar in the Church, but she wasn't worried about offending any of the Gods. The Old Ones would understand, and she didn't care for this new God from across the sea. All she knew about the Christian Church was that it came from the place where her silver bracelets had been crafted. No, Eoghan was right. It was better not to tell anyone, so that she could make her own decision about the future.

Eoghan walked quickly to his hut. He would saddle his favourite horse, say that he was intending to ride further than usual, and not return for a few days. Rae could go with him. Eoghan was worried, despite what he had said to Beth. He didn't know if he could trust her. Women were unpredictable at the best of times. Defying Duncan, his Lord and Father, was a serious mistake. If he was found out, the Lord's anger would be inflamed by Mora's harsh words. Women! They were so different. He chuckled when he thought of Beth kissing him in the Church. There wouldn't be any going back now. She would see it in time. Eoghan stroked his hunting knife. If the Monk needed a little help to go on his way, then so be it. He wasn't a match for the Lord's son, unless he could invoke the power of the Church to protect him which was doubtful. Durstan wouldn't be able to do anything about losing Beth, except whinge like the old woman he was. Eoghan decided in that moment that he would do whatever was necessary to marry Beth, and he would kill the Monk if he had to.

There was also the old man, her Uncle wanted to involve. Odhran, she called him. He wouldn't stand a chance with her. She wouldn't want to be touched by a man who smelt of age, and with death looking over his shoulder. Eoghan groaned. He would have to find a way, to see her again soon.

Beth went to her hut, and asked a slave to bring warm water so that she could bathe. Eoghan had charmed her heart. She would tell Durstan, she couldn't be with him again.

Chapter 21
Three Days Later

Future Plans

Duncan was pacing the floor of his brother's hut. Eidard and Durstan were watching him. "Mora has told me that you have become involved in the trouble which Beth has brought to our Hall. I'm disappointed, Durstan. We are already losing our roots to the Christians. That is enough in itself to disturb our Ancestors, and this girl has now threatened us with a blood feud we can't possibly defend. We don't have the men nor can we pay mercenaries. I certainly didn't invite her here. If it weren't for the laws of hospitality, and your sister's kindness, I would have turned her away before she came through the gate."

Duncan saw the stricken look on the Monk's face, and attempted to moderate his anger. "I listened to the tales told in this Hall by my Father and Grandfather. Their Fathers before them fought alongside Arthuir. The old King's bones which were laid to rest on Iona have become unsettled by these problems, and the way the Abbot conducts his affairs. I appreciate that you are one of his Monks, Durstan, but you are also our kin. If we aren't careful, there will come a time when we can no longer call on the spirit of the Old Gods for help. Arthuir fought many a dragon for us while on this earth, and we are falling behind now in our duty to the old Celts, to ensure their ways aren't forgotten. Columba's Christians were skilful in how they stole Iona from the Druids. They came disguised as holy men, but were in truth soldiers. They took the mysticism which our Ancestors' hearts loved, and Faisal is doing his best now to obliterate all that is left of it. We can't let this continue!"

Duncan sat down, wearily. "I'm afraid, Durstan, of this Christianity. It's becoming stronger all the time because of men like your Abbot. Some of the most powerful Lords in the south have taken an interest in it. I've heard Faisal preach that there won't be any need for life or throne to be sacrificed after seven years, if a King or Lord becomes Christian, even if the Gods are angry and send a famine. A tempting inducement indeed for a man to change his faith. Druid Brionach and I have talked at length of this. He fears too that the old path is dying. The Church is becoming too powerful, and their word continues to spread."

Duncan acknowledged Eidard with a nod. "My brother and I are of the same mind. It's younger people like you, Durstan, who can restore the natural order. Brionach should be with us soon. You must speak to him, and leave here as soon as possible. Let the new religion begin again elsewhere. I doubt we can now eradicate it completely, but it shouldn't be centered on the personal greed of men like Faisal, or at the expense of the Gods we revere. People will come to you, Durstan, if you offer them protection and a better way of life. I've heard how you speak of love, and honouring nature. I know something of this Roman Pelagius whom you follow. I talked to the King's advisors about it when I was in Mercia last. I prefer his ideas to the other one Faisal talks about all the time, St Augustine if I'm not mistaken, and he calls himself an Abbot. The amount of time I've had to waste on that man, to keep the peace hereabouts. He's so conceited he thinks to stand above me. Lord Duncan who owns the island on which he walks, as did my kinsmen before me. He seems to think that because he has our Ancestors' burial plots in the cemetery behind the Monastery, he is the keeper of our souls. He asserts that as God's right hand on earth he can be the only one to guide our spirits when they pass to the Otherworld. If we take up his faith, he'll intercede with the Christ God for us."

Duncan frowned. "The man is dangerous. He's a vindictive, self-centred toad! He will stop at nothing to keep what he has, and take more besides. I've heard too much already about this culture of fear he has created on the holy isle. Most can't deny him because of the power he wields. It stretches far across the sea. He has links to kinsmen in Ireland, and the political clout of Rome. His interests even go as far as Mercia. If we aren't careful, they'll meet those belonging to the Christian Abbot at Canterbury in the south. An alliance with him would make Faisal stronger again. You'll need to be wary when you leave here, Durstan."

Duncan drank the rest of his ale from a pot on the table nearby. He offered more to his companions. Eidard held his pot steady whilst Duncan refilled it, but the Monk refused. "It's the island which is holy, not Faisal or his doctrines," Durstan said, thoughtfully. "You can feel it when your feet touch the white sand. It's in the wind from the sea, and a Monk's eyes when they're unguarded. Faisal preaches against following the natural laws. How can that be? You're right, Duncan, when you say that he needs to be stopped. I can't go back to Iona, as a Monk. I made a mistake with Beth, but in doing so, she helped me reach that decision. I am bound by duty now to take her to the Abbot to ask for sanctuary, but I hope that I shall be able to leave again soon afterwards, with or without his blessing."

"It would help us, Durstan, if you could get Beth away from here quickly," Eidard said. "You must leave Iona, as soon as you have had an audience with Faisal. Her too, before she tries to tempt you further with a woman's magic."

Duncan nodded. "Beltane was the Druid's last hope for change," he said. "Brionach took the old ways back to Iona, but by ignoring the solstice and continuing as before, Faisal showed that it was of little consequence to him or his Christianity. There was nothing he or I could do afterwards, to persuade people to denounce him. It would have been too extreme a step for me to threaten men with being outcast, or even hanging, when they didn't agree. They seemed to be more afraid of defying the Christian God, so we failed."

Eidard put his arm around Duncan's shoulders when it became clear that his brother couldn't carry on. "We believe that you should start again in another place, Durstan," he said. "Somewhere Faisal and those of his ilk have yet to make a mark. You'll have the opportunity then to create change. Preach your message of love in creation if you will, but let those who choose the Old Ones continue to worship them without complaint. We have kinsmen and friends further south who will help you. They are also unhappy with the way the Church is trying to dominate us. They don't want Christianity to unify our islands. No one will be able to follow their true beliefs, if that happens, and your Christ is simply another God. Faisal hasn't given us any reason to think that He should be the only one we ought to follow. The Old Gods have looked after the

Ancestors and us, for as long as we have had memory and before. They deserve our continued respect."

"Go to the Monastery at Lindisfarne," Duncan said. "Speak to the men there, and Abbot Hygebald, if you can. Try to find out who will be sympathetic to your cause. When there's enough support for you, hopefully before Litha, seek patronage from one of the local Lords. Then build your huts, Durstan, as quickly as you can with a vallum for protection. It would be wise afterwards to carry on looking for more men to follow you, and live in the place you have chosen." He smiled. "I've listened to you, Monk, speak about your belief in kindness and love. That's what Faisal talks of too, but there's been precious little evidence of it on Iona while he has been there."

"We'll send word to Northumbria, that we support your interests," Eidard said, persuasively. "Believe in this, Durstan, and you can do it! Word will spread. People will ask to join you. There'll be some who are outlawed, but haven't committed so grave a crime. They'll have nowhere else to go. Consider them carefully. Men and women who are forced to live in the forest aren't always beyond redemption."

Duncan cleared his throat, and put his hand on Durstan's shoulder. "I can't leave here at the moment, but Eidard will come to you as soon as we've dealt with Aodh and Beth. When you see Faisal tell him that you wish to return to Mull, to carry on with your missionary work. He may let you leave again. If not, I'm certain you can make your own arrangements to disappear. Let him complain to me afterwards that you have travelled as far as Lindisfarne. He told you to convert men and women to Christianity, and which is what you'll be doing." Duncan grinned. "Although it won't be in quite the way he envisaged. It's fortunate that he has given both Andrew and you authority to baptize lost souls. It would have been preferable for you to have made the journey south by boat, but not with the Vikings to contend with. We don't yet know how to break down the strength of their shield wall or defy their blood eagle killing, but we'll find a way. Now, what do you say, Durstan?"

"I'll speak to Beth, and tell her that I will take her to Iona," the Monk said, decisively. "We've been avoiding each other since Yule, but she'll be pleased to hear that." His eyes were glittering with excitement. "I don't see why this can't be done. It hadn't crossed my mind to build an enclosure. It'll be a massive undertaking, Duncan, but I like the idea. I'll think about what's to be done, and leaving the Monastery will be the first step." Durstan paused. "I have a favour to ask of you, Duncan. I would like to take Ailan with me if she will leave here, and her brother too."

It was the Lord's turn to look surprised. "Whilst I'm delighted to hear that you'll end your entanglement with Beth, Ailan is handfasted to Branach. I'm not one to interfere willingly in my people's domestic arrangements. Nevertheless I won't refuse your request, Durstan, if she'll go with you. From what Mora says the marriage is an unhappy one, and I've seen her bruises. Take the girl if you must, the boy too. As for Eidard, he'll easily get the better of Kate and her daughter, given time. None of them are a match for men like us!"

Eidard grinned. "No one is blaming you, Durstan. Women have their charms. There's little doubt of that," he said, smugly. "Kate believes that she already has the upper hand with me, but I want their family land. I won't stop until it's mine."

Duncan laughed, heartily. "It seems that we are agreed.

I am grateful, Durstan, for your help in taking Beth to Iona. Let Faisal have her! My only reservation is that we are handing her to him on a platter. If he can convert her he'll think to have some say in her Mercian lands, but that is something Eidard can no doubt deal with later when he is married to the Mother. We can't fight Aodh, or this Odhran. No one would come to our aid in such an argument. We don't have a choice. It amuses me to say that it's unlikely Odhran will start anything with so powerful an Abbot and Church, but get that she-devil away from here quickly. She has discovered the power she can have over a man. There's no doubt Odhran will come for her." Duncan's thoughts had turned to Beth's hand on his thigh a few nights ago, when she moved closer to him in the doorway of the Hall. "All of us will be well rid of her, including Eoghan."

Duncan walked across the rushes to the beautifully carved chest which was against the timber wall. He knelt to open its heavy lid. He took out a thin strip of fox fur, and pushed aside the Monk's robe to tie it around the top of his arm. "Christian or not, this is rightly yours. My son and brother wear it, as do I. You are our kinsman, Durstan. I'm sorry not to have passed it to you sooner. I assumed Faisal wouldn't have approved of you wearing so noble a fur beneath your robe. Your decision today has changed everything, and it's a good match for your new tonsure. I prefer it to the Roman cut you had when you first came here. Hair shaved at the front belongs to the man you are now, and the rest hangs royally behind in a fine, black pelt. A circle cut from the hair on top has always seemed strange to me. When you have rid us of Beth and are away from here, seeking converts to your new faith, give it to them too. That would please Druid Brionach and the Ancestors.

It belongs to the old ways. When Faisal has gone you could even come back to us, as Abbot of Iona, with my blessing. You would be returning the holy island to our family."

Durstan's thoughts turned again to Ailan, and her delight in the old stories about Saint Columba. "Many believe that Columba was a better man than Abbot Faisal, irrespective of how the holy island was taken. He and his followers wore their hair this way, by all accounts. I've wanted mine for a long time to be the same, whatever Faisal makes of it. You are right, kinsman. So much needs to change, and it has begun."

Ailan walked as quickly as she could across the enclosure to Saille's hut, while Durstan was talking to Duncan and Eidard. The baby was growing heavier by the minute, and Branach and Oonagh would be back soon. She had managed to tell Saille that they would be able to talk later. Ailan was afraid that if Oonagh saw them, she would be forbidden to speak to Saille again on some pretext or another. She couldn't bear the thought of not seeing her friend, especially when she had also lost Durstan.

Saille shared a hut with Dacey, her five year old daughter. The girl was her mother's shadow, a delicate and inquisitive child whom Tam loved. They were often involved in mischief, chattering at every opportunity about children's affairs, and had enough common sense to keep away from Oonagh's watchful eye. Saille was tall and slim. The other women called her ethereal. Her long, brown, hair and soulful eyes reminded Ailan of the doe who had lost her stag in the forest. Any tunic of rough cloth hung well on her, with her Mother's agate brooch on her right shoulder. Saille had been a widow for six years. It happened almost immediately after Dacey had been conceived. Although she had come to the Hall as a slave, her handfasting had been a love match to one of Duncan's favourite men. This elevated her status. She wasn't expected now, to share a hut with anyone else. Ailan knew that the death of her Husband had been hard to bear. The sea had taken him from his coracle when he was with Cormac, fishing in angry water. Cormac had sworn an oath afterwards that there was nothing he could have done to save him. The Gods had sent an immense wave from nowhere, and overturned their boats. He managed to cling to his coracle when he swam to the surface, but Neil hadn't been so fortunate.

Saille had carried on looking after the children when the women went to Iona, or worked in the fields and kitchen. The Lord said that grief shouldn't prevent a woman from doing her duty. She had asked Duncan through Mora, if she might be left alone. She didn't want another Husband as yet, and possibly not at all. The Lord had by this time lost interest in the situation so simply agreed. That didn't stop the men, in particular Cormac, from trying to persuade Saille otherwise with their attentions. It was common knowledge that Oonagh was consumed with jealousy. Cormac had taken to visiting Saille's hut at every opportunity. Oonagh took her revenge whenever she could. She gave Saille the near-rotting fish which no one else wanted when Cormac's back was turned, and it was her turn to distribute the catch after the Lord's share had been taken. Saille didn't speak of it. She didn't want any trouble with Oonagh, nor was she interested in the older woman's man. Events had however escalated recently, making Oonagh more spiteful. She had seen

Cormac lunge at Saille when he had drank too much ale. She failed to notice the young woman push him away, and spit in his face.

When Ailan arrived, Tam was playing a complicated game with Dacey in front of the hut. It involved stones which the children collected before the snow had covered them. Saille put down her knife as soon as she saw Ailan, and went outside. Her arms immediately encircled her friend. "You're looking tired. Have you had any sleep?" She said, gently.

Ailan shook her head, and followed Saille into the hut. She sat on the straw next to the cooking pot, stretching out her legs to rest the weight of the baby on her thighs. "Nothing much has changed," she said, smiling sadly before she burst into tears.

Saille sank to her knees beside her. "What are we going to do? I'm so sorry, Ailan. No one should have to put up with Branach, or Oonagh. I wish Tam and you could stay here with Dacey and me. You'd be safe then."

Ailan wiped her face, with the back of her hand. "You've no idea how much it means to me, Saille, knowing that you are close by but I can't come to you. The Lord wouldn't agree to it unless Branach let me go. I doubt he'll do that. What can I do? I've lost Durstan to Beth, that's plain to see. Duncan has said that Branach is my husband, and I've taken his family too."

"The way you are living isn't right, Ailan," Saille said, angrily. "Can't Mora help you? She understands what it's like for us, and she is Durstan's sister. If you are right about the Monk being this little one's Father, she is the child's aunt. You are her kin. If anyone can persuade Duncan to change his mind, it'll be her. Even though she's a woman he listens when she speaks. I'm sure she would talk to Durstan for you, and make him understand."

"Is there any point, Saille? I know I can't be with him. I have a young brother to care for, and there'll be a baby soon." Ailan shook her head, sadly. "The Lord is unlikely to treat me well if I defy him by asking to undo my handfasting with Branach, even with Mora's help. You know what Duncan is like. It's always the man he favours. A few bruises here and there on a woman don't matter to him. Remember old Nairne? She found that out quickly enough when she complained about her Husband. Duncan admitted that he knew about it, but punishment still hasn't been passed. That was before last winter. It likely, as not, won't be. Nairne has had to carry on living with that man all this time. I can well imagine how it's been for her. Pah! Men aren't Gods, yet they have so much power over us. Where would they be without women?

"I know I should do my best to forget Durstan, but I can't," Ailan said, softly. Her eyes were filled with love. "He let me see a part of himself, deep within all the layers he's created over the years for protection, the special place in his heart which I can't leave behind. Like us, he's not had an easy life, Saille. He's my soul friend. Durstan has my heart."

Saille frowned, and said, angrily, "I can't believe that Oonagh is already talking about you going back to Iona to see to the Monks. The babe hasn't even been born. She can't leave you alone for a minute. The Abbot doesn't allow pregnant women on Iona nor does he want to see our babes. It frightens him too much when he sees a woman's power, and the life growing within us. Duncan told me to look after the children when they are weaned, not before because that isn't right. It's unnatural to go back to the island too soon. You need to wait until the babe is on solid food, and can be left safely with me!" Saille looked through the doorway of the hut. "The problem with Oonagh is that she has lost the ability to love. I can understand why when she's married to Cormac, given the way he treats her, but it's hard for all of us as women. I don't have any patience with her, Ailan. She should be on our side, not making things harder. It's the same, with that awful Beth."

"Saille, please don't talk about her. I feel even worse when I think of what she's doing with Durstan. She has everything, and I don't expect she realises it. Oonagh is a horrible, old woman. The Goddess must have abandoned her. She has forgotten that love is still there if we're kind. It does worry me sometimes, how I'll cope when the baby is born." Ailan half-smiled. "But I'm praying to Brigid every day, so maybe things won't be too bad? At least I'll be able to hold him in my arms. If only I had a better Husband…" Ailan sighed, as her arms encircled the child growing within her. "I daren't say anything to Branach. He would think I was disobeying his Mother. Thank the Gods, that I've had a little peace from them both this afternoon." She looked shamefaced when she said, "even though it's come at a high price. Oonagh insisting that it's time to go to Edgar's burial place again, and make an offering. Even then she leaves work for me to do, and if she's gone to Iona, Branach will watch to see it's done." Ailan frowned. "They are still blaming me for Edgar's death. They think that I tempted him. I ask you. She can't accept that he wasn't right. I'm not looking forward to them getting back today, Saille. Oonagh is always more unreasonable when she has been at the burial mound."

Saille looked at her friend, helplessly. "Things have to change, Ailan. You can't carry on like this."

"Saille, Saille, Dacey wants to see the baby." Tam shouted as he ran into the hut, followed closely by the girl.

Saille held Dacey whilst Ailan stretched out her arms to Tam, and said, gently, "hush, now. The noise is enough to frighten the Gods. You'll have to wait a few weeks to see the baby, but if you're very quiet you can find out if he's awake."

Tam pulled away from Ailan when he felt the baby's foot connect with his cheek. The women smiled at the look of surprise on his face. "He's only moving his arms and legs, Tam. It's what babies do before they're born, and the Gods send them to us. You would have done the same with our Mother when you were getting ready to leave the Otherworld."

"Perhaps you would both like a story?" Saille said. "Sit down, and I'll tell you about the creatures who play in the water around the islands. Tam can be their King. Dacey, you are the Queen who has an oyster shell necklace. Here, you can have these." Saille held out a handful of shells to the children. "If you hold a magic shell against your ear, you'll hear the sea. Make a wish, to find a pearl in one of them. I can see Tam riding his chariot through the waves, pulled by two silver dolphins. They are racing the others, riding fast through the sea. The King wins the prize, and the Gods are smiling on you both."

Saille wove her words well to entertain the children while she stirred the vegetables cooking in the pot. The small piece of fish which Oonagh had given to her would be added near the end. She wished that the Druid was with them. She liked his stories best, even more than those told by the scop. Brionach's tales were filled with magic, and enchantment. The words she was saying to the children were his from the last time he had visited the Hall.

Ailan touched her friend's arm gently, so as not to

break the spell. "I had better go," she said, kissing Saille's forehead. It was time to return to the work, Oonagh had told her to do.

Chapter 22

Druid Brionach's Tale

Brionach was on his way to the Yule celebration at Duncan's Hall, and had reached the oak tree half a day's walk from there. The Druid greeted his old friend respectfully before he slumped onto the dry earth, and rested his back against the mighty trunk. The oak would carry on, but the Gods had warned Brionach several times already that he had almost reached the end of this task.

The walk had tired him. He closed his eyes. A black crow cawed noisily in the distance, and the Druid let his mind focus on the energy centres in his body. The Gods were ready to speak to him again, so he opened each of them as he had been taught to do years ago. His thoughts floated in and out of the clouds, visiting the place where he could always find peace. The pool with the waterfall, and the cave behind. It soothed his soul. The lush, green, grass felt soft to touch. It smelt of early summer. Ancient trees moved closer, as he fell deeper into the recesses of his mind.

He had been a High Priest before the Romans came to the southern shores of these islands. The Druid could see it again, as it had happened…

The air was saturated with the scent of May blossom. The children were excited. They had been waiting all day for the ceremony to begin. Their spirits couldn't be contained any longer. Relief shimmered in the sunlight when the horn sounded, and it was time at last for them to take their places in the procession. The Elders wore the flower garlands with pride across their blue and white cloaks. A proud day to be named, Druid. Ethna, his daughter, was to be honoured. She was fifteen years old, and had been given the gift of sight four months ago. She didn't always want to listen to what the Gods were telling her, but it couldn't be stopped. Her Grandmother said that the feeling she experienced, of knowing before anyone else, was a privilege and wouldn't let her down. Nevertheless she would have liked sometimes to be able to run free in the meadow with the children, not stay inside a hut with the Elders.

Brionach heard his Wife's voice. "Ethna, child, are you playing in the Otherworld again? You are a long way from here. Come back! You have forgotten the flowers to lay on the altar when it's your turn."

Ethna's eyes cleared. She smiled at her Mother, took the daisies, and followed the crowd when the horn of plenty sounded again. Jared was staring at her. He often did that, and Ethna had started to feel anxious about it. Mother said that it was because she was visited now by the Moon Goddess once a month. He had sensed it. After the initiation she would be ready to join with him in the meadow at dusk, but Ethna was afraid. Jared was sixteen, and she had seen him torment a young goat two seasons ago until its breath was gone. She couldn't forget the memory, however hard she tried. She wished with all her heart that it was going to be Baen with her tonight. He was the kindest person she had known, and would often find the time to give her a flower or sweet treat. But the High Priest had said no. Ethna couldn't understand why he had refused. The Elders said it was for the good of the tribe. They wanted Baen to make a child with Sima who had been her friend. Ethna was jealous. She didn't like Sima anymore. She could feel love in her heart when she looked at Baen. Jared's eyes were fixed on her breasts. The heat rose to Ethna's cheeks. Mother had told her it would become easier once she had lain in the meadow for the first time, but the girl wasn't so sure. Baen was looking at Jared. Ethna sensed that he also didn't like him. Sima was fortunate. Baen would be kind to her later. He would help her become initiated.

The procession walked slowly through the wood. There was laughter, and friends jostling each other. Ethna tried to calm her fears. She could see the altar in the distance where the High Priest would perform the ceremony of light. It seemed a long time to have to wait again. When her turn came, the Priest raised the ceremonial knife. He walked around her inside the circle, saying the sacred words. Ethna saw coloured lights flashing at the corners of her vision. She could feel the trance beginning. A lone deer stood under the oak tree at the edge of the forest. The raven cried out a warning from high overhead. It was Jared! Ethna flinched. She could see him tearing at her robe and the blood flowing between them. They were covered in it. Ethna screamed. It was a high- pitched cry, and she felt herself being shaken roughly.

"Come back, child! You've spent long enough with the Gods today. It isn't time for you to stay with them," the Priest said, laughing. "It is done! Your spirit has been blessed, as Druid." Ethna glanced at her Father. She was confused and ashen faced, but went to stand obediently with the others. Sima looked at her spitefully, before she smiled across the clearing at Baen.

He was also lost in thought. His heart wasn't in this with Sima. She was pretty enough but it was Ethna he dreamed of, when the God's seed filled him with the need to make a gift of it to a woman. It was a pity he couldn't swop with that fool, Jared. Baen knew that he didn't care, so long as he had one of them, but the High Priest had ruled again that Jared was to have Ethna.

When dusk came, Jared touched Ethna for the first time in the meadow, and their blood was on Baen's knife. The people heard her scream as she had done earlier at the altar. Jared and Ethna's life force seeped into the earth beneath them, while Baen ran into the wood to the sound of Sima sobbing. He had sacrificed them all because of love.

The Druid's eyes opened with a start. He had been pulled back too soon. There must be danger. He heard voices through the trees, and breathed deeply. He glimpsed Lugh nearby. The God had come to travel with him to the place where a new life would be waiting. All was well. Perhaps Lora and he could be lovers, next time? The thought cheered him. Brionach took a mouthful of water from the animal skin at his belt, and his dizziness ceased.

The Gods had split their flame. Lora couldn't always remember. It frustrated him when she forgot that time was man's creation. Sometimes it would be in the wyrd that he was her lover, whilst in other lives they might not even meet. The Druid, or High Priest as he had been earlier, was jealous. His Lora, who was Ethna in that life, had loved Baen. The High Priest had sent her to a violent death because of the strong feelings he hadn't been able to control. Brionach knew that he was here now to redress the balance, but it wasn't of any concern. This was creation. The way the Gods helped us live and die, according to the wyrd.

It would be Odhran, searching the forest. Beth had good reason to be afraid of handfasting with him. Evil clung to the man as a second skin. He had walked too long in the darkness. The Druid tried from habit to create a cloak of protection, although he accepted that death was waiting. He felt a faint light cover him from head to toe, and the presence of a powerful Devil when Odhran came closer. "Where is she, my Lady Beth?" Odhran said, as he lunged at Brionach's throat.

A wren sang on the branch of a nearby tree, and the Druid stood watching from a distance. Odhran and his companions, all battle-weary men, were grouped in a loose circle around his body. "Where is she, Druid? I am told that she ran to Duncan's enclosure. Is that where I'll find her? Speak, old man! I've wasted enough time on this. I have little patience with being made a fool of any longer."

Odhran tightened his grip, as Brionach gasped for breath. "I won't answer you. If I can help her escape, I'm glad."

Odhran sensed that there was something otherworldly about the Druid, but he had killed many times in the past. He ordered two of his men to torture Brionach until he let them have the information. They chopped his fingers first, then took his eyes, but the Druid kept his word. Odhran's men cut him along his middle whilst he was still alive. They broke his ribs, to splay his lungs across both shoulders in a blood eagle style. Even though they weren't Viking, they believed that this would honour their Gods. It also satisfied a cruel wish to watch the Druid die under the oak tree. They didn't see Lugh waiting for Brionach on the branch, next to the wren.

Chapter 23

Fighting For Their Lives

The forest seemed quiet after the noise of the enclosure. Durstan was walking in front of Beth along the track through the trees. The snow had stopped falling, making it possible to reach the shore again. He pushed the stray branches aside to make the way easier for her, but they hadn't spoken for some time.

Kate had stayed at the Hall with Eidard. She intended to tell Aodh that they were going to marry as Christians. That would give them the protection of the Church. Durstan had baptized them both before he left, and received a promise of coins which he was to convey to the Abbot. He was to ask Faisal to agree to conduct the marriage ceremony, as soon as possible. Kate was hoping to be able to delay Aodh if he came with Odhran, until word could be sent from Iona that the arrangement was agreed. Alys had decided to handfast with Rae. Durstan wondered what had caused the rift between Beth and her. He suspected it concerned Eoghan. He had seen Alys kissing him at Yule.

Beth was feeling awkward about being alone with Durstan. Her thoughts were the only escape, and she collided with his back when he stopped suddenly. The weight of the snow had caused a small tree to fall across the sharp bend in the path. They couldn't go any further.

"I'm sorry, Durstan. I wasn't watching where I was going," Beth said, quietly.

He turned his head, and looked at her properly for the first time in days. He was startled. She was unkempt, and very dirty. It was so unlike the woman he had known intimately, that he couldn't help but grin. She often used a bone comb to untangle her hair, and potions on her skin. He had thought her vain. It surprised him when she agreed without argument, that their lovemaking couldn't happen again.

"I'm glad that you've found something to laugh at," she said, irritably. "I can't see that any of this is funny. I'm running away again in fear of my life, to a Monastery of all places. I don't know how I'll be received even if I arrive there in one piece, and you don't need to say any more. I know only too well I must have taken on the appearance of an outlaw's woman. I can't say I rightly know who I am anymore." Her face crumpled, and she looked down at the frozen ground.

"Beth, stop it! You're still Lady Beth, and you know it. This is nothing that a wash in the stream can't put right, some hot food, and sleep. You'll soon be safe, so be patient. I'll talk to the Abbot for you. I promised I would. I'll ask him to take you in. That's what you wanted all along, isn't it? The protection of the Church." Durstan said, in consternation. "If all else fails, we can hide in the caves on Iona for a few weeks until your Uncle and Odhran lose interest. It won't be the most comfortable place for you to be, but at least it'll give you the opportunity to decide what happens next. I'll do my best to persuade Faisal to help us. If you tell him that you'll become Christian, and make a sufficiently large donation to the Church from your inheritance which the King holds, I think he'll agree."

"I'm sorry," she said, softly. "I know you're doing your best. It's just…. The past few days have been overwhelming, and now I don't even have Alys." Durstan assumed that she was feeling ashamed, but Beth was thinking instead of her bedraggled appearance. She wriggled the toe of her boot against the hard earth. "Too much has happened recently. It's difficult to make proper sense of it all."

Durstan's heart weakened, despite his earlier resolve. "I'll always think of you in a special way, Beth, but it can only be as your friend. When you won't accept it, you're making it harder for both of us. There's Eoghan too," he said, looking at her with doubt in his eyes.

"I do accept it, but you're the same, Durstan. You won't tell the truth!" Beth said, with her hands on her hips, and her eyes flashing. "This is about Ailan. Isn't it? Not only your God!"

"Yes, I love her," he said, without any hesitation. "I don't know if I've lost the chance to be a part of her life. She has Branach now, and a baby soon to be born. Things have changed, Beth. Maybe too much, and for you too." He paused. "You haven't mentioned Eoghan, but I'm not a complete fool."

Beth lowered her arms, and looked sadly at Durstan. "You're right. I am in love with Eoghan, at least I think I am. The Gods alone know how that's happened, but it's over between us, Durstan. However this turns out, there was someone else for both of us. I would like us to be friends because of how our threads crossed in the wyrd. All the time we spent talking about life has made me look at who I really am, but it's about Eoghan now. That's if I see him again. It's strange how love works. We have to learn its ways, and hope that we have enough time to get it right. It's easy to see why people make so many mistakes."

Durstan saw a depth in her eyes which hadn't been there earlier. Would there be a time when he understood women? He felt much better suited to life's practicalities. "It is difficult," he said, abruptly. "It's a pity that Duncan didn't have enough men to stand up to Odhran. I feel guilty about leaving the Hall, without saying goodbye to Mora. I have no idea if I shall be able to go back." She would know by now that he was gone, and be calling him a fool. "I assume that Eoghan's disappearance has something to do with you, Beth? I saw a change in you when he'd gone. I'm glad that another man is waiting for you."

Beth was surprised. It was almost as if Durstan felt hurt by what she had done, but he said that he loved Ailan. She put her hand on his arm. "I'm sorry, Durstan. I didn't mean for this to happen, or to hurt anyone. I went to the Church to ask for Brigid's blessing. I was frightened. The Goddess answered by sending Eoghan to me. He thought Duncan would punish him for what had happened between us when we were in front of the altar, if I complained to the Lord. I didn't get another opportunity to speak to him. Duncan is angry with him about Edgar's death, but you've seen how Eoghan is. He gets carried away in the moment, and things happen. Duncan had warned him that his behavior was unacceptable for a Lord's son, and said that he was to leave me alone. I wasn't able to tell him my true feelings." Beth's eyes filled with tears.

Durstan groaned. "What have we done?" He kissed her cheek, gently. "Both of us still have time to sort everything out. My God and your Gods will help us, but nothing can alter that there was once a you and I, whatever the future holds." He put a hand firmly on her shoulder. "But for now, come on. We have to keep going. Odhran's out here somewhere. You are getting cold, and there has to be a way around this dead tree."

The Monk hacked at the undergrowth with his knife until another path was made, and they could rejoin the original track on the other side. The ground was icy in places. Beth walked behind him watching her step. Neither of them spoke. Durstan's thoughts were on Ailan, and God. Beth was thinking of Eoghan. It worried and excited her that she didn't really know him, yet felt that she did. Loud shouting from the direction of the shore interrupted their thoughts.

Durstan pushed Beth roughly down behind him into the low undergrowth. They had started to walk through this after leaving the cover of the trees. The barren clumps of heather, frozen grass, and rocks didn't hide them completely from the commotion further along the sand. A longship had been pulled onto the sand. Vikings were among the women, children, and Monks in the distance. Durstan and Beth looked on in horror. A Viking had snatched a small child from the sand. He seemed to be trying to tear her limbs apart, as he would have done a haunch of meat. He was shouting at one of the others who was laughing at him. The child's Mother punched the Viking repeatedly with her small fists, but which didn't have any effect. He threw the girl onto the ground when she ceased to amuse him. He trod on her and the weeping Mother, as he walked away.

Durstan's eyes scanned the beach quickly. Ailan was being pulled in their direction, behind one of the Norsemen. She was trying to hold the baby safely with one arm, and with the other, keep herself from falling. Tam was following a few paces behind them, seemingly not knowing what else to do. Durstan felt the bile rise to his throat. "Beth, go back! Do it now. The way we have come. I can't protect you from these men if they see you. For the love of God be quick, and careful how you go. I have to help Ailan!"

"But, Durstan, you must come with me. What if Odhran is behind us?" She said, protesting until he put his hand across her mouth. Sounds carried easily in the air, and every second counted. "Listen to me, Beth. Run! That's your only chance. You have to do it. You would be too great a prize for them." He saw her uncertainty, and hesitated. "More so than Ailan. You don't want to be taken as a slave. Do you? It would be far worse than any life with Odhran." Fear flickered through her eyes. He had to make her leave now, without further delay. He panicked, and in that moment, he kissed her lips roughly. "Here, my special friend. Take my knife. It will keep you safe." He didn't know how else to persuade her to leave him. The magic in his hands was in the knife. The Blacksmith's spell for protection had also been crafted into its blade and hilt. She understood the true value of the gift.

Beth grasped it tightly. "Durstan, what are you going to do?" She said, quietly.

"Help them, if I can," he said, across his shoulder as he left the undergrowth. He looked back briefly across the sand, but Beth had already gone. The Viking was still holding Ailan tightly by the arm. Durstan couldn't understand why he would want a pregnant woman unless he thought to have two slaves for the trouble of raiding today, but a baby? Durstan recalled with horror the cannibalism he had heard of in the winter months, and felt the vomit rise from his stomach. He turned to one side, to clear his mouth.

The Viking was making his way to the boat. The women

had arrived in their coracles from Iona after a day on the island. It was the first time they had been able to make the crossing for a few days because of the poor weather. This was what Ailan and he had been afraid would happen when they talked months ago. The men from the longship had caught the women when they landed. Ailan had for some reason been on the beach to meet them. No one thought they would be here so late in the year. Obviously the full extent of their sailing abilities, and courage or foolhardiness, had not been properly recognized.

Durstan clutched the wooden cross hanging from his neck. He prayed to God for safe deliverance as he ran along the sand. He could still see Ailan and Tam through the people who were trying to escape at this end of the beach. The Viking was pulling her along as he strode forward. Ailan was doing her best to remain upright. As he gained distance, Durstan could see the exhaustion on her face. The Viking still hadn't seen him. He taunted Ailan when she shouted at Tam to run, but the boy refused to leave her.

Durstan looked around for a weapon on the sand. He noticed a piece of driftwood, and grabbed it thankfully. He ran towards them, shouting as loud as he could in the name of God for protection, trying to divert the Viking. He called out for help from his Ancestors, and any of the other Gods who might be listening. Erik turned around. He was startled when he heard the Monk approaching from behind. Ailan found herself dragged almost full circle by this movement. She froze momentarily when she saw that it was Durstan, and managed to pull her arm from Erik's loosened grip. She realised that the Monk was giving them a chance. She took to her heels as best as she could, shouting for Tam to follow her. When they had gone a little way from Erik and Durstan, she stopped and turned to Tam. "Run, child! Hide yourself in the cave over there until this is over."

"But sister," Tam said, looking at her in confusion. He didn't want to leave her.

She took his small face into her hands. "Do as I say, please. Run, with the wind. You can do this for me, Tam. I can't leave him," she said, with uncertainty in her voice. But Tam had already started to run. He had seen how much she wanted to help Durstan.

The Monk hit the Viking's back with the piece of wood. Erik had staggered under the strength of the blow, but he was standing now with his hands on his knees, laughing at so feeble an attempt to knock him over. The wood was lying at his feet broken into two pieces. He spluttered, "I can't decide if you're a brave man, Monk, or simply stupid. You're no match for me!" He stopped abruptly when a shadow caught his attention.

"No, but you may be a better match for me," Roy said, with his voice a low growl. The Blacksmith was standing next to them, holding his knife in readiness. The Viking considered him carefully. He recognised a more worthy opponent. Giving a battle roar he ran at Roy who sidestepped, and lunged with the knife to graze Erik's arm. The Viking turned again to face him with anger in his eyes. He licked the wound slowly, not taking his eyes from Roy. The taste of blood invigorated him. He ran at Roy, hacking viciously with his own knife. The Blacksmith's magic wasn't sufficiently strong enough to defend him this time. Although he tried to step aside again, the Viking's weapon entered his chest. Roy fell to his knees as Erik withdrew it, and took several attempts to decapitate him.

Durstan and Ailan looked on in horror, as the blood gushed from the stricken man who was their friend. Both of them were incapable of movement. Ailan was still holding the rock in her hand which she had intended to hurl at Erik, as soon as she had the opportunity to do so. When the Viking turned to them again, she managed to throw it as hard as she could, catching him lightly on the leg. Erik grinned. Woden had returned her to him. He had also noticed Saille and Dacey from the corner of his eye when he had been stopped by Durstan's blow. They were half-hidden behind one of the low rocks. His chest filled with pride. The Gods had given him a choice today in recognition of his courage. If he had more men and longships, he would have taken them all.

Saille had been watching Ailan's progress along the beach. She wanted to help her friend, but didn't know how. Erik was standing in front of her in a couple of strides. He leaned down, and grabbed her waist to pull her towards him. Dacey screamed. "Well, well, this is an even better prize!"

Durstan's hatred for Erik consumed him. Roy was the Father he should have had. He realised too late how much he loved the older man. He did the only thing he could, and threw himself at the Viking. Erik's grip on Saille weakened for a moment, and she was free. Ailan ran across the sand to help her, but Saille was shaking uncontrollably. She couldn't move, while Erik was undeterred by Durstan. He pushed him away easily. The Monk fell backwards, and hit his head on the sharp edge of a rock. He lay lifeless beside the Viking's boot, as Erik's eyes searched for Saille. He wanted her. She would fetch a good price at the slave market when he had finished with her. It would be a long journey home to Gudrid. There would be plenty of time at the dry end of the longship. Her hair glittered in the sun. This one had the look of a Goddess. She reminded him strangely of Gudrid when she was younger despite being slight, and compared to his Wife's sturdy frame. Erik could taste the anticipation. He tore the front of her tunic in one easy rip, eager to see what was now his. It was enough. He slung Saille over his right shoulder, and grabbed Dacey's arm with his left hand. The girl would fetch a good price too. She was a pretty child.

Ailan bit his arm, and Erik dropped Dacey in surprise. Saille, realising that they were fighting for their lives, kicked Erik's back as hard as she could. Ailan snatched the girl free. She couldn't do any more for Saille, and dragged Dacey beside her along the beach in the direction Tam had taken. Erik guffawed. He slapped Saille hard on her buttocks as a punishment, causing her to scream and him become more aroused. Neither of them saw her Mother's brooch fall onto the sand. Erik hadn't enjoyed himself so much for a long time. It was a pity that he had become separated from the other men who would have liked the sport, but he consoled himself. He had the prize. This woman was the best. By the Gods, she even smelt good! They would be back again later for the others, without a doubt. This was all too easy. Land would come next which was what they really needed. It would mean that they wouldn't have to take these risks, sailing so far into the winter. Hunger had driven Erik and the others to it this time, but the crossing had been hard even for them.

He walked past Durstan who hadn't moved. Erik kicked his side, viciously. "It's your lucky day, Monk. I don't have time to finish this with you, and your friend's head has satisfied me for now." Erik chuckled, as he strode away with Saille who was crying quietly against his shoulder.

Tears were also falling down Ailan's cheeks, and the pain in her belly frightened her, but at least she was still holding Dacey's hand. She hoped that Saille had heard her, when she shouted that she would look after the girl. And Durstan? There were so many questions. She couldn't ask him for the answers. She didn't understand why he had done what he did today. It was foolish, brave, so like him. He may have lost his life because of it, and where was Beth? Ailan had seen Andrew on the edge of the beach, with some of the Monks from the Mull monastery. They had run away when the longship was getting ready to land, and the shore was too far from the Hall for any of their shouts to have been heard by Lord Duncan's men.

Ailan was praying to Brigid as she half-ran and walked with Dacey. She wanted Saille to be safe, and Durstan alive. She would have given everything she had to be able to turn around, but she couldn't risk it. The baby was suffering. She could feel him moving awkwardly, and Tam and Dacey were too young to fend for themselves. Branach wouldn't care. Ailan realized with a start that she was the only one who knew Tam had gone to the cave. He would perish tonight unless she went to him. It was unlikely anyone else would find him by chance. Everyone was dead, taken, or fleeing to the Hall.

There wasn't a choice. She had to see to the children. Dacey was still holding her hand tightly, whimpering as she ran. May the Goddess keep all of them safe! She would go back later for Durstan, after she had found Tam. She loved the Monk too much, not to try to help him.

Oonagh wouldn't be able to say anything about it. She was gone. She had seen one of them push a sword into her flabby stomach until the tip had come out of her back. Ailan dropped Dacey's hand and stopped running, so that she could retch into the rocks.

Chapter 24

Durstan

Durstan opened his eyes, and saw Andrew leaning over him. The ice in the wind blowing from the sea had revived him, but he was still only partially conscious. "I thought… I don't know… I can't see very well." Andrew could feel his heart breaking. God couldn't let Durstan die. He had already taken Osfric! He pulled his friend's head upwards so that it was resting on his lap, while his body protected him from the wind. The Vikings were gone, and the Monks from Mull were checking the bodies on the beach to see if anyone else was alive.

"I've had such a strange dream, Andrew. I was walking along a passageway. Someone was holding my hand. I don't know who it was, but they left me. I couldn't find the way by myself so I had to come back." Durstan said, as he struggled to sit up.

"Quietly, quietly! There's blood on the back of your head. You have to rest," Andrew said, anxiously looking across the beach for the other Monks. He needed help getting Durstan into a coracle, but they were too far away.

"What happens when we die? Was it my Mother who was holding my hand? There are so many Ancestors, Andrew. Brionach the Druid was talking about it at the Hall. I didn't know how to answer him," Durstan said, slurring his words. A wan smile lit his face. His skin was as white as the snow.

"Don't talk like that, Durstan! It's not time for you to join God's Angels in Heaven. Let me get you into a coracle, and back to Iona. Athdar has the herbs and magic to cure you. I'm not so certain of the care you'll receive at the Monastery here." Andrew began shouting for help.

"Tell me! I have to know." Durstan gave a low moan.

"I don't know." Andrew said, fearfully. "Please don't ask me. I need to find a coracle. It'll be dusk soon, and none of us knows the answer to your question not even Faisal."

"Ailan! Where is she? Give me your oath, Andrew, that you'll make sure she is safe." Durstan's voice was a harsh rasp. "Promise me," he said, coughing.

Andrew began to tremble. "I promise you, my brother, by God's holy will. Anything, but don't leave me."

Durstan closed his eyes and fell into a deep sleep. Andrew laid him carefully on the sand, then ran as fast as he could to the Monks who were searching the bodies near the water's edge.

The noise of the wind and sea was deafening. Tevin, the youngest Monk, had fallen backwards in his haste to move away from the woman he had found. She was covered in blood, and had been lying across a severed head. Her eyes were wide open, staring emptily at the sky. Andrew ran to the boy who was whimpering. He pulled him away from the corpse, and dragged him across the sand to where the other Monks were standing. Their faces also bore the marks of shock. Despite the revulsion and sickness he felt, Andrew went back to the head Tevin had discovered. He held his cross in front of him while trying to say a blessing. He knelt to close Roy's eyes. Andrew's sadness overwhelmed him. The Blacksmith had not deserved this.

He had a kind heart, and was a good friend to Durstan. He said a short prayer for his soul. When he stood up again, he felt that he had aged many years.

A large coracle had been left in the undergrowth near the trees. Several of Duncan's fishermen kept their boats there, and the Monks knew of the place. One of them carried the craft to the edge of the sea. Durstan was still unconscious so they carried him then to the boat, but none of them would row to Iona. They were afraid that the Viking longship would return. The Monks said that they would go instead to the Monastery on Mull, to spread news of the raid. Andrew was beginning to doubt the wisdom of his earlier decision, but there wasn't a proper infirmary here. Durstan would stand a much better chance of survival on Iona. "May God give my arms the strength to do this," he said, pleading with the sky to grant him this blessing.

Meanwhile, the Goddess alone knew how Ailan had managed to carry on. The baby was getting ready to be born. She would have to hurry. There was no one now to help her. Durstan hadn't been found, and Brigid was warning her of danger with the sound of ringing in her ears.

Tam had been waiting for her in the cave. She took Dacey and him back to the enclosure. Branach was sitting beside the fire in his Father's hut, worrying about Oonagh. His face was sullen. No one had told him of her death, and Ailan didn't have any inclination to delay. He would find out soon enough. He put an arm out to stop her, as she was leaving the hut. She mumbled that she would be back shortly, and hurried through the door. She prayed that he wouldn't use his temper on the children. Duncan had sent men to the beach as soon as he heard of the raid, but Ailan didn't believe that they had searched properly or they would have seen the Monk. She had to look for herself.

Her thoughts were in a turmoil, as she retraced her steps. Oonagh had told her to meet the coracles today. She was to help carry the extra food which the Abbot had promised the women they would receive, if they ignored the weather and went to work on Iona. The dead had been left on the sand. The animals would have their chance before the Lord's men had taken them to the cairn. The wolves were always more hungry at this time of year, and quick to find prey, dead or alive. The few people Ailan met on the track as she walked through the forest didn't have any news of Durstan. She had seen Beth with Eoghan at the enclosure and tried to speak to her, but had been pushed aside by one of the men. Most of the women were still in shock, weeping, or sitting quietly. The ones who would speak said that they hadn't seen her Monk unless he was one of those who ran away when the Viking ship landed. Ailan turned quickly away from them, but their curses still followed her.

She searched among the rocks. Durstan might be sheltering there, if he was unable to walk to the Hall because of his injuries. Ailan stopped when she saw Saille's brooch glinting in the last of the daylight. It belonged now to Dacey. She bent to pick it up, and held the amulet tightly. The pain inside her was getting worse. She would have to see to herself quickly. Otherwise the baby would be born here. She couldn't find Durstan. She had failed him. Ailan was deep in thought when a hand grabbed her arm. She turned around petrified. Her face crinkled in horror when she saw that it was Branach. It couldn't have been worse, if he had been a Viking.

"Why are you here, woman, and not at the fire with my cooking pot?" He yanked her long hair in a hefty tug, as if he needed to get her attention. Ailan held her head to try to ease the pain. Finally, something snapped inside her. Her voice became a shout from deep within. "Don't you touch me again, Branach. Do you hear me!"

His mouth fell open, in surprise. He lunged at her. "You dare to speak to me like that, Wife. I'll make you sorry, whelp that you are carrying or not. I won't ask you again. Why are you here on the beach? It's not unusual to see your face covered in tears and nose dripping, but what's caused it this time?" Anger and jealousy were surging through Branach's veins. He had heard that Ailan was asking about Durstan at the enclosure. He thought she would be here looking for him. He hated the Monk, and the feelings he knew his Wife harboured for him.

She didn't reply, and Branach pounced. He released her when she scratched his face with her remaining strength. She was fighting for the baby, and her life. Branach put a hand against the red weals. He stared at the blood on his fingers. Ailan said, breathlessly, "I want to break our handfasting, Branach. This can't carry on. I've grown to hate you, and you don't love me. You're nothing but a bully. There's no need to hit me, or hurt me every single day. Where's the love in that? I'm sick of it, the way I have to live with you. I'm having a child, and you're still at me."

"Don't be so stupid, girl. You're my Wife. I can do with you as I please." He retaliated, spitefully. "Lord Duncan said that you are, so you belong to me. Get you home now, to the cooking pot." But Branach was afraid. He hadn't seen Ailan behave like this in the past, and he didn't know how to deal with the change. She was normally meek, however badly he treated her. He was surprised to find himself aroused, and stared at her in fascination.

"I mean it, Branach. Saille's gone, and Dacey doesn't have anyone else. I know that there's no point asking you, to take her into our family. Pah! If you can call it that. You have barely said a word to Tam in weeks, and don't think that I haven't noticed how he cringes when you come into the hut."

"And so he should, Wife. I'm having to bring up a brat who doesn't belong to me, and a second one is almost here because you couldn't keep your legs closed. Edgar wouldn't have had any idea what he was doing. That pathetic Monk should have been enough for someone like you."

Ailan spoke, without any emotion in her voice. "If you refuse to let me go, Branach, I'll show Duncan the bruises I still have from last week. They aren't a pretty sight, believe me, yellow and black most of them. Lady Mora will speak for me too. She has seen often enough how you've treated me. I should have spoken to the Lord before now. He'll be angry. You've disobeyed him. It was part of our handfasting that you should respect me as a Wife, not beat me every day to please your Mother."

Branach's anger erupted. "You are a liar, Ailan. Don't speak of my Mother in that way. I'll be glad to see the back of you. Oonagh will be too, given what you've done to our family and my poor brother, Edgar."

She realised then that Branach didn't know, and she spoke slowly, as if to a child. "It won't matter to Oonagh what I do."

"What do you mean, woman, of course she'll be glad?" He shouted the words into the wind.

"She's dead, Branach. When Oonagh was getting out of the coracle, she fell on a Viking sword. She'll be lying with the others further down the beach, if the waves haven't taken her out to sea."

Branach dropped to his knees on the wet sand, and screamed. He could see from the look on Ailan's face that she was telling the truth. She turned and staggered away from him in the direction of the track leading to the Hall. The ringing noise in her ears was louder. She knew that she would die, if she fell on her way back to the enclosure.

Chapter 25

The Gods Are With Eoghan

Beth was sobbing when Eoghan ran across the enclosure. "What happened?" He said, holding her tightly in his arms.

"I fell on the track, Eoghan. I twisted my ankle. There's been another raid. A longship on the beach," she said, wiping the tears from her eyes.

"Did they hurt you?" His voice was cold, and the look in his eyes murderous.

"No! But Durstan has gone, and the Vikings were taking the women who had come back from Iona, killing the ones they didn't want." She began to cry again.

Eoghan shouted for one of the slave girls, to help Beth. He ran back across the enclosure then, calling for men to follow him through the trees, but the beach was empty when they reached it except for those who had fallen. He ordered them to search for anyone who might still be alive, and retraced his steps. Beth was sitting with Kate and Mora in the Hall. Her ankle had been bound, and her cuts were being tended by the slave. Mora was applying a herbal salve to the girl's arms, to heal the bruises. Eoghan didn't see the regret in his Mother's eyes. He was at Beth's side in an instant, and had taken her hand in his. "I thought I had lost you," he said, in a low voice. "When I came back to the enclosure, Father told me that you had gone to Iona for sanctuary with Durstan. I would have protected you, Beth. You know that. He couldn't have done."

She sighed, softly. "Eoghan, I had to go. Everyone thought it best. I didn't have any choice."

"Were they gone when you got to the beach, Eoghan?" Duncan said, as he hurried through the door. "The stragglers who escaped are still coming back to us, with tales of goodness knows what. I can see, Beth, that you at least are safe." He looked at her, with displeasure. "What have you done to my kinsman this time, girl?"

"Durstan was safe when Beth saw him last, but she left him on the beach to fight without a weapon. She came back with his knife," Mora said, spitting the words at her.

Eoghan's arms tightened around Beth as Kate said, in her daughter's defence, "this isn't her fault, Mora. She had to save herself. You know that. If she had been taken, I dread to think what would have happened."

"Kate, I am equally afraid for my brother. I didn't know he was going back to that awful Monastery, and now this has happened," Mora said, silently cursing Beth.

"We didn't find him with the dead on the beach, Mother, so he may well have escaped with his life," Eoghan said, coldly. He hadn't forgiven Durstan for the night he spent with Beth.

"I would like to speak to you in private," Duncan said, indicating that Eoghan should follow him.

"I'll be back soon." Eoghan whispered to Beth, before he followed his Father from the Hall.

Duncan went into one of the huts nearby. As soon as his son was half-way through the door, he began to shout at him. "I can't believe your stupidity, being smitten by that she devil. It's against all our wishes, and I thought we were rid of her. The spell she has cast on you is potent indeed. That needs to be broken. I have news of Odhran. He is nearby. The Abbot of Lindisfarne is a good friend. He owes me a favour. Take her there! He'll likely keep her if we can't get her to Faisal, and I don't think we dare risk a sea journey again. If anything happens to Beth while she's in our care, we may still be the subject of a blood feud for having deprived Aodh of his niece's marriage prospect. She'll be the Church's problem once she's inside the Monastery. I'm hoping that their magic will be strong enough to come between you and her, Eoghan. I want you to return here safely, and before you ask me, your Mother agrees. You're used to riding in all weathers and, frankly, I'm not bothered whether Beth is. If you take good horses with several men you shouldn't come to any harm unless of course you meet Odhran. You'll have to be careful, my Son. I can't stress that enough."

Eoghan saw the hard glint in his Father's eyes, and realised that it would be pointless arguing. The change of plan would at least give him an opportunity of spending more time alone with Beth. A lot could happen before they reached Lindisfarne. Perhaps she could be persuaded to handfast with him once they were away from here? A Christian marriage might come later, if he could get her with child fast enough which shouldn't be a problem. "Yes, Father," he said, obediently, much to Duncan's surprise.

They left the Hall at first light, and followed the river's path for most of the day. Eoghan and Beth were riding between the trees at the front of five men. The gushing water prevented any opportunity of conversation. He glanced across at her. He hoped that they would soon find a safe place to camp for the night. He could have taken her on his horse but she would have refused the offer, and the animal was tired. They all were. It would be cold out here tonight, without proper shelter. Eoghan consoled himself with the thought that Beth would be lying next to him. He shouted encouragement to her across the short distance between their horses. "You are beautiful, my Lady, even when you are tired and pursued by the Devil. Do you not love me a little?"

Beth smiled, at his teasing. Eoghan was trying his best to keep her cheerful, and forget the pain in her hands and limbs. "Perhaps I could learn, my Lord?" She was pleased to see annoyance flash across his face before the smile returned. He shouldn't expect to have all his own way with her.

A stray branch caught Beth's cloak, and Eoghan was at her side in an instant. "Here, let me. You'll tear the cloth if you pull it." His hand grazed hers, and he brought it quickly to his lips to kiss her fingers gently. One of the men riding behind them guffawed. He made a comment to the others that the Lord's son would have the Lady bedded before the day was out. A glare from Eoghan silenced the man. He dropped Beth's hand, and didn't see the triumph in her eyes.

They rode on in silence through the dense trees at the river bend, and entered a clearing unexpectedly. Men were camped there. The babbling water had drowned their noise. Eoghan quickly realised his mistake, and shouted to the others. "Turn your horses! Turn your horses!" Beth tried, but was caught by the first of Odhran's men to reach her. He grabbed the reins, pulling them hard. She lashed out with a whip, but the man took it easily from her hand. His other hand was on her leg when Eoghan knocked him to the ground with a hefty kick. The man was up in an instant, and the riders forced at knife point to dismount.

"Well, well, well. I have searched far and wide for you,

my Lady, and here you are. You have come to me as a bride, of your own free will." Odhran stared lasciviously at Beth, as she watched Eoghan struggling. The man he had knocked to the ground earlier had his boot behind Eoghan's neck, to hold him down. A knife was pointed at his back. The Lord's son could barely move, but he could still speak. He said, in a hoarse voice, "Leave her alone. I am to be handfasted to the Lady."

A look of pleasure crossed Beth's face while Odhran laughed. His men joined in the mirth. "Perhaps you would like to tell me what you are intending to do, if I don't? I would also like to know your name before I kill you."

Beth struggled harder with Durell, the man who was holding her arms, and she screamed. "Eoghan!"

"Aah, I have my answer. Thank you, my dear." Odhran smiled at her. "Let me guess. You are my old friend, Duncan's boy," he said, warily. He was delighted to see Beth again, but this young man could be a problem.

"My Father will send men to find you, if any harm comes to us. Honour dictates that he should. You know that, old man. If you kill me, you'll find yourself in the middle of a war. The Lords who support him dislike murder. They'll side with Duncan if the need arises."

Odhran's face darkened. He hadn't expected this. "Your threat doesn't leave me with a choice. I will fight you honourably for the Lady. A whelp like you won't be difficult to kill, and I'll beat your backside first." Odhran's men shouted in support of their Lord until he held his hands up for silence. He called another order across the clearing. Four of Eoghan's men were stabbed, and the fifth had his throat cut.

Beth looked away in horror. She felt the world slipping. She would have fallen had Durell not caught her, and pushed her down to sit on the frozen ground. She was temporarily blinded by the glint of sunlight on Odhran's blade. "I see now how it is," he said, looking from Beth to Eoghan.

Odhran told the man who was holding Eoghan to release him, and return his weapon. A dark anger raged through the Lord's son when he faced his opponent. Their eyes were fixed on each other. "No! Go back. This is my fight," Odhran said, when one of his men moved to his side. Eoghan began to circle him. Odhran lunged and struck the first blow. He moved so fast that the blade seemed to flash by itself through the air. Eoghan deflected the sword instinctively with his own, and managed to punch his adversary as he stepped to one side. Odhran was furious at the insult. He rallied fast. The two men appeared equally matched in skill. They fought blow by blow for several minutes until Eoghan became wrong-footed when he stumbled on a tree root. His opponent wounded him in the shoulder. The Lord's son fell backwards with a groan, as Odhran withdrew his sword.

Blood spurted from the wound. Eoghan felt lightheaded. He put his hand across it to staunch the flow, but his life force was trickling between his fingers. The shadow spirit at his side whispered softly in his ear. Eoghan could see Beth from a far away place. She was struggling again with Durell. He was holding both her arms tightly so that she couldn't escape. Beth kicked him hard on the shins. He looked as if he would let her go, but slapped her instead across the face. Eoghan fought to remain conscious. The world was tilting. He could hear a voice, saying to him, "fight on, Eoghan! You must do this…"

Beth was sobbing, and Odhran sensed victory. He raised his sword to strike the final blow. As she screamed

Eoghan's name, Odhran was blinded by bright sunlight on the blade. He faltered, blinked to clear his vision, giving Eoghan the opportunity he needed to thrust his sword into the other man's abdomen. The Gods were with him. He pushed the blade in deeply with his unwounded arm, turning the sword as he did so. Duncan had taught him well when he was a boy. Eoghan could use either hand for sword fighting, with equal ability. It had been a childhood game he had played often with his Father, but there wasn't any room for mistakes this time. He pushed against the sword with all his remaining strength until Odhran fell backwards. A black raven flew overhead as cloud obscured the sun, and the world became dark momentarily.

Beth succeeded in pulling away from Durell, and ran to Eoghan who had fallen to his knees. Odhran lay on the ground nearby. His eyes were open, but sightless. Her Father, the Druid, would have said that the raven was an omen. The bird had come to collect Odhran's soul. Beth looked warily around the circle of men which still enclosed them, but Durell was already kneeling in front of Eoghan to offer him his sword. The other men followed with their allegiance, and stayed on their knees before their new Lord.

Beth tore her cloak, to wrap a piece of cloth tightly around Eoghan's shoulder, and cover the wound. His back was resting against the trunk of a large tree as he sat on the ground, accepting oaths from Odhran's men. He smiled at her. Perhaps this would be a good opportunity to ask his Father again? There wouldn't be any need now for them to travel to Lindisfarne. The Monk had gone, and Odhran's men obviously didn't want to become outlaws. If Duncan offered them a place at the Hall as was likely, they would stay on Mull with Eoghan's agreement. There wasn't any guarantee that these men would get the opportunity to serve another, and they had offered themselves to him in the old way when he had killed their Lord.

Eoghan leaned forward with difficulty, to kiss Beth. His eyes were full of promise. "You are my woman now, my Lady. I will protect you, as I said I would." The young Lord's eyes closed, and he passed into unconsciousness.

Chapter 26

Ailan's Magical Charm

The stars glittered in the sky above Iona, as Durstan lay on the pallet he had left a few weeks ago. Andrew sat beside him with his hands clasped in prayer. He didn't realize that his friend was regaining consciousness. "I've been so angry with you, Durstan. The spells those women cast made you forget me, your anam cara, but I'm sorry now for what I said."

He wiped his eyes with the sleeve of his robe. "You might not live to see the season change, and I'm frightened, Durstan. I've already lost Osfric." Andrew's voice quivered. He was exhausted. He had struggled the day before, to row through heavy seas from Mull to Iona. His arms and legs still ached from the effort. One of the Monks on the island had noticed the coracle in difficulty, and raised the alarm. Several had braved the icy water to swim to them, so as to be quicker than finding boats. The first Monk to reach the coracle took the oars from Andrew's frozen hands, and others pulled it along behind them with a rope until all of them were safely on the sand. They carried Durstan to his hut where he was given a powerful potion. Athdar told Andrew to pray and talk, to tempt the young Monk's spirit back to them. He had done so throughout the night, while the Abbot kept his distance. Faisal was with an important visitor from Rome.

Aelfric the Saxon had however looked in on them earlier. He smirked before he turned away.

Durstan opened his eyes. He was blinded by the light and a dull pounding inside his head, before the haziness in his mind cleared sufficiently for him to recall floating in a coracle with Andrew. It was too dark to see anymore... No wait! He did remember. The Viking raid… and everything began to tumble into place. Ailan had escaped, but not Saille. May God help him… Roy… A low moan escaped from Durstan's lips. He moved a hand upwards to shield his face from the daylight which was coming through the doorway. The movement caught Andrew's attention.

"Thank God!" The older Monk's face was filled with joy, as he helped Durstan sit up. He held a pot of water against his friend's cracked lips. Most of it ran down Durstan's chin onto the sheepskin which was covering him before he fell back onto the pallet with a groan, clutching the side of his head.

"I have a headache strong enough to please Woden, but that's not sufficient cause for complaint." The tears in Durstan's eyes felt like sharp stones.

"Sshh… You must keep calm! We are supposed to have faith, but…" Andrew didn't finish the sentence. Durstan had fallen asleep again, so he resumed his place beside him. When Durstan opened his eyes later, the hut was partially lit by a low fire casting shadows around the walls. Andrew was eating a thin vegetable soup, one of the others had brought for him. He shared the few spoonfuls which were left with his friend, and gave him more water.

The pain in Durstan's head had receded to a low ache, and the food helped settle the sickness in his stomach. "All this is my fault! I've broken my vows, and have gone against everything I've been taught. Faisal says that we'll only find God through obedience to the Church. I'd do anything to have Roy here now. He was the Father I should have had when I was growing up." Durstan hesitated, "… but then, I can't give up Ailan. I know I can't." Andrew held him, as he sobbed in anguish.

"Sshh, Durstan. You're hurt, and need more time to recover. Don't think of it now."

"It's all so mixed up, Andrew. Do you know about the Roman, Pelagius? One of the missionaries who visited Iona last year told me about him when I mended his sword. Pelagius believed that God is in our love for each other. Why hasn't the Abbot mentioned him? Before this happened I thought that if Pelagius was right I couldn't have committed the sins Faisal would say I had. Perhaps those who refuse to worship our God aren't evil after all, if they know of love?"

"Don't say those things, Durstan! It doesn't do any good," Andrew said, fearfully.

"I've decided to leave the Monastery. Lord Duncan wants me to. I know that I've failed as a Monk. If I'd been more obedient to Faisal's Church, kept my vows, God wouldn't have taken Roy or hurt Ailan and Saille. It is all my fault, Andrew. I can't stay here."

"No!" Tears slid down Andrew's cheeks, as his eyes pleaded with Durstan.

"Please don't, Andrew. I'm not proud of what I've done. I've wronged two women, most of all Ailan. When she didn't come back to Iona, it seemed easier to carry on as before. I should have followed her, found out why she had left, and made sure she was alright. Those are the things you do if you truly love someone. Faisal's endless talk of chastity goes against nature itself. How can anyone who has taken part in the Beltane solstice pretend afterwards that it didn't happen? Faisal doesn't have any compassion. My soul is with Ailan. I love her dearly."

Durstan paused. "I want to spend my life with her, Andrew. I have no idea whether she'll agree to it, given the way I've behaved. There's Branach too, but I have to see her again to find out."

Andrew was astounded. "You can't do that, Durstan. You have made your vows to God, and all of us are guilty of sin. The Abbot has told us that many times. I wish you had learned more of the Bible, and read the manuscripts. You would know for certain then that the Devil is present among us. God sent his only son to suffer so that we could be forgiven for our sins. There's no need for you to go, Durstan. I can't believe you are thinking of it. You must give up this notion of Ailan."

Durstan smiled, sadly. "I can't Andrew. It's not right. She is in every breath I take."

"And what of the other one, that Lady Beth? Your eyes were all over her when I left the Hall. You didn't need to tell me what it meant. I thought she was the one who would be your Wife if you had to choose, and were intent on sin?" Andrew said, bitterly.

Durstan moved awkwardly on the pallet. "I was wrong. May God forgive me again. I am not one of the blessed Saints, Andrew. It makes no difference. I can't give up fighting for Ailan. Please understand. You were the same about Osfric. I saw your eyes on him many a time, and Beth isn't an ordinary woman. She's far outside my experience. The amber beads from the Baltic she has on her belt, and silver armlets that the Mediterranean men brought to the mainland to trade. I was fascinated by her, flattered that she looked at me. I'd never seen the like of her or such jewels before. It wasn't until later that I found out her reasons. There was nothing to the love Beth talked of, not as I feel for Ailan, and I understand now that physicality is only a part of it. Beth thought that I could bring the protection of the Church to her. She doesn't have any understanding of God's ways, or men like us who serve Him, but we've made our peace. Eoghan is the one for her, not me. He will have to protect her, if she goes with him." Durstan's eyes were shining. "Ailan on the other hand, will always be with me in my heart. She has been every single day since I met her, except for the short time I was blinded by Beth. I'm truly ashamed of that now," Durstan said, the last words with difficulty. His breath had become ragged.

"Rest, Durstan! We'll talk about this later. I'll come back to sit with you, as soon as I've told the Abbot that you're recovering. He said he was to be informed immediately there was any news, and I didn't tell him earlier that you had spoken. Lie still, while I'm gone. I'll bring Athdar too, in case you need another potion. You'll see sense when your mind has fully recovered."

Durstan grasped his friend's arm. "Faisal is wrong in how he treats us, Andrew. Duncan said that he'll help me escape, and travel south. I want you to come with me. We can start again in a different place, with other men like us. We have learned a hard lesson being here, but I'm certain now that love is the most precious gift we have received from Him. It should be the basis of our beliefs, Andrew. I learned this from Ailan, not our Father Abbot. It's the love between people, the kindness and compassion, which is most important not an ache for gold or power. Think of the bell, and Osfric. How much you loved him."

Andrew turned his face away, and began to cry. Durstan stretched up awkwardly, to touch his arm. "I'm sorry, my old friend. I want you to come with me, and not stay here at Faisal's mercy with your sight leaving you. God must have had good reason to part your path from Osfric's. It doesn't mean He's forsaken him, or you. Don't be afraid of what I'm saying. I still believe in our Christian God but in a different, better, way."

Andrew wiped a hand noisily across his wet eyes and nose. "Paul said something similar about the Abbot. We have talked too about the Vikings. They'll come back, Durstan. Faisal will have us trying to defend ourselves next time, even though it's obvious to any fool they are the stronger men. Our only hope is to make them see violence isn't the way. When they trade in the warmer months they don't live by the sword or knife, but the Christian God alone knows if I can forgive them for Osfric, and now Roy."

"It'll be unwise to be here when they do come back, Andrew. As soon as I can row, I have to cross to Mull, to see my sister and Ailan. She may not want anything more to do with me but if she does, we have a chance. Duncan has agreed that I can take her from the enclosure, if she'll go with me to Lindisfarne. There's the opportunity of a better life there, Andrew. Think of it! I didn't imagine that I would leave here, but so much has changed. Now I really can't stay. Come with me. Faisal will without a doubt refuse to allow us to go, but we'll find a way." Durstan smiled, and winced when Thor's hammer began to pound again inside his head.

Andrew frowned. "There's something which you should know, Durstan. Lady Mora sent one of Duncan's men to Iona at dawn, with a slave girl, She was asking for you. It was Lora, if I'm not mistaken. They had learned from the Monastery on Mull that I'd brought you here. The girl said that she had Ailan's most valuable possession with her. A holy relic which her Grandmother had given to her.

A piece of cloth, no less, from the blessed Saint Brigid's robe. The girl insisted it was to be put under your pillow while you slept, so that her Goddess could heal you. Faisal refused to allow it. He said that you were resting safely with the Christian God and His Angels, so were not to be disturbed. You didn't need a woman's charm when you were in our Heavenly Father's hands. Durstan, every Monk here speaks well of you, and Faisal doesn't like it. You risked your life on Mull, without a weapon or the magic in your knife, and Ailan must love you to have sent so powerful a charm to keep you safe. Even I am aware of that." Andrew patted his friend's arm affectionately. "I don't agree with your decision, but go to her as soon as you can. You won't find any peace until you do."

"Thank you, Andrew. Your words mean a lot to me. It would have cost precious little for Faisal to be kind to Lora, especially if he believed the cloth was simply a powerless charm. This is what I've been saying about him. I want no more of these Roman ways. Please come with me."

Andrew shook his head, sadly. "I've been thinking too, Durstan. When I could still copy passages from the bible into our manuscripts. I noticed that Faisal doesn't always accurately repeat the teachings of Jesus or his disciples. It didn't feel right to question it before now but, as you rightly said, so much has happened to change things. There's a whole world beyond Iona, and the Norsemen have shown us how easily it can touch our lives."

Andrew hesitated. "I would like to go to Lindisfarne with you, and Ailan too, but I can't. I'm sorry, Durstan. The Abbot will welcome you both. He is a kind man, much like the sound of your Pelagius. I made a lot of friends when I was there. I have been worried about them since the Viking raid last year. I heard that there were many dead, but I haven't been able to find out who is still alive. It matters to me. Faisal could have helped me, but needless to say, he didn't. Perhaps you could somehow send word of it? I would be grateful to know, and that you are well. You will always be my anam cara. I'll worry about you, even though you'll be with God whatever you are doing. I won't breathe a word of your intentions to the Abbot before you leave. You are right to choose a time when you won't be seen. Aelfric the Saxon has started to drink his fill of the Abbot's wine every night. Maybe that will give you the opportunity you are seeking?"

Durstan began to object, and Andrew held up his hand to stop him. "No, Durstan. My sight would only be a problem to you. I'm living more in shadow now, than in the light. If I'm here, I can at least pretend to see what I can't. The others will help me pass it off. I would also like to go back to Mull. On a good day, I can see enough to teach the older boys at the Monastery how to write some of their letters, even though I may not be able to create a manuscript."

The look which passed between them showed the love within their friendship. Durstan tried again to sit up, but the effort was too much. He fell onto the pallet, coughing. Andrew held him, as he put the pot of water to his lips. Durstan drank thirstily. As soon as he could, he said, "I assume there'll be little point in trying to get you to change your mind, Andrew. I wish your decision had been different." He closed his eyes. He couldn't keep them open any longer. The skin around them was deeply etched in black.

Andrew kissed his forehead gently before leaving the hut. It was snowing in light flurries, and the wind whipped the Monk's robe around his legs. He felt a sense of relief that a decision had been made, even though it meant that he would lose Durstan. Osfric might still manage to return to Iona, one day. He would be waiting for him when he did. He stretched his arms upwards to the white sky, and looked across the turbulent sea in the direction taken by the Viking longship. He shouted into the wind. "May God go with you, Osfric, for I can't."

Andrew stood motionless until the snowflakes almost covered his robe. When the cold reached deep inside him, he made his way into the Church to pray. The Abbot could wait, to hear the news of Durstan's recovery.

Chapter 27

The Only Truth Is Love

"I know that we can't change the threads of the wyrd or the Sun and Moon in the sky, but can't we begin again?" Durstan said, hopefully. The flecks of light in Ailan's eyes were the same as he had seen at Beltane.

She didn't reply. She was too afraid to break the spell. It was difficult to believe that Durstan was still alive, and with her now inside the Church at the enclosure on Mull. His gaze didn't waver when Beth's shadow crossed his face, and Ailan refused to think of her. He was all that mattered. Lora had run to tell her that the Monk was praying inside the Church. She had dropped the cloth she was folding to see him with her own eyes, and it was true. Durstan was talking with his God.

She could hear the pain in his voice when he said, "I'm sorry I have hurt you, Ailan. Please forgive me. There can't be any excuse for what I've done. Everything was always about you." Durstan paused, to find the right words. "If you are thinking otherwise, I do love you. Eoghan is for Beth, not me. They are to marry. The Lord has given his permission."

Ailan couldn't keep the tears inside any longer, and Durstan put his arms around her shoulders. He pulled her close against his chest whilst kissing her hair. "I'm truly sorry. I wish the last few months could be erased from our lives. I didn't know until I came here what had happened to you after Beltane. It's all my fault. I should have left the Monastery, and looked for you. Please can we talk about it? I can't accept that loving you is a sin."

When her tears became quieter and Ailan was listening to him again, Durstan carried on speaking with more confidence. "I want to tell people about Christ, and for you to come to Lindisfarne with me. My life lost meaning when you weren't in it. I refuse to be shut away inside the Monastery any longer. I'm a Celt, and a Monk. There's no reason why I can't also be a man. I want to make a difference to other people's lives, so that they can see as I did that the only truth is love. It should be the foundation of all our lives. You showed me that, Ailan. When we talked about Columba, I saw that he was a man who knew how to fight for what he wanted. A Celt, and from what the scops say, his miracles helped many. They came from the love he had for others, and he was right. It was always going to be easier, if everyone followed our Christian God."

Ailan turned to face him, angrily. "I'm trying my best to understand, Durstan. You say that you love me, yet all you can talk about is your beliefs. Mora said that you know what happened. Have you any idea what it's like for me? I've lost a child. The birth cord was fastened around her neck. I blame myself for it. If I hadn't been running around so much before she was born, and resting as the women had told me to, the baby wouldn't have strangled herself. I wonder though what sort of life she would have had, if she had lived? What sort of life does any woman have, if she isn't born with the privileges which your Lady Beth has?"

Durstan felt confused. He knew that he didn't always speak eloquently, but he had sworn his love to Ailan. He was trying to hold her in his arms, and she had pushed him away. "I'm truly sorry, my love. I should have been with you. I can't forgive myself, but what about Branach? Didn't he help you?" Durstan said, desperately. He realised his mistake when he saw the contempt in Ailan's eyes.

"When I couldn't find you on the beach, Branach came to look for me. I told him that I wished to break our handfasting," she said, in a lifeless voice as Durstan's heart soared. He had been waiting for her to mention Branach. "I didn't see him after that. He'll be off somewhere crying for his Mother, or lying dead in a ditch for all I care. Lora has been seeing to Tam because I couldn't leave my bed for days. Cormac has gone too, so that makes the whole family. He'll be drunk, no doubt, trying to come to terms with Saille having been taken. That he has lost the chance of her. No, Durstan! It was Lora, a slave girl, who was with me when I needed help. She held my hand when the birthing crone cut the cord, and took the baby to give to the dogs because she couldn't take a first breath. Are you satisfied, now that you know everything?" Ailan's eyes bore into his, like iron.

"Your sister has spoken to Lord Duncan. I can have Saille's hut until he chooses another Husband for me, if I don't take one myself. I knew already that your kinsman had little patience with women. He says we are only here to work and birth. We should start work again as soon as the child is out. Men have to keep fighting in battle, even when injured. An enemy won't excuse them the deathblow because of a broken limb. He is obviously of the opinion that a woman's life has become too easy, and I thought we had everything, last Beltane Eve. Didn't you feel the God and Goddess were with us, Durstan? It was so beautiful, and then…" She faltered, unable to carry on. He tried again to hold her in his arms, but she pushed him away.

"You had taken off the wooden cross you are so fond of wearing, but later when the light was coming back, I saw the indentation it had made on your skin. It was still there, as if your God wouldn't let you go. I was frightened, Durstan. Mora found some work for me to do on Mull, but that was the real reason I didn't come to you after Edgar. I thought your God might be punishing me. He is powerful, and you are a part of Him. After a time I thought I must have been mistaken, that you didn't love me after all. You stayed on Iona, and didn't think to follow me here. That's not what someone in love would do. When Duncan offered me to Branach, it seemed the only way out. I didn't have anyone else, and I knew by then that I was going to have a child. Branach was the best I could do." She finished speaking, with a sob.

Durstan felt even more confused. This was Ailan talking to him, and yet what she had said didn't make any sense. "You thought the mark on my skin was a magic trick performed by God? That's only a superstition, my love. Here, let me show you." He took the cross from around his neck and pressed it firmly against the soft flesh of her arm. Ailan cringed from him. She struggled to move away, but Durstan held her firmly. It was too important that she understand this. "Look now! If you are right, you also belong to my God, even though in His mind you have always done so. There isn't any dark magic here. A crucifix is an amulet which a Monk wears, along with a robe and sandals. The indentation could happen to anyone, the same as the scent from the violets on your body at Beltane filled my hair and skin with their perfume. Love was the only magic that night, Ailan, and it's still there between us."

Durstan kissed her lips, tenderly. She responded, reluctantly at first, then hungrily to the pressure of his before he broke away. It hadn't been long enough since she had given birth. Durstan was beginning to understand the meaning of being in love. "Ailan, sweetheart, you don't know how pleased I am that Branach has gone. Come with me now. It isn't safe here. The Vikings will be back, raiding along the shoreline. Too many have already been killed or injured, and so far they have only come a few times. It isn't for us, or the children. Duncan wants me gone for his own reasons, and I need to put distance between the Abbot and myself. We can't match the Norsemen's fighting skills when they jump from the longships. They attacked Lindisfarne last year. I heard that they took everything from the Church, the Monastery's coffers, and jewels from the book covers. I can't see why they would go back there again. They've already had their fill, but if I'm wrong and it does turn out that we need to move further south, there are other places we can go which will be well away from the sea."

"Durstan, I need to talk to you about the baby," Ailan said, patiently. "You still haven't told me how you feel. What happened wasn't my fault. You need to know that. Do you think it was, and that's why you aren't speaking of it? It didn't happen because I encouraged Edgar in any way. He didn't know what he was doing. It was awful. He broke my arm too," she said, sadly. "I had to let him do it. There was nothing I could do to stop him. I tried to think of something else while it was happening because it's you I love. I prayed to the Goddess every day after that for you to be the baby's Father. Branach may have been told by Duncan to handfast with me because of what his brother had done, but it wasn't a love match. I want you to know all of it. You are saying that you want to be with me but I can't go through the possibility of losing you, not again," she said, earnestly. "You may as well know too, that I did try with Branach at first. I thought I had to. You had left me, but it was perfectly clear early on that he wasn't for me. I didn't love him, not even for a second. I couldn't because it's always been about you, my Monk. I've never stopped loving the man I sat beside on Iona, listening to the depth of his voice, as we watched the light shimmering on the sea."

Durstan's heart was overflowing with love. "Please don't say any more, Ailan. There's no need. I don't know how to answer you, other than to tell you that my God will help us. We need to spend time together, to become as we once were. It'll probably not be the same again. We have both changed, but there's no reason it can't be better. It's me who has to beg your forgiveness, for not having had the strength to go after you when I should quite clearly have done so. You have nothing to be sorry about, my love. Don't ever think that. As for Edgar and Branach, they are nothing to us now apart from the past, although I can't stop being angry with them for what they did to you. Christian charity says that we should forgive each other, but I'm presently a long way from that." Durstan kissed her forehead gently.

"But Beth is so beautiful, unlike me..." Ailan said, unable to keep the jealousy from her voice.

"Ailan, sshh... She's to marry Eoghan, and Rae is to have Alys. Mora caught Duncan fumbling with the girl's clothes at Yule. He has no more say in it, if the peace is to be kept between them." Durstan burst out laughing. "My poor sister. How she suffers with her wayward Husband. When will Duncan learn, or her for that matter?" Durstan said, shaking his head. "I've spoken to my kinsman, and I have his permission. You are free, Ailan. Tam and Dacey too. I want to travel with you as my Wife, if you'll have me by Christian marriage, or a handfasting if need be. It makes little difference. It's the love between us which matters the most."

Ailan's face had reddened. "You can't even say that she isn't beautiful, Durstan, or that you think I am the better woman. You are the same as all of the other men. I hate you for what you've done. You only want me now because you can't have her!"

Ailan pushed past him and ran from the Church, leaving Durstan feeling confused in front of the two altars.

Chapter 28

May Woden Go With You

It was a bitterly cold morning, too icy for more snow to fall, and the best anyone could expect for a journey at this time of year. A small group of men and women were huddled together by the enclosure gate. Durstan was standing next to a large, black, horse. He was wrapped in a fine new cloak which Mora had given to him. The green and gold of the dyed wool contrasted strongly with the white landscape, but none of it could remove the pain from his heart.

"I've tried to talk to her, Mora, but she refused to listen. I said that Beth meant nothing to me. If Ailan won't believe me, that's the end of it. Duncan has said we must leave this morning. Faisal won't wait much longer before he sends men, to force me back to Iona. I left without his permission. No one does that. He'll assume that I have come here to you, even if he hasn't got it out of Andrew. If I'm not at the Hall when they come, they may not follow us. Duncan has promised to delay them with food and wine, plenty of it. What did Ailan say when you spoke to her?" His eyes were pleading for a different response this time.

Mora's heart reached out to her brother. She took his hand inside her own, wishing that the world could be otherwise. "I'm so sorry, Durstan. She barely spoke to me.

She listened when I told her that you would protect her, but she is punishing herself for the loss of her child. Ailan's been hurt. She's jealous too of Beth, and your God. I told her that I thought she would regret the decision she has made not to go with you once she is feeling better. She didn't answer." The Monk grimaced, and Mora squeezed his hand. "Don't worry about her, Durstan. Ailan is a survivor. She is also missing Saille, and can't forgive herself or you for the time being. You can't undo Beth, but if you could have given up your God for her, perhaps it would have been different?" Mora paused, to search his eyes. "I can see that you won't be able to do that."

"If only there was more time, Mora. I am sure I could have persuaded her. The worst part is, I know that she loves me."

Mora sighed. "I think you are right, Durstan, but you also know now how women are." She glanced at Duncan who was talking to the men he had chosen to travel with the Monk. None of them had wives or were handfasted, but Farlan was close to one of the girls at the enclosure. He had told Mora that he didn't want to leave her. Even if he had felt able to say this to his Lord, it wouldn't have made any difference. One woman was mostly as good as another in Duncan's eyes. Mora found it difficult sometimes, to believe that he had kept her heart with his for so long. "I was thinking about asking Duncan to tell Ailan that she had to go with you, but it would have been wrong. She isn't a slave, and should have some say in who she beds."

Durstan looked hopeful. "Yes, but…"

"No, Durstan, it's not right. She has refused you." His eyes filled with sorrow. "I promise you that no harm will come to her. Your safety is the most important consideration, and you mustn't go back to Iona. Faisal wouldn't let you leave again, not now. Do as Duncan has said, and hurry! May the Gods and our Ancestors go with you, to ensure that it's not too long before we meet again." Mora embraced him. The charm she had sewn into the seam of Durstan's cloak carried Woden's blessing. She had prayed over it many times, for the magic to be strong enough to protect her brother.

The men were already on their horses when Durstan slid easily into the saddle on his. The black stallion didn't make a sound. It was used to being handled roughly by Eoghan. Durstan patted its mane. As he sat upright, he caught sight of Lora at the back of the crowd. She had an arm around Ailan's shoulders, and was whispering to her. Several runny-nosed children were weaving in and out of the people, while Tam and Dacey stayed close to the two women. Durstan couldn't hear Lora urging Ailan to go with him, or her reply when she asked Lora how her future would be. It was in the slave's eyes when she said, "all will be well, Ailan. Druid Brionach told me so."

Beth was standing next to Eoghan, near the front. Her eyes shone when they met the Monk's. She smiled and waved before turning again to the Lord's son. If only she was Ailan… Durstan shook his head, trying to remove the thought from his mind. He bent to kiss Mora for the last time. The horse struggled beneath his thighs when Duncan clapped its hindquarters, and shouted, "may Woden go with you, Durstan." His voice was joined by similar cries from the onlookers.

In a flash of half-light, and movement at the back of the crowd, Ailan began pushing through the people in front of her. Durstan could hear her clearly. "Let me through, please. Let me through." Suddenly she was at the side of his horse. Their eyes met in understanding, and desire.

"Take me with you, Durstan." Without any hesitation, he pulled her up behind him onto the horse. She kissed his neck, and put her arms around his waist. He felt himself drowning in the scent of her skin, the memory of Beltane. Ailan whispered, "I'm still angry with you, but I love you too much to lose you. This is our chance."

One of Duncan's men pulled Tam upwards onto his horse. Farlan took Dacey. They rode behind Durstan through the enclosure gate, to follow the path to Lindisfarne. Ailan's arms stayed around his waist, and Durstan knew without a doubt, that the Christian God had meant for this to happen.

Author's Note

Thank you for reading, The Monk Who Cast A Spell. I hope you enjoyed the story. There'll be more books coming soon... in the Durstan series.

In the meantime, if you would like to keep in touch, please sign up for my free newsletter to receive a short story from me every month. There are lots of different characters and plots to enjoy.

You'll be the first to learn about my new books and stories, what inspired me to write them, and much more.

So please sign up now:
https://www.sharonbradshaw.com/newsletter/

You'll also find me on:
https://www.facebook.com/sharonbradshaw0/
https://twitter.com/SharonBradshaw0

Printed in Poland
by Amazon Fulfillment
Poland Sp. z o.o., Wrocław